SHIVA'S FIRE

SUZANNE FISHER STAPLES

Shiva's Fire

FRANCES FOSTER BOOKS

FARRAR STRAUS GIROUX

NEW YORK

Copyright © 2000 by Suzanne Fisher Staples
All rights reserved
Distributed in Canada by Douglas & McIntyre Ltd.
Printed in the United States of America
Designed by Filomena Tuosto
First edition, 2000
1 3 5 7 9 10 8 6 4 2

Title page photograph of Shiva Nataraja, eleventh century,
used by permission of Giraudon / Art Resource, NY.

Library of Congress Cataloging-in-Publication Data

Staples, Suzanne Fisher.
    Shiva's Fire / Suzanne Fisher Staples. — 1st ed.
        p.   cm.
    "Frances Foster books."
    Summary: In India, a talented dancer sacrifices friends and family for her art.
    ISBN 0-374-36824-4
    [1. Dance—Fiction.   2. India—Fiction.]   I. Title.
PZ7.S79346Sj   1999
[Fic]—dc21   99-10626

This book is for
my mother, Helen Brittain Fisher,
and my father, Robert Charles Fisher,
whose curiosity and enthusiasm infected me early, and
from whom I have learned there is always a way

ACKNOWLEDGMENTS

I am deeply grateful to the following people for graciously helping in many ways: pointing me toward information, guiding my travels in India, telling their stories, and, most important, spending many hours discussing the complexities of Hindu belief and mythology and answering my many questions about bharata natyam, the most sublime form of Indian classical dance. Thank you to Perinkulam P. Ramanathan, T.S.K. Lingam, Villy Gandhi, Neelakant and Vasantha Patri, Iqbal Athas, Suma Perumal, Sadhana Gupta, Kala, Mr. Chandrashekar, and the late Protima Bedi. While I would not have been able to write this story without them, any mistakes belong entirely to me.

My thanks to Gregory Maguire for his wisdom and friendship, and to Virginia Morgan for lending a discerning eye. Thanks to Elaine Chubb, whose copy-editing skills, perseverance, and judgment leave me in awe. And my thanks and love always to Frances Foster for her forbearance, vision, and wisdom.

AUTHOR'S NOTE

The village of Anandanagar and the district and former princely state called Nandipuram are fictional places in the South of India.

All names and all Tamil, Hindi, and Sanskrit words are spelled phonetically, and spelling may vary from one source to another. A glossary and pronunciation guide appears on pages 271–76.

NOTE

To know India's spirituality is to know India. To the Hindu, God is One but His manifestations are many. A person facing calamity turns to Ganesha, the remover of obstacles; a student facing exams looks to Saraswathi, goddess of knowledge; the businessman's deity is Lakshmi, who grants wealth; and so on.

Lord Shiva, unseen director of the world's drama, performs His cosmic dance in the heart of each individual. He dances the world into and out of being, his fire consuming inflated egos, greed, anger, jealousy, lust, and all aspects of darkness. He dances in the play of children, the wars of nations, the movements of stars, in earthquakes, conflagrations, and deluges, in a drop of water, in the raging torrent. To dance with Shiva is to know freedom from the cycle of birth and death.

—*Perinkulam P. Ramanathan*
Cultural Coordinator
Indo-American Cultural and Religious Foundation

SHIVA'S FIRE

One

Meenakshi arose early the day Parvati was born, for the infant in her womb had not allowed her to sleep during the night. Tiny knees and elbows thumped Meenakshi's sides in an odd, slow rhythm: *tai-taiya-tai, tai-taiya-tai*.

She did not know her daughter would arrive amid a change in the course of natural events, that fish would swim among the stars and birds would soar beneath the waters.

Meenakshi yawned and tied her sari around her swollen middle. She moved quietly to let her husband, Sundar, and their sons sleep while she went to the temple to offer prayers. Flies buzzed lazily in the leaden heat, and a trickle of perspiration rolled down the side of her face.

On a metal tray she arranged a coconut, bananas, and a champakam blossom with a fragrance as delicate as the pink at the base of each white petal. She laid another blossom at the feet of the statue of the dancing Shiva, which Sundar had carved of sandalwood and placed in a niche in the wall.

Meenakshi arched her back to ease it, and a pair of hands clasped her from behind and quieted the thumping against her ribs.

"You think he'll arrive today?" Sundar asked. Meenakshi turned and laid a finger against her husband's lips.

"Shh-hh, you'll wake the boys," she whispered, and pulled him out into the pale heat of the morning. "I told you," she said, smiling, "this one's a girl!"

"But how can you be so sure?" Sundar asked, his head cocked to one side. Meenakshi smiled again and patted his cheek. He sighed and reached for the pail to milk the water buffalo while Meenakshi went to the temple.

For many weeks early in Meenakshi's other pregnancies, she had felt ill and was unable to eat. But this time everything tasted sweet and delicious, and she felt especially alive and healthy. She found herself daydreaming as she worked in the fields among the other women of the village of Anandanagar, planting rice and sugarcane. And her eyes filled with tears every time she saw a particularly beautiful flower or an unusually magnificent sunset.

Often Sundar asked, "Why are you smiling?" Almost always she was unaware that she had been smiling. But throughout her pregnancy she had felt inexplicably happy.

Meenakshi hurried to the temple at the edge of the village to perform her puja before her sons awoke. She wanted to feed them and her husband before Sundar had to leave to tend the elephants. This was a festival day, but her husband was chief of the Maharaja's mahouts, and he and a few other mahouts could not be spared from looking after the elephants while everyone else attended the feast.

It was the Maharaja Narasimha Deva's birthday. While most ordinary people did not mark their births on a calendar, a maharaja's birthday was one to celebrate. This year the Raja's birthday would be especially joyous, because the Maharani was expecting a child, and the priests had predicted a son. Meenakshi did not want to miss the feast, but she was certain this was the day her infant would arrive. The gentle thumping resumed against her ribs: *tai-taiya-tai, tai-taiya-tai*.

Before India's independence some forty years earlier, the Raja's father had owned the forests of teak and sandalwood that spread from one end of Nandipuram to the other. The government of India owned the forests now that the rajas no longer ruled, and the Maharaja Narasimha Deva was the government's agent for the timber. As a religious leader and the beneficent employer of many of his father's former subjects, he was supreme in the hearts of his people.

Each year the people gathered on top of the hill outside the Raja's palace as flutes warbled and the throaty voices of mridangam drums answered each other back and forth across the tree-covered valley. The Raja was weighed in his ceremonial robes, and the equivalent in gold was distributed to charities and the poor, to schools and temples throughout the region.

According to legend, the first clap of thunder of each year's monsoon was the signal that the gold had been fairly weighed and the gods were satisfied with the Raja's generosity. And the South of India, which had been parched through the long dry season, would prosper by four months of fruitful monsoon rains.

Meenakshi walked awkwardly, holding the offering before her. She smiled, thinking she must look as round as the gentle water buffalo she passed along the way. Monkeys scampered beside her, chattering and bickering over which of them should go first.

She arrived just as the priest, Mr. Balaraman, rang the temple bell. He wore an unbleached dhoti of soft cotton on his hips, three sacred threads over his left shoulder, three stripes of pale sacred ash across his forehead, and his graying hair tied in a loose knot at the top of his head. On legs as gnarled and creased as the trunk of the sacred peepul tree by the temple door, he stood before the stone likeness of Nandi, the soft-eyed bull that carried Lord Shiva from place to place. Incense burned in a brass dish, and perfumed smoke filled the inner chamber of the temple.

The priest took Meenakshi's offering and laid it beneath the kneeling Nandi's nose. Meenakshi tipped her face toward the priest, and he dipped his finger into a pot of red powder and gently pressed a small dot in the center of her forehead, a third eye through which to see the world more clearly.

Meenakshi ran her hands through the smoke from the censer and rubbed it into her face, then turned to hurry cumbrously back along the row of coconut palms to her thatched house at the edge of the village.

She poured four cups of buttermilk from the sweating clay pot in the courtyard, and whisked a pinch of salt into each lassi. Venu, who was born just as the monsoon spread across the South of India two years earlier, and Venkat, who had been born at about the same time two monsoons before that, stepped from the darkness of the mud room, rubbing at eyes stuck shut with heat and sleep.

"When will the birthday celebration begin?" Venkat asked, squinting up at the sky, where the clouds had begun to roll gently, turning from the pearl of dawn to a deepening gray. A pair of clean but tattered shorts hung about his thin hips. His little brother stood naked, but for a black string around his waist. A small silver disk with the likeness of the elephant-headed Ganesha, which was meant to bring good luck, dangled from the string.

"Just never mind. It will be soon enough," Meenakshi said, not meaning to speak sharply to her son. In the heat that came before the monsoon rains, women had to bite their tongues to keep from scolding their children for no reason at all. Some were even tempted to talk back to their husbands.

The air was hot and wet and expectant that morning, and the smoke of a hundred wood fires hung over the village as women prepared special morning meals. The rich smells of idli steaming and spicy sambhar bubbling mingled deliciously with the smoky haze and the sweetness of jasmine and sandal-wood and a breeze heavy with unspent rain.

Outside in the thorny thicket of acacia that separated the village from the fields where the women worked each day, a brain-fever bird shrieked its maddening ascendant call: *sweeeeip-sweeeip-sweeeip-sweeip-sweip-swip-swip-swip!* Meenakshi sat back from the fire where she was frying puri and brushed hair from her forehead with the inside of her wrist. The dough puffed up and sizzled in the hot oil. Sundar sat beside her, cleaning his teeth with a thin stick from the branch of a neem tree. He spat into the fire.

While her sons ate, Meenakshi hurried to feed the water buffalo that stood contentedly inside the courtyard, for she had much to do before Parvati's arrival. She went to the well and filled two red earthen jars with water, bending slightly to one side because Parvati sat upside down in her middle.

Meenakshi returned to find Sundar talking to his sons and carving a likeness of Ganesha from a piece of sandalwood. He turned the pale golden wood this way and that, flicking away tiny bits of sawdust with his gouge as he worked.

"You will go to the festival with Uncle Sathya," Sundar said. "I will come home tonight, after you are asleep. By then you will have a sister."

"Will you bring her home with you?" Venkat asked. Sundar threw back his head and laughed.

"Nay, son," he said. "Your mother will stay here and get her."

"But why can't you come with us?" Venkat asked.

"Because someone must look after the Raja's elephants," Sundar said. "I must do it, just as my father did, and just as you will do one day."

"And will I miss the feast, too?" Venkat asked. Sundar laughed again.

"Not for many years," he said.

Sundar had a tender affection for the gentle elephants, who returned his devotion with an uncanny knowledge of what it was he wanted them to do and enthusiastic performance of their work. He inherited this affinity from his father, who also had taught him to carve, and that was where his true talent lay.

Sundar awoke early each morning and went to work on the family farm before leaving to tend the elephants. All day they hauled sandalwood trees felled by cutters with axes to the riverside to cure. In the long evening hours after the elephants' work was done, Sundar sat among them and kept the fires burning. The elephants were hobbled with chains attached to logs that kept them from wandering far.

For in a time when tigers were endangered throughout India, and the rest of the world as well, in Nandipuram they still crept to the edge of the forest, sleek and golden and glowing with menace, their bellies just inches from the ground. From the center of the stable yard Sundar saw their eyes and long sharp teeth glint beyond the firelight. To pass the time in a way that kept his mind from the tigers, Sundar carved sandalwood statues of Shiva, Ganesha, Nandi, and other Hindu deities to sell to pilgrims who visited the ancient temples of Nandipuram. His carvings were elegant and graceful, and he became well known particularly for his statues of Nataraja, the dancing Shiva.

There were stories that people passing a niche in a certain wall of the village at an odd hour of night sometimes caught a glimpse of a Shiva Nataraja dancing there amid flickers of flame. But if they stopped for a closer look, they saw that they were mistaken, that the statue—which had been carved by Sundar—stood still, and perhaps the fire was simply a reflection that glinted from the wood in the dim light of a lantern beside the lane. Real flames or not, the statues Sundar carved were special in some way that was difficult to define, even if one did not believe statues could dance, and the demand for his dancing Shivas grew and grew.

Sundar stopped talking when he saw Meenakshi. He folded the sandalwood Ganesha into a soft cloth and dusted off his tools, wrapping them in cloth pouches, which he tied together with string. He put the carving and his tools into a cloth bag.

"Priya will be here if you need help," Sundar said, setting his bag aside. The old ayah was a good midwife. He drew Meenakshi inside their small mud house and embraced her. "I'll take the boys to Sathya," he said, brushing the hair away from her face and looking into her eyes. "It will be good to have a daughter to help you with your work." He pulled away then, and went outside.

Meenakshi watched him go, holding a son's hand in each of his own, the cloth bag slung over one shoulder and across his back, toward his brother's house at the other end of the village.

Meenakshi poured water into a plastic basin and washed the breakfast dishes. She swept the courtyard, and went to the field to walk in the hope that she could dislodge her unborn child in time for them both to attend the ritual weighing of the Raja. She was pleased that her baby was to be born on such an auspicious day.

In searing heat under a leaden sky, Meenakshi walked. She sang and she held her aching back and she walked. She heard noisy throngs pass by the trees along the dirt track on their way to the celebration, happy voices and the jangle of silver bangles and ankle bracelets. And still Parvati did not arrive. And Meenakshi cried with disappointment, and she walked.

At about midmorning, when the white wet heat began to press downward like the heel of a giant hand, a crow alit in a palm tree at the edge of the field. Many palms stood between the fields, guarding the edges of the family plots, swaying, the wind clattering lightly through their fronds. Monkeys sat among them and ate bananas stolen from the trees below.

Meenakshi leaned against the trunk of the palm tree in which the crow sat to ease her back, which was stiff and sore from bearing the weight of her infant. The crow cocked his head at her.

"Do you have a seed for an old beggar, sister?" the crow asked, peering down from his perch. In that very same moment Meenakshi felt the first pang that signaled the baby's impending arrival.

"Go away!" Meenakshi said, pulling her sari forward to shade her face from the sun. Overhead the clouds tumbled and rolled in a fast-paced dance across the sky. Meenakshi stood still a moment, rubbing her back and waiting for the pain to ease. "Anyway, it's not planting season," she said to the crow. "I have no seeds."

She gathered the end of her sari over her shoulder and set off again, looking for a quiet place to bring her child into the world. The crow flew down from the tree and hopped toward her with his lurching, stick-legged gait, over the furrows in the rich red soil.

"But I'm starving," he said, cocking his head in the most beguiling way a crow can manage. The sun shone brightly for a moment, turning his feathers from dull black to a shimmering blue-green. "Surely that's not an issue you can ignore!"

Meenakshi stopped mid-stride, and the sun shone on her face in another brief moment of illumination. An otherworldly, faraway look played about her dark eyes. The crow thought that Meenakshi had reconsidered and would take at least a crumb for him from the pouch at her middle, if only to stop his pestering.

Instead Meenakshi stumbled to her knees and rocked forward to rest her hands on the ground.

"Get away," she gasped.

"Starving!" said the crow. "You can't ignore a poor . . ."

"I have other things to worry . . ." But Meenakshi was

unable to finish her sentence for the pain. The crow cawed indignantly and dove at her shoulders.

"What could be more important than a starving brother?" he croaked. He alit on the ground beside her and pecked at her hand splayed before her, then flew up and dove at her head.

Meenakshi tried to stand. But the pain staggered her, and she felt a rush of alarm as she leaned farther forward, stretching her back to ease it. The births of her two sons had not come on with such sudden intensity. The crow continued to peck at her. She ignored him and crawled slowly toward the purple-blossomed jacaranda tree at the edge of the field, and squatted with her back against its smooth gray trunk. The crow retreated to a branch over Meenakshi's head and watched the whole time, cawing petulantly.

With a mighty surge of water and a startling clap of thunder that signified the Raja's gold had been weighed, Meenakshi's infant made her entry into the world.

Meenakshi told Parvati the story of the day of her birth many times as the child grew.

"Ah, Parvati," she would say when she reached this point in the story. "I don't know if the crow caused our troubles. But at least you were born, straight and fine and lovely!"

Parvati always wondered whether her mother hadn't left something unspoken when she ended the story. Might Meenakshi have thought the trouble had started because of Parvati's refusal to arrive in time for the Raja's birthday celebration? Her mother never wavered from blaming the crow.

But make no mistake. Parvati's arrival, whether an accident of timing or the cause, coincided with the worst calamity to inflict wind and water upon Nandipuram in living memory.

Two

Meenakshi sat for a while, inspecting the infant and wiping her dry with a corner of her sari. The rain had begun to fall in great, swollen drops, sending up puffs of reddish dust. Meenakshi's first look into her daughter's face took her breath away. The infant's eyes peered deep into her own, with a more penetrating and intense gaze than any Meenakshi ever had seen. And the infant was beautiful, with a full head of softly curling dark hair and a deep cleft in her delicate chin.

The mother rested and recovered, and by that time the rain had begun to fall in great sheets of water. Meenakshi wrapped Parvati in the end of her sari and crawled to a grove of palms, taking shelter under a large banana leaf. Several monkeys had also taken refuge there. Together they watched the parched earth accept the water, which soon began to churn the ground to mud.

Tears fell from Meenakshi's eyes. Perhaps it was relief that the difficult birth was over and her child was whole and beautiful. Or perhaps it was a premonition of what would follow. The tears were the first of a torrent Meenakshi wept that filled the river and flooded the land.

Meenakshi cut a banana leaf with her knife and held it over her head as she made her way back to the village, her infant bundled in her arms. The rain had turned into a wall of water, and before they were halfway home the wind had shredded the banana leaf to brilliant green striplets. Meenakshi couldn't see more than a few inches in front of her. She pressed Parvati against her breast to keep the rain from stinging her daughter's delicate new skin. Meenakshi ran along the path, for her feet knew their way without the assistance of her eyes.

It was late afternoon when Meenakshi arrived in the village among a crowd of families, who ran with their bright festival clothing plastered against their bodies.

Priya, the old ayah, was already in the courtyard of Meenakshi's house, scurrying back and forth, dragging string cots and jars of milled wheat and lentil flour and rice and bundles of firewood under shelter.

"Something is wrong!" Priya said, her voice crackling with fear. She took the infant from Meenakshi's arms. "Look at the sky!" Priya pointed a crooked dry finger at the sickening green pallor that spread across the sky and darkened in the brief moment before Meenakshi followed the ayah inside the house. It was true, Meenakshi thought, the sky was not the normal bruised bluish-black of the early monsoon.

Priya sat on the edge of the cot and inspected Parvati. As Meenakshi searched the shelf for a clean towel, the old ayah's sharp intake of breath caused her to turn back. Priya was still as a sandalwood statue, staring into Parvati's eyes.

"Such a beautiful child," Priya said softly, her long teeth shifting in the front of her mouth. "Born on such a day . . ." The old ayah looked up at Meenakshi from beneath papery eyelids. Meenakshi's eyes still streamed with tears. "Her life will be either extraordinary or terrible," the old woman muttered, thrusting the infant back into her mother's arms.

The rain did not frighten Parvati. Her arms were round and fat, much more typical of an older infant, and she moved her tiny fists before her face and looked into her mother's streaming eyes.

Venkat and Venu ran into the courtyard just as Priya left.

"Amma!" Venkat shouted. His voice was high with alarm. Venu held the hem of his big brother's shorts in his fist and stumbled along beside him, his other hand sheltering his eyes from the driving rain.

"Here, son," Meenakshi answered, and she held Parvati out for her brothers to see. Venkat peered into his sister's face, and then looked up into his mother's brimming eyes.

"She sees me!" he said in amazement.

"Of course," Meenakshi said softly, wiping absently at the tears on her face with the back of her hand.

Above the hammering of the rain, Meenakshi heard shouting. It was not the joyous clamor that usually greeted the monsoon, with children dancing and women singing, their eyes cast heavenward. In most years everyone was thankful for the end of the hottest, driest season, when water grew fetid in canals and cisterns. These were shouts of alarm as the storm grew in magnitude and intensity.

Sundar's brother, Sathya, stuck his head inside Meenakshi's doorway. He saw the infant wrapped in the towel in his sister-in-law's arms.

"Her name is Parvati," Meenakshi said. Sathya nodded.

"I must get back," he said. "Send Venkat if you need help."

"We will be fine," said Meenakshi, and Sathya hurried away. She laid the infant on her back on the string cot and handed Venkat a towel to dry himself.

"You must sleep," Meenakshi said, taking another towel and rubbing Venu dry. "When we wake up, the storm will be over."

"Amma," Venkat said, "it was the best feast ever. They gave everyone a huge leaf heaped with sweet rice. When the rain came, the people dropped the food and ran because it has never rained so hard!"

"Go to sleep now," Meenakshi said, wiping her face.

"Why are you crying, Amma?" Venkat asked. Meenakshi did not know herself. A kind of dread had come over her.

Venkat tried to tell her more about the celebration, and

Venu wanted to talk, too, their soft high voices tumbling over each other. But Meenakshi was too exhausted, and she hushed them and went to lie beside her infant on the cot.

⟶

At about the same time that Meenakshi's sons had come home that afternoon, just four furlongs away her husband and the other mahouts took the elephants out beyond the sheds where the harvested wood had been stacked to cure, into the forest to cut grass and low-growing shrubs for fodder.

The mahouts stopped by the edge of the river, where they brushed the damp leathery hides of the large, tranquil beasts, and let them loll about in the rain, which the elephants greeted happily, with trunks upraised.

Sundar was troubled by the terrible green light in the sky, and he ordered the mahouts to bring the elephants inside an old fort that they often used as shelter from bad weather. The fort's walls were made of huge blocks of silvery granite from the Deccan Plateau that had stood through centuries of storms, and Sundar thought the animals would be safe there. Then the men ate their own supper of sambhar and rice that had been delivered from the Raja's kitchen, and went to sleep early, the elephants dozing off around them. Some slept on their huge sides, snoring gently like giant babies, and others nodded off where they stood, their young ones under their bellies.

Sundar's first inkling that all was not well came a short time later, not long after dark. The elephants strained at their hobbles and milled about, snorting and trembling, awakening

Sundar from the sound, untroubled sleep of a man who did physical labor. Only then did he hear the wind as it rose from a whistle to a wail.

He pushed open a wooden door to look outside. All around, the lightning flashed in a constant pulsing of purple, illuminating the sight of hundred-year-old trees tumbling into one another as they tore from their roots with a sickening groan. The impact of the ancient trees landing made the earth jump.

The sight of it made Sundar's heart thud against the inside of his chest. He shut the door and leaned his back against it. The stone walls held, but the tree trunks crashed about like so many matchsticks fallen from a broken box.

A large female elephant who had been snorting and shuffling restively lifted her trunk and trumpeted for her infant. Sundar didn't notice, because all the elephants were trumpeting in fear by then. He moved among them, attempting to calm them. The lost little one did not answer its mother, and she trumpeted again and again in a maternal panic.

One by one the elephants broke loose from their hobbles and thundered back and forth in their terror, trampling Sundar into the dust until there was little left of him but shards of bone and pieces of his dhoti and pale blue turban. The other mahouts, who had fled to save themselves, came back when they were unable to make their way to the village through the storm. They collected what remained of Sundar, laid his pieces on a cot, and covered them with his shawl.

A short time later, when the wind slowed to gather itself

for another assault, they carried him to his brother's house in the village.

⟿

Meenakshi lay on her cot with Parvati nursing at her breast, a shawl covering them, and fell into an exhausted sleep. She did not hear the screaming of the wind or the groan of wood as palm trees were uprooted and tossed over the village. She did not hear the collapse of the thatch roof and the mud wall at the end of her room.

Meenakshi did not awaken until Sathya came to take her and Parvati and the boys into his more substantial house for safety from the storm. He had also come on the terrible mission of telling Meenakshi what had happened to her husband.

From the front, Meenakshi's house looked as if it was shut up tight. Sathya could not see the broken wall and collapsed roof at the back. Venkat and Venu huddled together on one small cot, while Parvati and Meenakshi slept on the other.

Sathya pounded against the door, calling, "Meena, sister! Meenakshi! Wake up!" Meenakshi slept so soundly and the wind roared so loudly she did not hear his banging on the door.

At last Venkat came to his mother's bedside, holding Venu on his hip. He shook her by the shoulder. When finally she rolled toward Venkat she saw that his eyes were large and round with fright. And behind her sons she saw the flash of lightning and the water streaming where once there had been a wall.

"Amma!" he said. "Uncle has come. Wake up!"

Meenakshi awakened fully with a start, which the infant felt, and her tiny heart began to race in concert with her mother's. Meenakshi leapt up and, drawing a shawl about her shoulders, waded through ankle-deep water to unlatch the door. Sathya nearly fell inside, rain streaming from his hair and mustaches.

"Meena!" he gasped. "Something terrible has happened." Meenakshi's hands flew up to her face, for, frightened as she was by the sounds of the storm, her heart knew instinctively what her brother-in-law had come to tell her. She saw in a flash her future—in which the main reality was the simple horror that she would never see Sundar again; that he would never hold Parvati in his arms; that her children would grow to adulthood without a father.

Three

Without saying a word, Meenakshi turned deliberately and took an old dhoti of her husband's from a peg beside the cot. She shook it slowly and held it to her face for a second, then lifted Parvati into it and bound the infant tightly against her chest. She moved so very slowly, and Sathya was wild with impatience. He carried a lantern, but the wind had blown it out. Meenakshi's movements looked fractured in the flashes of lightning.

"Hurry, Meenakshi," he said, his voice quavering. "We don't have time." But as if she hadn't heard, Meenakshi bound Venu to Venkat's back, using a tattered shawl, also belonging to Sundar. Then she gathered half a sack of rice and half a sack of lentils.

"We must run for our lives!" Sathya hissed through his teeth. But still Meenakshi's movements were deliberate and slow.

Silently she worked, lashing the sacks to the great gentle buffalo, whose eyes slid from side to side in terror though she stood still in the covered end of the courtyard. Sathya sensed it was futile to attempt to persuade Meenakshi to leave the beast behind, and so he helped her.

When they had finished, Sathya unfurled two umbrellas, handed one to his sister-in-law, and gathered Venu and Venkat under the shelter of his own. Meenakshi refused the umbrella and ran back through the door of her ruined house. Sathya followed her.

"Are you mad?" he demanded. "We have no time!" But Meenakshi ran to the wall above her bed and grabbed up the dancing Shiva statue that Sundar had carved and thrust it into the bundle that contained Parvati tied tightly against her chest.

The rain beat at them first from one side, then from another. Lightning flashed constantly in rhythmic purple bursts, and by its light they saw waves on the river that only hours before had been the lane through the center of the village, lined with shops under open awnings and carts of ripe yellow mangoes under clouds of flies.

Together they made their way, slogging knee-deep in the muddy water, toward Sathya's house, which sat atop a gentle rise at the other end of the village. Every few seconds a gust of wind knocked them a step backward. All around them people ran in the opposite direction, away from the bazaar and away from the river, hauling on bridles and tethers of terrified animals that bawled and rolled their eyes. The water had not risen beyond the foot of the hill, and Sathya's house atop it was dry.

Sathya's wife greeted them at her doorway—the grief-stricken Meenakshi, with Parvati lashed against her breast, and her two sons, who cried because their mother's anguish frightened them nearly as much as the storm, and Sathya, whose face was grim. Their clothing was plastered against their bodies and their hair streamed with water.

Auntie, her own infant daughter wrapped in a shawl and lying in her arms, hurried them inside. She peered into the bundle that was Parvati and the infant peered back at her. The depth of her gaze shocked Auntie. Her own infant, who was named Chitra, was sickly, which her mother attributed to her being female. All three of Auntie's sons had flung their arms out when they were small. Chitra lay quietly, and barely moved. She was difficult to rouse, even to suckle, and when she was awake, her eyes were unfocused and cloudy. But Parvati looked deep into Auntie's eyes, and Auntie had the eerie feeling that the infant could read her thoughts.

"Oh!" was all that Auntie said. And she withdrew into herself for a moment. It was not normal for a child to look into one's eyes so piercingly, Auntie thought. A seed of knowledge planted itself within her—with that first glimpse—that Parvati was to blame for the terrible trouble that already had claimed Sundar and would afflict not only her family and the village but the entire population of Nandipuram.

⁓

Sathya had been the elder of two brothers, and he was known as the cleverer. Sundar, it was said, had been the strong, quiet one—the one people trusted. As a child, Sathya had solved complicated mathematical equations. So impressed was the village schoolmaster that Sathya was sent to the university at a tender age, his tuition paid in full by the government. He joined the Civil Service and lived in a bungalow in the city of Bangalore, many miles away.

Sathya's wife was a village girl, and it turned out that she could never be happy in the city. So Sathya had built Auntie a house of Deccan stone in his humble ancestral village of thatched mud huts. The highland stone was speckled with dots of black and tiny flecks of mica that winked and sparkled in the sunlight. It was a sturdy house, and the only house of any grandeur in the village. People viewed Sathya with a mixture of envy and pride that he was one of them.

Sathya stayed in Bangalore and came home once a week to see his family. But Auntie did not like living in her house of Deccan stone without her husband. And Sathya did not like city life at all—he was homesick for his family, his village, and the farm that he and Sundar had inherited from their father. So Sathya retired early on a modest pension, and came home to live with Auntie in the village, resuming work on the family farm with his brother.

⁓

Auntie tucked Venkat and Venu in beside her own three sons, who shared a wide string cot at one end of the bedroom. Then Auntie rewrapped her infant daughter in a soft gray shawl and placed her in a small swinging cradle beside the stones that Sathya had piled to shield the fire he'd built to defy the deep darkness of the storm. Meenakshi unlashed Parvati from her chest and carried her to where Auntie sat in the sheltered corner of the courtyard beside the fire.

Rain poured into the center of the courtyard, drumming on the paved floor. The wind grew stronger, but carried the rain away from them. The storm showed no sign of abating, but for the moment at least they were dry.

Auntie took Parvati into her fleshy arms and held the infant slightly away from her body, and looked down at her. The infant's cheeks were full and round, not at all like Chitra's cheeks. And the tiny dark eyes found Auntie's eyes and held them solidly and directly, until the woman looked away.

Auntie's first impression was reinforced: this was not an ordinary girl child. She laid the infant across her lap and held her there firmly with one hand. She looked at Parvati from the corners of her eyes. If Auntie had known the baby's mind was recording the events that unfolded around her that day with a comprehension that was unheard of for a newborn, she would have been even more unnerved.

Poor Parvati had no way of knowing that her perceptive abilities were any different from other infants'. What the baby already understood was that the events of the day of her birth had wrought a terrible change in her family's world, and that her aunt, at least, held her responsible for all that had happened.

Sathya led Meenakshi to the corner where the courtyard wall met the house. There, covered with a tattered shawl and pieces of a ruined dhoti, atop a narrow cot, lay the small lumpy heaps that were all that was left of Sundar's body. Shadowy flickers from the fire played across the folds and drapes of his makeshift shroud. A withered clutch of marigolds lay at one end the formless thing on the cot.

"The mahouts brought him to us just after the river began to spread inland," Sathya said softly. Meenakshi knelt beside the head of the cot and flung her arm across the slack space occupied by her husband's remains. The buffalo came and stood over them, and Sathya went back to where Auntie held Parvati on her knees as she rocked her own daughter's cradle with her bare foot.

Sathya had to shout above the storm as he told Auntie of the destruction he'd seen on his way to fetch his brother's family.

"The water poured out of the doors of the shops," he said, "as if——" He stopped in mid-sentence to listen to a high-pitched sound. Pieces of tile from Sathya's roof flew up and over the courtyard, and the wind hurled other tiles downward, smashing them on the floor.

Sathya rushed inside and hauled the sleeping boys out of their bed, roof tiles exploding all around them. He motioned toward a deep fire pit in the center of the courtyard, where Auntie had made soap before the Raja's birthday celebration. Auntie grabbed Parvati, and in the same motion bent forward and scooped her daughter up from the cradle with her free arm. She ran toward Meenakshi and thrust Parvati into her mother's arms. Auntie tugged at her sister-in-law, but Meenakshi did not want to leave Sundar's cot.

"Come, Meena," Auntie shrieked into the wind. She shoved Meenakshi toward the fire pit, which she had covered with woven grass mats to keep it from filling with rainwater before she left for the festivities. Meenakshi went unwillingly and silently, looking back over her shoulder at her husband's shrouded remains. Sathya and Auntie shoved and dragged all of their family members into the soap pit, which smelled acrid, of dead fire and wet ash, and pulled the woven mats over their heads.

That was when the full force of the cyclone struck. The wind lifted the mud and dust and trees and water, air and clouds and fire and darkness, and mixed them in the ferocious beating of a single element—cyclone. It raised the hair on their skin and caused their ears to ache, and their breathing to stop. They all felt certain they would die. The pressure of the storm held the mats down like the lid on a jar of pickles.

Meenakshi sheltered Parvati in her arms and rested her head against her. They felt rather than heard the rest of the tiled roof of Sathya's house fall in. And in lesser tremors, the walls went, one by one.

It's difficult to say whether they slept, or perhaps their senses were so profoundly assaulted by the storm that they had ceased to function. None of them remembered how much time passed or precisely when the storm abated.

Gradually they became aware that the wind had died and

settled into an eerie wail, and they heard the steady drumming of rain on the mats over their heads. It was not the sound of wind in trees or wind in thatched roofs or wind turning the curves of village lanes but of wind blowing over an open plain. By comparison with the ferocity of the cyclone this wind seemed benign.

Slowly they climbed from the pit, hardly able to believe they had survived. The children cried and the adults tried to hush them. Somehow the sun had risen again, though it was hidden behind layers of gray, teeming clouds. By an inexplicable coincidence of nature, one corner of Sathya's house remained standing—two bits of outside wall with a triangle of roof sheltering it. Timbers and stone littered the still-standing corner of the courtyard. Sathya took a splintered beam and pulled it aside, and another piece of the roof crashed down beside where he stood.

There, behind the timber, under the triangle of the sheltering roof, Sundar's remains still lay—by some minor miracle—undisturbed on the cot, the buffalo stunned but still standing beside him.

Sathya was awed that anything stood at all—and that the buffalo had survived a storm so other-earthly. His eldest son, Mohan, reached to touch the beast to be sure his eyes did not deceive him. Otherwise there was nothing recognizable in sight—not a tree, not a house, not a fence, not a single living being—only a sea of lapping brown water as far as they could see from the top of Sathya's hill.

The storm had destroyed everything: the village, fields,

forests, and crops. Entire families and flocks of sheep and cows and goats and chickens simply disappeared, snatched up by the wind and flung away.

Since there never had been a cyclone in Nandipuram, the people had been taken totally unaware. But in truth there was little anyone could do against such a storm.

The rain fell harder, and Sathya feared they would be caught in a rising flood if they did not find higher ground. He motioned to his wife, who gathered the others together and herded them into the corner of the shelter beside Sundar's shrouded remains and the water buffalo. Sathya went away, hushing Auntie's protests.

The rain steadied into what seemed like a normal monsoon downpour. Once again they lost all sense of time, and it was difficult to know how long they huddled there in the miracu-lously still-standing corner. The air was filled with water—water falling from the sky in thick curtains and rising again in brown clouds so thick that breathing felt like drowning.

Several times during the day, Meenakshi held Parvati to her breast, where the infant nursed hungrily. Auntie eyed her sister-in-law suspiciously. How could a grieving wife—thin and frail as she was, who had eaten nothing in more than a day, and who had suffered such a shock as the death of her husband—how could she have enough milk to satisfy an infant? The other children cried that they were hungry. There was nothing for them to eat but the raw rice and lentils still lashed to the buffalo's sides. There was no wood for a fire to cook over, and no place dry enough to make one.

After some time Sathya came back. He was muddy and wet, and his eyes were tired.

"The rain has slowed some, and the water is not so deep," he said. "The village is gone. But there are other survivors, and there is shelter and food on the hillside near the palace. I think we can walk there."

"But the children . . ." said Auntie.

"We can carry the infants and the others can ride the buffalo," Sathya said. "Mohan and I will take the cot with Sundar's body. But we must hurry. If the rain begins to fall heavily again, this hillock could be swept away, and us with it!"

Sathya lifted Venu and Venkat and his two smaller sons onto the buffalo's back and lashed them there among the bags of food and the cookpot. Sathya and his eldest son carried Sundar's remains, each holding an end of the cot above his head. Meenakshi carried Parvati, and Auntie carried Chitra.

And so together they made their slow, sad, sodden way down the small hill, into the water. At the bottom of the hill the rain and river waters swirled around the thighs of the adults, almost to the belly of the buffalo. The mud sucked greedily at the bottoms of their feet.

A torn tree limb with a chicken roosting in its branches floated past among logs and the intimate ruins of people's lives—a kitchen basket with flat and soggy puri half covered by a white cloth, a straw doll with round black beads for eyes, a bright orange scarf, a blue plastic washbasin. A small bed lay wedged against a jagged tree trunk, its sheet trailing in the water's flow.

Their progress was slow as they pushed through the driving rain and the current of the flooded river to the foot of the very large hill atop which stood the Opal Palace and Fort of the Maharaja Narasimha Deva. They looked up at the white marble walls, crenellated and magnificent, with delicate domes and arched turrets. The palace and fort appeared undamaged, regal as ever, protected by the gods, who had spared little else.

Above them the air was crowded with the great feathered bodies of vultures, circling endlessly, looking for corpses that had been washed away. The enormous birds perched, malevolent and majestic, on the parapets of the palace and on the poles that supported the canvas shelter the Raja's soldiers had raised over the parade ground, where, only the day before, the Raja had celebrated his birthday among his people. One vulture hopped brazenly up to a group of children who sat at the edge of the shelter to see whether they were edible yet. A woman came shrieking after the thick-bodied bird and it hopped lazily away, as if to say there was time to wait.

About half of the shelter was made of red, blue, yellow, and green pandal, gaily embroidered tents that normally were set up for feasts and celebrations. The primary colors throbbed against the gray-brown of the floodwaters below and the blue-gray sky above. The rest of the shelter was made of drab army tarpaulins and tents the color of the mud at their feet.

The pandal filled quickly with the drenched and exhausted remnants of families. By the time Sathya and his clan arrived, they could find barely enough room to huddle together beside the cot bearing the rumpled heap of Sundar's remains.

The men thumped the undersides of the pandal with bamboo rods to keep the water from collecting and leaking down on everyone. But leak it did, and for the first weeks of Parvati's life she never knew what it was to be dry.

From the moment Meenakshi learned of her husband's death she had kept a vigil of silence—even her tears were shed quietly—and the one thing about those terrible hours after Parvati's birth that the infant could not remember was the sound of her mother's voice. Meenakshi's face was drawn and pale, and she moved through the encampment like a ghost, as if her feet didn't touch the ground.

She fed Parvati and wrapped her away again in her shawl, she milked the buffalo and cooked rice and lentils under the shelter of the pandal, but she never said a word. She fed her sons and collected rainwater and looked over to the head of her husband's cot, where she longed to keep watch beside him.

But there was no time for grieving, and Meenakshi was as busy that day as everyone else trying to learn how they would survive. Meenakshi had been one of only a few people with the presence of mind—even in her grief—to gather up food, and the people who took shelter on the side of the Raja's hill were very hungry. Most had not eaten since the day before, when they had celebrated His Excellency's birthday.

Meenakshi cooked pot after pot of rice. She dipped her metal measure into the woven brown bag that she'd brought lashed to the water buffalo's side, dumped it into rainwater heated over fuel provided by the palace, and sprinkled in some lentils from the other bag. She scooped it out again when it was cooked, heaping cupful after cupful into each outstretched bowl or plate or bare hand that presented itself. Meenakshi did not even pause to consider where all of the rice and lentils came from. She'd brought two half bags, and two half bags they remained, as one pot was cooked, and then another, throughout the day.

The seemingly endless supply of Meenakshi's rice and lentils, which no one thought to comment upon in the pressing need of that terrible first day, was looked back upon later as the first of many small miracles that surrounded the family amid the tragedy that followed the cyclone.

All during that day Meenakshi's dark eyes stared straight ahead, never blinking, never moving from side to side or up and down. Her eyes seemed no more than vehicles for tears.

In normal times Sundar's body would have been cremated the day of his death, and his ashes scattered in the river. As soon as Sathya saw his family was settled he went into the crowd that had gathered at the makeshift camp to find a familiar face. Mr. Balaraman, the priest and caretaker of the small temple that Meenakshi had visited the day before in Anandanagar, returned with Sathya and talked to Meenakshi for a while.

"We must release the deceased before the sun sets," Mr. Balaraman said. Meenakshi said nothing. She stood silently before him with her head bowed. Mr. Balaraman found the other priest who had fled with him from the temple, and they led the small, dignified procession down the hill, through the rain, to the edge of the floodwaters.

It was a treacherous walk of only a few dozen yards from the bottom of the hill to where the water flowed, brown and strangely calm, toward the sea, far away beyond the hills.

Sathya and Mohan and two other men from the village of Anandanagar quietly bore the body of Parvati's father on his cot over their heads. Venkat and Venu came next, looking brave and solemn. Meenakshi stumbled after them, weeping silently, her head bowed, supported in the arms of village women, one of whom also carried Parvati. Auntie carried her own daughter, and her smaller sons came behind, followed by a group of mahouts and carvers who had known and respected Sundar and had heard his soul was about to be set free into the light.

Since there was not enough dry wood, there was no question of cremation. But a piece of paper was produced and twisted into a thin taper. Someone from the village pushed Venkat's shoulder, urging him forward to light it. Uncle Sathya guided Venkat's hand as he touched the thin yellow flame to the sodden dhoti that was his father's makeshift shroud, as if lighting a funeral pyre on the cremation ghat beside the river. The small purifying flame spluttered and died against the wet cloth. Venkat's eyes were large and round and solemn, and all the while he looked across Sundar's body and up at his mother, who slumped against the women, the end of her sari drawn loosely over her face.

Meenakshi broke away from the cocoon of arms that held her, a terrible wail wrenching itself from somewhere deep within her. She flung herself across the cot and her poor husband's sparse remains until the women pulled her back again. Parvati saw it all and remembered.

Mr. Balaraman stood to one side, bald and bare-chested but for the cotton threads that ran across his shining wet shoulder and looped over his right hip, the sacred threads of the upper castes. A faded smudge of sacred ash blurred across his forehead. The second priest stood opposite him, on the other side of the mourners. Their voices rose and fell as one in a melodic chanting of sacred verses.

Mr. Balaraman nodded toward Sathya, and he and Mohan tipped up the end of the cot. Sundar was borne away, shroud and all, on the sucking brown water.

Up and down the river other groups assembled in a similar fashion to release the bodies of their family members, praying and chanting, the women wailing.

The river contained many corpses that day—the bodies of cows and monkeys and goats and sheep and human beings bobbed along, side by side, amid the beams of houses, entire trees, an occasional jatka still attached to its horse. It seemed almost as if Sundar joined company more lively than that which he left behind. His family and acquaintances watched, and each of them felt small and alone, like an insignificant fleck in the large and swirling universe.

The evening of Sundar's funeral, Meenakshi returned to life. She sat on the ground and pressed moldy wheat flour and water into wafers to cook over the fire. Her eyes blinked and moved the way other people's did. But they did not fill with tears as they had since the monsoon rain had begun to fall.

When Meenakshi stopped crying, the rain stopped for a while. Until then Parvati had known only the sound of the rain and her mother's crying. The next morning Meenakshi took Parvati into her arms and smiled down at her daughter. The child's gaze was so intent and serious that Meenakshi laughed. Parvati smiled back at her mother, and the future no longer looked like the blackness beyond that minute. It was something to live for.

Four

A rumor spread throughout the camp that during the cyclone the wife of the Raja had given birth to a sickly male child who was unlikely to live. Since the Maharaja had only daughters, the birth of an heir to carry on the traditions of the former kingdom would, under ordinary circumstances, have been marked with unprecedented celebration. But the birth of a weakling would-be heir in a time of terrible despair was almost an unbearable thought to the people of Nandipuram, who already had more woe and sorrow than it seemed they could manage. And so news of the birth of the tiny Yuvaraja barely registered amid the mourning and suffering.

The Raja ordered more rice, chickpeas, lentils, flour, and

firewood delivered to the refugees—they were all that was left of his people. Families set out pots to catch water for drinking and cooking and bathing. A few, like Parvati's family, had managed to save a buffalo, and milk was shared all around the camp. Life for the refugees settled into a grim routine.

A kitchen was set up with a common fire in the middle of the camp where the refugees took turns preparing the food that had been given by the Maharaja. The pots were filled with a watery stew and distributed, one to each family. People sat in scattered circles, and ate hungrily but politely. Those who had no bowls ate directly from the pots. Each person waited a turn until the pot was empty again.

Auntie tried to feed her daughter. She held Chitra to her breast long after the infant was asleep, jostling her and trying to make her suckle, but the infant grew weaker by the day. Still Auntie held her and encouraged her to nurse until tears streamed down her face.

Meenakshi's milk flowed plentiful and sweet. But when she held her arms out to take Chitra from Auntie to feed her on whatever might be left in her breast, Auntie pressed her lips together and shook her head.

The patter of rain on the pandal became the most familiar sound to Parvati. Blue powdery mold formed on the tent poles, and black spots appeared on the tent walls, and the musty smell of damp and mildew seemed perfectly normal to her.

And so did her mother's pleasure when she looked at her daughter seem perfectly normal, and welcome, after Parvati's first two days of life had passed in the shadow of Meenakshi's sadness. At night, after everyone else was asleep, Meenakshi washed Parvati with the last of the water from cooking the evening meal. She left the infant unwrapped afterward, her arms and legs free for some time, and gazed with wonder at the perfect small body.

"There is no one to provide money, to make decisions, to look after us," Meenakshi whispered close to her daughter's face. "And yet I feel we are safe. God will protect us."

Meenakshi sang softly to Parvati in the night. She sang songs of Krishna, the handsome blue-skinned god who played his flute and entranced the young girls who kept the village goats. She told her the stories of Shiva, how the river Ganges flowed from his hair, how he crushed the demon of darkness beneath his feet, and kept the earth spinning as he danced his dance of eternal destruction and re-creation. And Meenakshi told Parvati about how kind Sundar had been to her, how she had loved him.

Night after night the two lay together, and Parvati gazed at the red and blue and yellow triangles and stripes sewn into the tent above them. She had no other knowledge of her father, except as the lifeless form that they had dumped into the river as the priests chanted.

Auntie watched Meenakshi and Parvati, and her suspicions about her sister-in-law and niece deepened. It was not normal, Auntie thought, that a new widow should look so happy, her skin so radiant and her eyes shining—more like a bride than a widow. It pained her that Meenakshi did not show more respect for her dead husband.

Whenever Auntie looked at Parvati, she had the distinct impression that Parvati could read her thoughts. Meenakshi also had that impression, but unlike her sister-in-law's, her thoughts were of the sort a person would not mind so much having read. It was disconcerting, but once she became accustomed to the infant and her knowing look, Meenakshi rejoiced at having borne such an unusual child, and her heart continued to mend.

Several days after Sundar's funeral, Meenakshi brought some cooked rice to where the Viswanathan family was camped. They sat together talking quietly among themselves. Two of the smaller children chased around the outside of the circle of their relatives.

"Namaskaram," Meenakshi said, pressing her hands together and greeting them warmly, for the Viswanathans had always been kind to her. There was no reply. "We had some rice left," she began. Mrs. Viswanathan pulled the end of her sari down to hide her face and turned away from Meenakshi. One by one her daughters and daughters-in-law did the same. Meenakshi leaned forward to offer the rice again, and Mrs. Viswanathan turned aside without uncovering her face.

No one would look at Meenakshi, and she backed away, unable to comprehend why they behaved so strangely. Meenakshi began to notice that when she walked among other neighbors and acquaintances from Anandanagar, they turned away from her. In her presence they fell into a hush. They stared frankly at Parvati. People stopped offering them food and solace, and Meenakshi began to feel uncomfortable among her neighbors. Not only did many avoid her but the women hid their faces and the faces of their babies when they could not help walking past the widow and her daughter.

Auntie kept silent. When Meenakshi spoke to her sister-in-law, the reply was a grunt. Only Sathya was kind to Meenakshi. But even he looked uncomfortable in his brother's widow's presence.

Just when it seemed nothing worse could befall the people of Anandanagar, disease struck. First some of the elderly survivors stopped eating food that grew fouler with each passing day of rain and wet air. And it soon became evident more was wrong than that, when the children of the village grew listless and weak.

First Venu fell ill. He writhed on the string cot, clutching his stomach. He was unable to swallow anything, and Meenakshi sat up late into the night, slipping spoonfuls of water between his swollen lips.

Then one of Sathya's sons—the middle one, Satish—was sick. Sathya sat by his son's bed. Day by day Satish grew weaker and thinner, until finally one day he simply disappeared. Auntie beat her breasts and wailed into the night.

"Why my son?" she cried. "Why me?" Meenakshi tried to hold Auntie in her arms and murmured softly to console her. But Auntie pushed her away roughly, and Meenakshi left her alone with her grief, sitting nearby in case her sister-in-law should need something.

Sathya sat silently, saying nothing, his head down. Auntie

was consumed with grief for her middle son—he'd been so sweet, so full of fun, the light in her life.

And then Chitra died. The morning after her brother's death the poor, thin infant with the withered face of an old woman did not awaken.

"You!" Auntie shrieked, pointing a finger at Meenakshi, who sat nursing Parvati. "You breathed her air, you fed that—that child!—all there was to eat. You took the lives of my children! *My* children!" Auntie collapsed against Sathya.

"She doesn't mean it," Sathya said, tears streaming down his face. "She doesn't know what she's saying."

"It's all right," Meenakshi said.

For the first time Parvati was left alone with her brothers and two cousins, Mohan and Mahesh, on a blanket in the clearing the family occupied in the camp, while Auntie and Amma and Uncle went out with Chitra wrapped in a shawl. Chitra had been a tiny thing, quiet and still, with large dark eyes. When they returned, Auntie sat on the floor and cried, rocking back and forth, her head rolling as her body moved. And Parvati realized that Chitra, too, was gone, her eyes closed forever.

Parvati lay on her back that evening, rhythmically kicking her arms and legs into the air. Somehow she had been the cause of even more destruction, although she hadn't meant to be, any more than she had willed the cyclone into being. In the vague way that very small children have of sensing things, Parvati worried that they might take her out, as they had Chitra, and that they would not bring her back, leaving her somewhere, still and lifeless in a shawl.

Day by day the gruel got thinner and thinner. Flesh drew taut over muscle and bone, faces stretched into gaunt grins of hunger. With the exception of Parvati, for her mother's milk continued to flow thick and sweet, though no one could say exactly why this was so.

Food from the Maharaja Narasimha Deva slowed to a trickle. The Raja sent his men to tell them the palace food stores had been depleted. The meager resources of Sathya's family were being used up, and for miles around there was nothing to buy to feed hungry families.

It was said that hunger and disease had taken up residence in the palace, too. The infant son of the Raja had fallen ill with the disease marked by a cramped belly and wasting flesh. Fears grew in the former royal household that the son of their beloved Raja would not survive.

Then, by what some of the villagers saw as another small miracle, Venu began to recover. His stomach stopped rejecting everything that went into it and his fever broke, and soon he was wanting to play with his cousins.

The day Venu got up from his bed, Sathya and Auntie and Meenakshi talked late into the night, whispering in the tightly drawn circle of their few possessions in the camp near the Raja's palace. Auntie cried, and Meenakshi and Sathya fell silent. Over Auntie's protests they had decided: When the time came to leave the camp, there was nothing to do but combine the fortunes of the two families and rebuild the house of stone and live in it together.

Finally the river retreated and confined itself once again behind its banks. And the survivors of Anandanagar returned to the village to see what could be salvaged of their lives. Sathya and Auntie and Meenakshi and the children came back together, the family fewer by two children, leading the water buffalo.

At first they thought they had come to the wrong place. Instead of palm-thatched roofs over mud and dung walls there was nothing but the stinking corpses of people and cows and goats and dogs and chickens and monkeys that had drowned in the floods. They did not lie upon the soothing green grass that had always surrounded the village, or under the gently waving palm trees that had marked the boundaries and protected the houses. The bodies were half-buried in a heavy sludge of drying mud that bolted up and cracked under the power of the sun, which shone with a terrible ferocity when the rain stopped for a day or two.

The first task was to collect the bodies for burning. The Raja sent his men with Sundar's elephants to gather burnable wood that lay scattered far and wide by the storm. The elephants returned, straining against their harnesses, dragging bundles of logs lashed together, sending up clouds of dust behind them.

The men of the villages stacked the logs into funeral pyres higher than the heads of the elephants, and laid the disintegrating bodies of their friends and relatives atop the wood. The huge communal pyres burned for days, their black smoke curling and twisting upward in spirals. The rain came and extinguished the fire, leaving bodies half-burned. The dust and crusted earth turned to mud once again. And the smell of charred wood and flesh hung over the villages of Nandipuram for weeks afterward.

As assistance began to flow in from neighboring districts, the Raja resumed sending food to the people of Anandanagar and the other ruined villages. The Raja's men also delivered tools and baskets and cartloads of dung and straw for the villagers to mix with dirt and water to rebuild the walls of their houses. There was no thatch, and so the new roofs also were made of mud. The men mixed the mud in the center of the village, and the women carried round, flat baskets filled with the muck atop their heads, back to where their houses once stood.

Bit by bit the village was rebuilt. But the place that grew up where the old one had been was a wretched place. The floods had taken everything—even the land had washed away, so there was no decent soil in which anything might grow for some time to come. With nothing taking root in the earth, the powdered mud was caught up in the wind—the gentle breeze that once blew across the villages carrying the scent of sandalwood from the forest and jasmine from the hedge along the road. The dust now penetrated every pore of every miserable person until even their teeth were dun-colored.

Cousins of Sathya and Sundar who lived outside the devastated area came with donkeys and tools and bales of straw. They set to work with Sathya and his sons to rebuild the house of Deccan stone. When it was finished, they added a room of mud and dung and straw to the back of the house for Meenakshi and Venkat and Venu and Parvati to sleep in.

The monsoon rains welled up again and Meenakshi's room began to crumble. There was not enough buffalo dung to make cement to repair it properly, for their one water buffalo produced only so much dung, and that had to be dried and used as fuel for cooking. Before long Meenakshi and Parvati had to sleep huddled against the stone wall that adjoined Sathya's house in order to stay dry. Venkat and Venu moved inside the house to sleep in the wide bed with their cousins.

In the night Meenakshi and Parvati often heard Auntie pour out her bitterness on the other side of the wall.

"That wretched child is so greedy—she's the only one among us who is healthy. And where does Meenakshi get her milk? She eats nothing herself. Her breasts are flat as mine. I've lost another tooth. Mahesh's arms are so thin I can circle them with two fingers. We're feeding your sister-in-law and her child and starving our own children!" Uncle tried to hush her, but Auntie wept through many nights.

Meenakshi held Parvati against her, covering her daughter's ears to keep her from hearing. But Parvati heard and remembered. After Auntie's anguish had spent itself, Parvati and Meenakshi slept with one eye open. In the middle of the night they heard the rain fall very close to where they lay. And once again Parvati did not know what it was to be dry.

On the wall opposite the bed beside the hole that got wider and wider as it rained and rained, Meenakshi had carved a niche. In it she placed her most valued possession, the sandalwood image of Lord Shiva, one slender leg lifted gracefully before him as he danced within the halo of the eternal fires that had given birth to all the earth.

At night after Meenakshi was asleep, Parvati's eyes focused on the dancing Shiva at the center of the shining halo of fire. The statue's feet moved furiously, and the earth spun beneath them, and the fire danced and reflected from his raised arms. In one hand he held a small drum. A cobra wound around that arm, and a second hand held a dish of fire. The palm of the third hand faced forward, and in its center sat the third eye of enlightenment. The fourth hand curved in the graceful arc of the dance.

Parvati did not know the formal symbolism of Shiva—that he was god of destruction, in which all things are created anew, and also that he was lord of dance—or that a statue made of sandalwood couldn't really dance. As she lay beside her mother, she simply gazed with wonder at the beautiful statue as he danced his enigmatic dance among the flames.

Sathya prevailed upon Auntie to swallow her bitterness. He was kind and generous with Meenakshi and her children. He and Auntie shared what food and water they had with their in-laws. But Auntie shared only out of a sense of duty. She pressed her lips into a thin line when Meenakshi and she worked together, seldom speaking to her sister-in-law. And Auntie avoided Parvati altogether, refusing to pick her up or help with her care in any way.

The food was plain: rice and dried lentils, with no seasonings. Everything else they were used to eating had washed away. Mail service had been suspended, and along with it, Uncle Sathya's pension payments. In any case, they were unable to get to a bazaar where these things might be available. There were no fresh fruits or vegetables, no salt, no sugar, no spices of any kind.

The buffalo ate only pieces of straw and bits of broken baskets the boys found in their scavenging in ever-widening circles around the village. Finally little nubs of grass began to take root here and there in the dried mud. The buffalo ate them quickly, so they had no time to thrive. The great gentle beast grew thinner by the day, yet like Meenakshi she produced plenty of sweet fresh milk, on which the family survived.

The animals of the forest had either died in the storm or been driven away by the floods. Those that returned were nearly starving, preying on the weak. In the night the villagers heard the cries of deer as they were killed by tigers. And then early one evening a child from the village was taken.

Some weeks after Sathya and his family moved back into the village, Sathya went to the district capital to look for work, for it had become all too clear that his family could not rebuild the farm, even when his pension resumed, without an income. Meenakshi and Auntie had built a small fire of buffalo dung and set a pot of water to boiling for rice. The sun lowered toward the horizon, where it lolled like a giant opalescent bubble, its light filtered through the haze of the pulverized mud that still hung in the air. Parvati lay on the ground, atop her father's dhoti, her tiny round arms and legs beating freely at the air.

Suddenly from the direction of where the forest had been they heard the sound of pounding feet—and screaming.

"Subash! Subash has been taken!" shouted a thin little voice. The dust that had just settled from the day rose again as people came from their fires to see what the commotion was about.

"He was coming back from the river with water," said Subash's sister, who stood amid a growing crowd at the foot of the hill upon which Sathya's house sat. The girl was breathless from having run all the way to the village, and she had difficulty talking. "The tiger was like a streak of fire, he came so swiftly," she said. Then she began to sob. The neighbors made soothing sounds as she went on crying for a while.

"He hit Subash from behind with such force it knocked his water jars high in the air, and they shattered. The tiger took Subash by the back of his neck and carried him off in his jaws like a mouse. Subash kicked and screamed, but the tiger would not let go!"

The men of the village set off with torches and staves and sickles, their tools the only weapons they owned. Later that night, when they returned, the men told of a trail of blood, a tattered dhoti, and otherwise not a sign of the tiger or of the unfortunate Subash.

Two days later, another child was taken.

Five

The tigers crept closer than they had ever come before. Every night Meenakshi and Sathya and Auntie and the children were awakened by a hungry roar. Meenakshi was afraid to sleep, for the hole growing in her wall left them exposed. She brought things she'd found stuck in the mud during the day to block the hole: a piece of a cot, a branch broken from a tree, shards of pots, palm fronds. But in her heart Meenakshi knew these things offered little protection.

One night a large tigress lay very near the corner of Uncle Sathya's mud courtyard wall, waiting for some unfortunate villager to come out to relieve himself in the darkness. But everyone was too frightened to leave the safety of their houses, and the tiger grew frustrated. Meenakshi and Parvati heard her pant as she lay waiting.

Weak with hunger, the tigress gave a small cough, and the bone-rattling *chuff* reverberated inside Meenakshi's chest, and she felt as if the powerful beast dwelt within her own body.

Fear of the tigers drove the villagers into a state of desperation. And so it was that the Maharaja Narasimha Deva visited the district collector and asked permission to organize a hunt for the child-eating tigers.

When the rajas were sovereign rulers, a shikar was an occasion for lavish entertainment. But in modern times the government protected tigers, and hunting them was forbidden—except upon occasions like this. The collector asked the Raja to invite a few marksmen to join Indian Army sharpshooters from a post near Bangalore.

The Raja ordered only the most necessary preparations to be made for his guests. Normally the open space around the palace pulsed with a profusion of color before a hunt, with elaborate, many-chambered tents set up for visitors. But on this occasion only a few dull rows of military bivouac tents sat like sentinels at the foot of the hill to accommodate those who lived too far to travel home at night.

Visitors began to arrive in a straggling procession. The guests were shocked and sickened into silence by the death and chaos they saw as they passed through Nandipuram. Many of them had suffered flooding in their own lands, but nothing like this.

Some of the visitors arrived by automobile. Several guests

came by elephants they'd brought to join the hunt. They wound their way among the strange new ravines carved by the floods in the wild and barren plateau that once was a majestic forest. Now it was a place where only scorpions and tigers could survive. Instead of laughing faces with soft eyes, the visitors saw people with spindly bones and parched eyes.

Early the morning of the hunt the dew hung heavy on the tents. The mahouts brought the elephants for the huntsmen, who waited on elevated platforms shuffling their feet, talking soberly. The elephants sank to their knees before the platforms and the mahouts climbed up and sat on their necks. The khaki-turbaned sharpshooters and the Raja's guests, wearing topees to protect their heads from the sun, settled into the bolstered howdahs. Bearers handed up shotguns and baskets of food and bottles of water.

They set out amid the groan of wood against elephant hide, the squeak of leather harnesses, the smoky voices of the mahouts, and gentle snorts as the elephants cleared their trunks.

The beaters spread out silently, like a human net across the ruined forest. The heat rose with a shimmer through a mist that portended rain. The beaters wore white turbans, and many wore masks painted with fierce faces on the backs of their heads to discourage the tigers' attacking from behind, which was often the way of man-eaters.

When the net of men had drawn around an area a mile across, the beaters clashed their cymbals and beat their drums and blew bamboo whistles, working up to a din that would frighten the tigers from their hiding places.

At the end of the day the buffalo staked as bait still stood sleeping in the heat, whisking her tail at the flies that lit on her shiny black hide.

On the second day the shikaris assembled and the beaters fanned out again, this time to the south of Anandanagar. When the beaters had tightened their circle, a tiger roared a loud and fearsome roar, as pervasive as thunder, and the entire shikar fell silent.

The mahouts dug their toes into the skin behind the elephants' ears and urged them deeper into the ruined jungle until they came to a mass of fallen tree trunks lodged in a ravine. A second roar came from the tangle of timber. The elephants trembled, and it felt as if the earth shook, with the roars of the tiger thundering through their bodies and the quaking of the elephants beneath them.

The lead elephant, which carried the Raja, rolled up her trunk and sucked on the end of it and swayed back and forth with fear. The Raja spoke to the mahout, who thumped the elephant on the head with his long curved pike. The animal moved forward obediently, sides still quaking, offering herself, the mahout, and the Raja as bait.

The elephant's front legs went rigid just as the tiger sprang out from under the pile of logs and clawed his way up her trunk. On the elephant next to them the Raja of Rajpipla put the stock of his fine English shotgun against his cheek, took careful aim, and put a ball of shot through the tiger's magnificent orange-and-black head. The cat paused in his ascent of the elephant's trunk, and Rajpipla fired again.

The tiger fell backward just as he reached the elephant's forehead, nearly face-to-face with the mahout. The tiger held on for a millisecond longer, the claws of one huge paw embedded in the muscle of the elephant's trunk, before he fell dead at her feet. They all stood frozen for a moment. Then the elephant relaxed her trunk, and heaved a great sigh, and her quaking ceased.

"Hut!" the mahout commanded. He placed his bare foot into the fleshy crook of the elephant's trunk, and she lowered him to the ground. He slid his hand down her trunk as he went, gently touching the deep red holes left by the tiger's claws, as if his fingertips could heal them.

At the end of the second day of the shikar only the one tiger had been taken. The trackers returned with the tiger hanging topside down, his paws lashed together over stout poles carried on the shoulders of ten bearers. The enormous head of the cat lolled and bumped the ground. Blood dripped from his triangular pink nose, and his fur was matted and bright crimson around a gaping hole in the side of his neck. The tiger had grown so thin from hunger his ribs stuck out like cookpots on either side.

The following day the heat had risen and steam poured from the cracked earth. Large clouds of flies buzzed around the hunting party, making everyone miserable. By afternoon a deluge forced the hunters back to the palace and the hunt was called off.

That evening the shikaris drifted away as quietly as they'd come. There was no feast, no dancing, no music.

In the long days and nights that followed the terror of the tigers, the village strained toward normalcy, a dark and quiet cloak of grief enfolding its inhabitants.

As people passed through the crooked lanes at night on their way from working to reclaim fields or digging new wells, the sound that grew most familiar from open doorways was the weeping of women. Children played quietly alone or in pairs, and happiness was a stranger in the cyclone-ravaged villages of Nandipuram.

Each morning Meenakshi fed Parvati at her breast and ate a thin paste of moldy rice before feeding her sons. There were no flowers and fruit for offerings, and so going to the temple seemed pointless. Meenakshi saved a bit of rice from her breakfast, offering it in her puja before the Shiva Nataraja statue in her room. Then she wrapped Parvati in her dead husband's dhoti, and joined Auntie to meet up with the men and women who gathered in the center of the village.

As they walked, Meenakshi thought of other mornings that seemed long ago, not just weeks before. She remembered the air was warm and damp and expectant, and the smoke of a hundred wood fires hung over the thatch-roofed huts as women prepared their families' morning meals.

Life was simple but good in the days Meenakshi remembered. She and the other women of the village walked to the fields, their hoes over their shoulders, singing. They looked like a meadow of flowers with their bright saris drawn up over their heads, the ends secured between their teeth as they planted and harvested. Meenakshi hurried home in the evenings, anticipating Sundar's return for supper. Afterward he sometimes took Venkat and Venu back with him to the edge of the forest to feed the elephants.

These days the women still wore the saris they had wrapped about themselves the morning of the Raja's birthday celebration. Now their garments were the color of the mud and dust that permeated their skin, their fingernails, and hair. The tattered remains of their clothing clung loosely to their protruding ribs and hips.

In earlier times the women gossiped as they worked, and the murmur of their talk and laughter hovered like a mist over the fields. Now they worked in silence, the only sound the chunk of their hoes against the dried mud. Before, two women left the fields at noon to return to the village to pre-pare rice and vegetables and lentils and tea. They carried it steaming in tin boxes suspended from either end of bamboo poles back to the others, and shared it at the edge of the fields.

Now they worked throughout the day without food or rest and were weak with hunger by the time they headed home in silence. There was scarcely enough food for two meals a day.

Each day Meenakshi left Parvati tied in her father's dhoti to a string cot in the shade of a ruined wall that stood beside the field. She propped the statue of the dancing Shiva within Parvati's view. She and Auntie hooked the water buffalo to the plow and Meenakshi guided it, pulverizing the dried mud into soil. As she worked, Meenakshi kept her eye on Parvati, who spent her days with eyes fixed on the statue, willing its feet to move. But the Shiva Nataraja never seemed to dance during the day.

By the time Meenakshi returned, the infant had worked her arms and legs free. She beat at the air with her feet and rotated her hands in complex patterns in an effort to induce Lord Shiva to dance.

One evening, as Meenakshi and Auntie returned to Sathya's house, a clod of dried mud struck Meenakshi in the back.

"Witch," someone hissed through clenched teeth. Meenakshi turned, but whoever had thrown it ducked down behind one of the rebuilt walls that lined the village lane. Meenakshi looked at Auntie, who made a small, satisfied growl in her throat without raising her eyes from the footpath. It didn't matter who'd thrown the mud at her, Meenakshi thought. Her own sister-in-law might do the same thing if she had the chance.

Another time a woman whom Meenakshi had known all the years since she came to Anandanagar as Sundar's bride accosted her as she walked with her small brass pot of water to her toilet at first light.

"We should turn you out of the village," the woman said, spitting each word out with hatred.

"Why?" Meenakshi asked. "What have I done?"

"Your infant brought this destruction," the woman said. "You and your children steal food from your in-laws. You're evil. Nothing but trouble has plagued us since that child was born!"

The woman spat in the dust at her feet and stalked off, with Meenakshi staring after her. Meenakshi wondered how long she and her children could survive in the village with such darkness.

Then, amid the grief and anger and pain that had engulfed Nandipuram, Sathya's family's fortunes improved. Although he had not been able to get back his old position—or anything that approached his exalted status before his retirement—he was offered work as a clerk in a government office in the district capital some forty miles away.

Each morning he polished his spectacles, hooked them behind his ears, picked up his briefcase, and secured the crook of his black umbrella over his forearm before saying goodbye and walking to the bus in a crisp new dhoti and stiff brown sandals he'd bought on credit from a newly stocked shop in the bazaar.

He walked almost an hour to the main road to wait for the bus. And then he rode the bus for another hour into the city, where he boarded still another bus that took him to the government office.

When he returned in the evening he had a bundle of rice, some vegetables, and even sometimes a piece of fruit.

The villagers plowed the dried mud into a field of powdery soil. They built canals from the river to the field and berms to hold back the water. They opened the gates and flooded the land, then planted rice seedlings supplied by the Raja. After many weeks of work, the land was coaxed into a brown-and-green patchwork of sprouting rice.

In the first year they had two good crops. The violet plumes of the sugarcane waved over the villages as they had in other years, and the rice paddy produced enough rice for everyone.

Six

Nandipuram began to look like many other poor rural districts, the treeless land divided into fields with people working at harvest and planting time, farmers driving their buffaloes and cows along the road to pasture.

By the time the next year's monsoon arrived, the people of Nandipuram had produced enough rice and sugar to sell. With the money they bought fruits and vegetables and spices and lentils. They bought buffaloes that produced sweet, rich milk. Once again they looked forward to spicy, coconut-flavored vegetable stews and steamed dumplings, and their health began to improve.

In the second year Sathya bought two palm trees and

planted them outside his stone house, and a jasmine vine that he planted beside the gate. It climbed the courtyard wall quickly, and bloomed in the first month. The entire village enjoyed its perfume. Nandipuram came to seem less alien than it had just after the cyclone that had so profoundly changed everyone's lives.

Parvati grew to be a child of sunny disposition, great charm and cleverness, and excellent health. Her mother took delight in her. Because of the terrible circumstances in which Parvati was born people continued to regard mother and daughter with fear and suspicion, and the village children were not allowed to play with Parvati. Her own cousins would have nothing to do with her. And so she tagged after her brothers, who tolerated her in the way older brothers do. Sometimes other boys refused to play cricket with them unless they sent her away, and she would sit watching from a distance.

But Parvati was content to entertain herself. As soon as she was able to stand she played at dancing, holding up one leg until her thigh was parallel to the ground, just as she had observed the Shiva Nataraja statue's leg. She lifted her chin to look out, as Shiva Nataraja did, as if peering into a place beyond this world. But the fire failed to materialize, and Parvati's balance was precarious, which was normal for a two-year-old child. And more often than not she ended up in a dusty heap in the middle of the courtyard.

Meenakshi was the only person who gathered Parvati into her arms to comfort her. And since her mother was away in the fields working most days, Parvati picked herself up and brushed the dust from her knees and tried again. Her brothers laughed at how she never gave up. Other toddlers bumped along after the chickens and other small animals, playing at the work the adults did. Parvati played at things that seemed bizarre—standing on one foot, her arms raised in poses that everyone found laughable.

Her cousins Mohan and Mahesh joined the village boys who tormented Parvati, switching at her legs with sharp-edged reeds from the river's edge.

"Dance!" they'd shout at her. "Let us see you dance!"

Venkat could not bear to see the boys taunting his sister. But when he told them to stop they turned on him with their sharp switches and ugly words.

One evening after dinner, when the boys sat with Uncle Sathya in the courtyard, Venkat decided to speak. Parvati played in the courtyard while her mother and Auntie cleaned the dishes and pots.

"We are cousins," Venkat said mildly, looking Mohan in the eye. "You should keep the other boys from teasing Parvati. Instead, you join them!" Venkat's voice cracked, but he continued to gaze at his cousins steadily.

"Is it true?" Uncle Sathya asked, looking from Mohan to Mahesh and back again. Mohan sighed sharply. "Is it?" Mohan nodded reluctantly. Uncle Sathya stirred the powdery dirt of the courtyard with a stick, and sat thinking quietly for a moment.

"It's your duty to look after your cousin!" he said. "Do you understand?" Mohan nodded again, and Uncle Sathya looked at his younger son, who did everything exactly as Mohan did. "Mahesh?" Mahesh nodded solemnly.

Afterward the cousins did not join their village friends in teasing Parvati, but neither did they defend her against them.

Often Parvati sat beside the hedge playing with the monkeys, who accepted her as one of their own. One female even allowed Parvati to hold her infant in her arms, and Parvati sat with it in her lap like a doll at the side of the track, waiting for her brothers to walk home with her. But, given the child's odd ways, no one thought that this was particularly remarkable.

On a clear sunny afternoon in the autumn after Parvati's fifth monsoon, Meenakshi took her children to stand in line to watch the procession from village to village on the last day of the festival of Dussehra. Thousands of people gathered for the festival, their sandaled feet stirring the dust as they waited expectantly.

In the years since the cyclone had destroyed the forest, the Maharaja Narasimha Deva and his family had celebrated neither the royal birthday nor the Dussehra festival. The Raja gave what he could without fanfare to temples, schools, and the poor. He had declared he would not rejoin the Dussehra procession until his son's illness ended. The people of Nandipuram took the royal family's participation this year as a sign that the Yuvaraja's health was good, and they were filled with joyous anticipation of better times ahead.

As the sun lowered, thousands of little clay oil lamps were

lit along the procession route, and they winked and twinkled as dusk came on. The dust muted the dwindling sunlight, and the air felt like soft fingers on their faces.

From a distance, explosions crackled and boomed overhead in bright fiery sprays of color. The ancient drums of the house of Narasimha Deva boomed, and the crowd fell into a hush as the procession drew near. Venkat lifted Parvati to his shoulders so she could see.

First came rows of camels, gold and blue tassels on their reins and saddles bobbing to the rhythm of their ancient gait. Next came an honor guard on foot in white churidar trousers and long slim jackets of brilliant blue. Men walked on stilts that made them twenty feet tall, and local dignitaries rode in palanquins carried on thick bamboo poles by bearers.

Toward the end of the parade came the Raja's elephant. A helmet of gold and silver set with colored gems covered the massive dome of his skull. On tusks as long as Venkat was tall the elephant wore gold caps, at the end of which hung tassels made of strings of jasmine and wisps of tinsel. His oiled skin gleamed darkly, and painted flowers wound up his trunk and spilled over onto his ears. The elephant saluted the crowd, lifting his majestic trunk in namaskaram as he went.

The Raja sat under an umbrella of tasseled silk in a velvet-lined howdah on the elephant's back. Before him sat the Yuvaraja, who wore a long gold brocade jacket and an egg-sized emerald medallion on his turban. It was the boy's first appearance in public. His eyes were outlined in black with oily kajal, and in his pale, solemn face they looked enormous.

The Raja and Yuvaraja smiled and waved, and fathers hugged sons in the crowd, and people wiped away tears of joy. Seeing the liveried elephants and the royal jewels and the small Yuvaraja sitting with his father made it almost possible for the people of Nandipuram to forget the hardships they'd suffered.

Atop the hill, overlooking the parade, the Raja's palace was illuminated—every graceful arch and dome and turret—by small electric lights.

Afterward Venu and Venkat and their cousins talked of the spectacle at the palace grounds of the demon Mahishasura being burned in effigy amid the show of colored fire in the sky. What Parvati remembered about that day was the lonely Yuvaraja riding with his father atop the elephant.

And she especially remembered this: after the Raja's procession had passed, from somewhere beyond the crush of dhotis and brightly colored saris that pressed on them from all sides, she heard the moan of a harmonium as it tuned. Her heart began to race. Then there was the magical trill of the strings of the veena, like rings of water spreading outward on the surface of the pond at the edge of the village. She strained to see, but too many legs and thighs and hips stood between her and where the musicians prepared their instruments to play.

Parvati tugged against her mother's grip, but Meenakshi held tightly to her wrist, dragging her along until the music was somewhere behind them. Parvati was desperate to get to the source of the magnificent chords. She gave another mighty tug just as a crowd of people pushed against them, and she was free. Meenakshi screamed, a terrified sound that tore from her throat, but her daughter was gone, headed back toward the source of the music.

"Parvati!" her mother called, panic making her voice as hard-edged as metal. "Parvati! Where are you? Venkat! Venu! Find your sister! Quickly! Go!" Parvati felt sorry for causing her mother distress, but only for the briefest moment. And then she heard the magical spangle of another chord as it rippled out into the soft evening air, and her mother and brothers and the festival were completely forgotten. She ducked her head and slipped behind a pair of legs, and darted toward the place from where the music came, and she could no longer hear her mother's voice calling her.

Just outside the wall surrounding the temple—the same temple where her mother and Auntie performed their pujas—sat a troupe of four musicians. Behind them the temple stood like a craggy little mountain, ancient and many-peaked. One man tapped and patted his hands on skin stretched taut over the ends of a long mridangam drum, coaxing a rhythm from it that darted and flitted like the voices of children at play.

Another older man sat cross-legged behind a veena, a huge instrument that looked like a large, stemmed gourd with strings stretched its length, twice as high as the sitting man's head. A third man held a bamboo flute to his lips, and the sound it made danced along the top of the music created by the other instruments. A woman with her sari pulled forward to hide her face pumped the harmonium box. Eventually the woman began to hum, and her voice expanded into a melody that Parvati recognized from somewhere—she could not quite remember where or when she'd heard it before. At the top of each phrase the woman's voice quavered and then tripped over itself before plunging downward in a way that made Parvati dizzy.

But most extraordinary of all was a young woman—a girl, really—who danced just as Parvati had seen Shiva dance in the niche in the wall above her cot each night.

The girl wore a jade green sari with a silver border, the loose end of it pulled up between her legs, across her back, and over her shoulder, then snugly gathered in around her waist to flare out over her hips. The tips of her fingers and toes and the sides of her feet and palms were dyed a brilliant crimson, so that she appeared to glow as she moved her hands and feet. She wore her thick black hair braided, intertwined with jasmine blossoms that continued in a fragrant rope reaching to the backs of her knees. As she twirled, the end of the rope snapped out behind her, leaving kisses of jasmine in the air.

She wore rows of small, shiny brass bells on leather cuffs around her ankles. The bells marked the staccato rhythm of her feet as she slapped them to the packed-mud ground. Her eyes turned up and looked expressively outward to another world in the same way that Shiva's did.

Meenakshi found Parvati there a long time later. But the child did not know how long she'd stood transfixed at the edge of the crowd watching the dancer and musicians.

"Parvati!" Meenakshi said, her voice a harsh whisper

against her daughter's ear. "Don't ever do that again . . ." She knelt and peered into Parvati's face.

"What is it, child?" her mother cried, alarm rising in her voice. "You're as blue as Krishna!" She shook Parvati by the shoulders until her head snapped from side to side, and she felt dizzy. Parvati had been so intent on the music and the dancer she had forgotten to breathe.

Meenakshi dragged the children home, her sons protesting that they wanted to stay and see the sword dancers, the sparks flying from their blades. Meenakshi held Parvati firmly with one hand and Venu firmly with the other. Venu held back and dragged his feet, and finally he sat in the middle of the street. His mother picked him up and carried him, still crying and lashing out with his arms and legs.

When they got home, Meenakshi sent Venu and Venkat to sleep with their cousins. She sat her daughter down before her and lit the oil lamp on the table near the bed. She spoke in a low voice so that Auntie and Sathya would not hear. And she looked at Parvati in a strange new way, with a tight squint at the outside corners of her eyes that her daughter couldn't quite identify—and which unnerved her far more than her mother's scolding.

"You must not run away from me like that, Parvati," she said. "Someone could steal you and sell you in the bazaar. It happens." The child said nothing. But fear pranced in tight little circles inside her chest. Meenakshi begged her to promise, and at first Parvati refused. But her mother looked desperate, and finally Parvati nodded her head.

"I promise, Amma," she said. But Meenakshi wore the strange expression for days afterward whenever she looked at her daughter.

⁓

In the days and weeks that followed Dussehra, an awareness arose within Parvati like a bubble to the surface of the pond until it was all she could think about. She had been born with music in her bones, a knowledge as natural and essential as knowing how to breathe and swallow, and she assumed it was the same with the musicians and the dancing girl.

She wanted nothing more than to dance among the flames like Shiva Nataraja, who destroyed the universe and at the same time danced it into being again. She knew instinctively that music could accomplish miracles, that it made all things possible. Seeing things in this way, Parvati was certain that music could deliver her mother and brothers and herself from poverty.

Some time later—it was perhaps in her sixth hot season—she decided to test her still-developing belief in music and its power.

One day her mother and aunt had shredded coconut and pressed it in a twisted white cloth to extract milk for flavoring the rich spicy dishes they made for the family to eat when Uncle Sathya came home each evening. When they were finished with the coconut milk, they left the fire burning while Meenakshi went to the bazaar to buy more lentil flour. Auntie went to see a cousin who had given birth that morning at the other end of the village.

Parvati was out with her brothers, who were playing cricket near the village well. She had been watching for just such an opportunity. She waited until she saw her mother and aunt pass by, then slipped away from the boys, which was not difficult to do when they were absorbed in a game of cricket.

When she came into the empty courtyard, the fire still burned. She removed the scarf she wore and laid it on the ground. It was a lovely bright pink cloth with silver threads woven through it and silver spangles in a pattern on the ends. Uncle Sathya had brought it to her from the market. She did not want to ruin it in case her idea about music proved wrong. She looked out the gate to make sure no one was watching.

And then she leapt into the fire.

A loud and joyous music very like what Parvati had heard at Dussehra burst into the air above her head at the same instant that the flames enveloped her. It began with a rapid descent of the scale on the veena, a sound that reminded her again of ripples fanning outward on the pond at dawn. The music was so loud it blocked out all other sounds. She did not hear the dog bark in the lane or the parrots squabble over berries in the bushes outside the courtyard or the cicadas screeching in the sugarcane.

The flames felt like little caresses on her feet and legs, and their tickles propelled her feet to move faster and faster. She whirled and lifted her legs and arms. She knew she looked as perfect as Shiva Nataraja dancing in the niche across from her bed each night, as she had seen him a thousand, thousand times. It was as if the flames transformed her, and the world seemed filled with endless possibilities.

Then suddenly she was snatched upward with a sharp jolt to her shoulder as Meenakshi plucked her from the fire by one arm, lifting her clear of the flames. The lilting music was shut off in mid-strain, as if a giant knife had cut it through the middle. And in its place were the screams of her mother, who beat at Parvati's feet and legs with her hands, then cradled her daughter against her, sobbing into her hair. She bent over the child in her lap to examine her feet.

"What were you doing?" Meenakshi cried in a fearful hysteria.

"Dancing like Shiva," Parvati murmured softly, for her mother's anger and shock frightened her.

"What!" Meenakshi shouted at Parvati. Then, seeing how pale and still the child was, she asked more softly, "What did you say?"

"I was dancing like Lord Shiva," Parvati repeated. Meenakshi grabbed her and pressed her close to her chest for a moment, and she cried into the child's hair.

"Parvati, Parvati! You might have been killed!" she said, and the fear tightened around her voice and squeezed it into anger. She looked at Parvati's ankles and at the bottoms of her feet again. But no burns marked the skin—there was not a single mark anywhere on the child's body. The skin was not red—it looked completely normal, brown and smooth. Parvati's dress had not caught fire—it was not even singed. And clearly the girl was not in pain, for she had been laughing with joy as she danced. This made Meenakshi even angrier.

"Our life is not difficult enough that you should throw yourself into the fire?" she demanded. She was angry with herself that she had left her daughter in mortal danger. Her breath was heavy and she watched Parvati in that strange new way, with her eyes crinkled at the corners.

And from that time onward, Parvati was not allowed to dance. She was not allowed anywhere near the fire. And worst of all, her mother put away the statue of Shiva Nataraja so that Parvati couldn't watch him dance at night, and there was to be an end to this nonsense, which had taken a rather bizarre turn, as Parvati heard her Auntie say to her mother.

Over and over again Meenakshi insisted that Parvati promise not to go near fire, and not to dance, and to forget about Shiva. Parvati did not want to distress her mother, and so she promised, and she intended to keep her promise.

Seven

The strange phenomenon of Parvati and the fire became well known, and in the months that followed, grown men and women stared at her legs and feet. They crowded around her whenever she came out of the courtyard, so that her mother kept her in the house, even in the heat in the middle of the day.

But Parvati grew bored and she nagged, and Meenakshi needed her to help with chores. And so finally she sent the child out to fetch firewood and water. And eventually she allowed her to play with her brothers again outside the courtyard. And life returned to normal. Or so it seemed.

One morning Meenakshi went down to the river to wash

clothes. While she scrubbed the soaped clothing against the flat rock at the edge of the river, Parvati watched the fish swim, farther out from shore. They were long dark shadows in the murky green water, which flowed slowly there, at the wide spot before a bend around the hill where the Raja's palace sat.

Suddenly the chatter among the women stopped and Meenakshi turned to see what it was that had captured their attention. Sitting on a large, half-submerged rock was Parvati, hugging her knees and looking into the water, her back to the others. All around her sat birds of every description—gulls from the river, softly cooing doves, bobbing sandpipers, shy cranes on long legs, shrugging pelicans. The fish gathered in front of the rock by the hundreds, their mouths gawping at the surface of the water. Some of them leapt into the air. And water snakes lay still in the water, their heads raised, and other creatures that lived in and around the river had collected in a circle around Parvati as if the child had been talking to them. Her mother ran to her and pulled her to her feet. But it was too late.

The women finished their work quickly and walked back to the village in silence. Around their midday meals they told their husbands and mothers-in-law of the spectacle of the child and the animals. The story spread and the details were exaggerated until Uncle Sathya came home one evening and repeated what he had heard: that a child in Nandipuram had caused the fish to swim in the sky, and the birds to soar beneath the waters.

Auntie and Meenakshi lived and worked together under an uneasy truce. They seldom spoke, and incidents such as the one that involved Parvati, the birds, and the fish tended to upset the household's delicate equilibrium.

One day Auntie came home from the bazaar with a huge and beautiful shining fish. She cleaned it and cooked it with black mustard seed, curry leaf, and coconut milk—a dish that Sathya was particularly fond of. As they ate that evening, everyone commented on how delicious it was. Parvati said nothing, but the piece of fish she'd been served sat untouched before her.

"You will eat your fish!" Auntie said softly but forcefully. Auntie took it as a personal slight when Parvati refused to eat the food she had prepared. Parvati looked at her aunt and then at her mother.

"What does it matter?" said Sathya. "She doesn't like fish."

"It was expensive and I took special pains to prepare it," Auntie replied. "You will eat it."

Parvati looked down and her brow furrowed.

"I love to see the fish in the river," she said. "I love to watch them move. I don't want to eat—"

Auntie leaned forward and pinched Parvati's cheeks hard, forcing her mouth open. With the other hand she picked up a piece of fish from Parvati's plate and shoved it between her lips. The child's eyes grew round and her lips moved and she fell over onto her side and flopped about, exactly like a fish just after it has been taken from the water.

"Enough!" said Meenakshi, rushing to the child. Uncle Sathya helped Parvati to sit up again, but the child's mouth continued to gawp like the mouth of a dying fish, and her mother took her to bed.

Over the next two years Meenakshi learned to live with the knowledge that her daughter was not like other children. In spite of everything, she loved her even more than her sons. Meenakshi withdrew from the rest of the village and concentrated only on her own children. She asked Venkat and Venu to be extra careful with their sister, not to leave her alone. The boys were allowed to play with the other children, but they were always to keep an eye on Parvati, who in her eighth year had grown tall and slim like her father.

Meenakshi's self-sufficiency drove Auntie to tell people outside the family that her sister-in-law was an ingrate. But Meenakshi did not care. All Meenakshi wanted was to be left in peace to raise her children.

Parvati longed for the Shiva Nataraja statue. Not a single day went by without her thinking of running her fingers over the fragrant waxy sandalwood and watching the flames come to life. She visualized the dance in her head. She sometimes amused herself for hours, a faraway look on her face, an occasional twitch of a finger or foot, until her mother noticed.

"Daughter!" her mother would shout, and Parvati realized Meenakshi had spoken her name several times. "You are a terrible daydreamer," her mother would say with a sigh.

And then another miracle occurred, one that changed Parvati's fate and that of her entire family.

One day Meenakshi put aside her other chores to prepare dinner as usual, about an hour before Uncle Sathya was due home. She called Venu and Parvati from their play and sent her son with the pot for water to set to boiling for rice. She asked Parvati to go to the woodpile near the village well and bring kindling for the fire.

Fuel had been scarce in the years since the cyclone. The Raja regularly dispatched his men to collect wood donated from other districts. They came with elephants dragging huge loads in from the main road and distributed large communal piles at the edge of each village.

As the children left to do their errands, Meenakshi asked Venu to wait for his sister, and to walk back with her from the woodpile.

Parvati walked slowly, humming to herself a song that had been running through her head. It was a strange and haunting tune, and had it occurred to the child to wonder where the music had come from, she would not have known.

A group of boys were playing cricket beyond the wood-pile. Her older cousin Mohan bowled, and her brother Venkat was the batsman.

"Don't get near the woodpile!" one of them shouted. Parvati stood with her hands on her hips and cast him a defiant look.

"And why not?" she asked. Venu tugged at her arm.

"Come with me, Parvati," he said. "Please don't make trouble." But Parvati wanted to know about the woodpile. She stood waiting for one of them to speak, her hands still on her hips, and finally one boy answered.

"Because a large cobra has taken up residence there, and she demands the life of one child before she will allow the village to take wood again." The boys shouted with laughter. "Unless you want to be that child, you'd better keep away!"

"Come, Parvati," said Venu, dragging on his sister's arm again.

But she shook herself free of her brother and took another step closer to the woodpile. She would not let them keep her from doing what her mother asked!

"Truly!" said Venkat, stepping forward. He leaned on his cricket bat while he talked. "For once be sensible, Parvati, and stay away! There's another woodpile over there." He pointed into the distance, toward a small pile of straggly sticks and broken palm fronds that would not burn long enough even to heat the pan.

Parvati turned toward the woodpile before her and laid a shawl on the ground. Venu took her hand again and begged her to stop. She hushed him and he backed away from her to stand beside Venkat, Mohan, and the other boys. Parvati took a piece of wood from the pile and the boys began to shout excitedly.

"You're mad!" they yelled. "Don't you believe us? We saw the cobra just a moment ago! She's enormous!" Venu began to cry, and Venkat put his arm across his younger brother's shoulder to comfort him.

Somehow it never occurred to Parvati that the snake might harm her. She simply knew that it would not. As she reached to take the next piece of wood from the pile, which stood twice her own height, the largest and most beautiful gray-and-brown snake Parvati had ever seen slid slowly from under the firewood, looking straight into her eyes.

Venu cried out and Venkat shouted, "Get away, Parvati—run!" But the two boys were too frightened to come to her assistance.

The cobra was enormous—at least as long as the woodpile was high. It came straight toward Parvati's bare feet, but the girl stood her ground. The snake slithered sideways, without appearing to move at all, until it lay between Parvati and the woodpile. Venkat left Venu's side and slowly raised his wooden cricket bat up over his head to bash the snake and save his sister's life.

"Wait!" Parvati said softly, putting her hand out to stop Venkat as he was about to bring the bat down on the snake. Parvati's eyes remained locked on the snake's as it glided smoothly into a coil, raised its body to Parvati's full height, and spread its hood in a magnificent flange around its head.

Venkat was directly behind the snake and could see the two round markings on either side of the back of its hood. Parvati was transfixed by the eyes in the front of the snake's head, and her brother by those in the back. Venkat's mouth remained open and he dropped the cricket bat. The other boys, who had gathered to watch the snake make a meal of Venkat's sister, began to back away. Venu stood still, his arm across his eyes.

"Run for your life, Venkat," said one boy, backing away and following his own advice. But Venkat was immobilized.

The others set up a din of shouting and screaming and turned to run in a gaggle down the lane toward the center of the village. Some laughed that Venkat's prideful sister would finally meet her undoing. Cousin Mohan let the others go, and stayed to watch.

Had they stayed, the other boys would have been disappointed. As Parvati stood watching the cobra, she heard the fanning out of the first chord of the music that had become so familiar to her. Her arms and legs lifted and her dance began.

The cobra's head began to sway, following Parvati's every movement in the same exact rhythm. Parvati danced until the music reached its conclusion with a final shimmering chord of the veena.

Venkat, Venu, and Mohan stood transfixed, as if their bodies were powerless to do otherwise. When it was over, Venkat's jaw snapped shut and his eyes came back to life. The cobra lowered its head and glided slowly back under the woodpile. Parvati bent and took as much wood as she could carry, laying it on the shawl she had spread on the ground.

Venkat helped her lift the load of wood, and instead of placing it on her head he put it on his own. Venkat and Parvati walked home wordlessly, their arms swinging at their sides. Mohan came behind them. Venu ran to fill the water jar and carried it back atop his head. The boys never mentioned the cobra and the dance to Meenakshi and Auntie, for they knew that such talk produced a storm of bad feeling in their house, and they could all do without that. Parvati took their silence as complicity.

But that very same evening Uncle Sathya returned home with the story of the cobra and his niece on his lips. As such things do, the tale had spread in those few hours to villages far distant at the other end of Nandipuram, and Sathya had heard about it the moment he stepped down from the bus on his way home. Meenakshi's face took on that tight, strained look once again.

Before long the stories of the miracles that surrounded Parvati grew larger than the miracles themselves and were told in a variety of embroidered details, so that it sounded as if there were many more incidents than actually had happened.

And then one day a famous master, Guru Pazhayanur Muthu Kumara Pillai, came to the village from Madras, a long distance away, to see the child.

The Guru was a small slender man, with a childlike face that was so round and smooth and devoid of wrinkles that it seemed somehow to have alit on the wrong body. His long white hair stood out from his head like a halo. His shoulders stooped and his long legs were bent with the tautness of aging tendons. His knobbled knees creaked as he walked. His long hands seemed more related to his cherubic face, and they moved with a lightness and grace that were almost other-worldly.

The Guru came shambling into the village under the shade of a huge black umbrella one still, hot day before the beginning of the monsoon season that marked Parvati's entry into the world nearly twelve years before. He wore a softly draped, pure white homespun dhoti and jibba and his head was bare. His glasses were thick, and they distorted his eyes behind them. A striped cloth bag that held his water jar and bowl hung over his shoulder. He asked for Parvati and was directed to Sathya's house on the hillock overlooking Anandanagar.

Auntie was sitting in the courtyard cleaning a fish. Sprouts of graying hair had sprung out about her face, and fish scales glistened on her forehead and arms.

The Guru peered shyly over the courtyard wall and knocked on the open wooden gate. Without looking to see who it was, Auntie called out impatiently, "Come! Don't stand there—come in!" Auntie was not accustomed to being polite to other villagers, for she regarded herself as of a superior station to everyone in Anandanagar.

But when there was not a satisfactory answer to her command and the Guru knocked lightly again, she looked up to see him standing before a growing throng of urchins who had gathered to find out why the master had come to their village.

The Guru, a follower of the Mahatma, Mohandas Gandhi, was well known in Nandipuram. He and his late wife, Lakshmi, were two of a handful of masters who had revived the ancient art of bharata natyam, a classical dance form that had fallen out of grace during the time of British rule. The Guru was regarded as one of the heroes who had saved the sacred art and taught it again in its traditional form. Lakshmi had been well known and much loved, one of the finest dancers in all of India.

The Guru's students were known as devadasis—servants of the gods—whose lives were dedicated to their art, performing and teaching throughout the South of India. And the Guru was immediately recognizable because he was also famous for his mismatched face and body, and for traveling humbly about the countryside in his search for new devotees. Many families wanted their daughters to become dancers, but the Guru selected only a few each year to study with him at his gurukulam near Madras.

"I'm sorry to trouble you," he said. His voice was light and youthful, more like his face and hands than the rest of his aged body. Auntie leapt to her feet when she saw it was the Guru. She straightened her untidy hair, then bent quickly to touch his feet.

"Excuse me," she said, her voice alarmed, for here was a man worthy of respect. "Please, come in. Please. Meenakshi! Meeee-eena! Bring coffee!" she hollered toward the open door of the house. "Hurry! Hurry!"

"Please, please," the Guru said. "I've come to see the child Parvati. I don't want to be a bother—"

"Nay, nay, nay." Auntie's voice rose as she scurried to find him a seat and at the same time to wipe the fish scales from her hot and glistening face and arms. "Meenakshiii-iii!" she shrilled after her sister-in-law.

Meenakshi came running, wiping lentil flour from her hands with a cloth. She, too, looked alarmed, as if she was afraid Parvati might have done yet another inexplicable and frightening thing. When she saw the Guru, her face froze into the same strange look resembling fear as when she'd plucked

Parvati from the fire and when she heard of the cobra in the woodpile and on a growing list of other occasions.

"Welcome," she said simply. "Please sit." She motioned him to the small cot Auntie had dragged across the courtyard to the fireside. Auntie fetched a thick white ceramic cup and saucer and poured hot coffee and milk, which the Guru accepted but did not drink. Meenakshi sat across the fire from him on a small wooden stool.

At that moment Parvati came running to see what the commotion in the courtyard was about.

"Parvati," Auntie said, "go cover everything in the—"

"She should stay and listen," the Guru said. "This is about her. It concerns her future, and I want her to understand what it is that I've come to ask of you."

The Guru moved over and made room for Parvati to sit beside him on the cot. She hesitated, but he patted the hemp strings and insisted. Parvati was unaccustomed to such polite and respectful treatment, particularly from a grown man. She looked from her mother to Auntie—it was most unusual for a strange adult to come visiting, not to mention such an august adult as the Guru. And that a child should hear of important doings . . .

She sat down beside him slowly, hung her bare legs over the wooden side of the cot, and tried to hide her dusty feet.

Meenakshi sat staring into the fire, listening to the Guru.

"I first heard of your daughter two years ago," the Guru said, "but I wanted to see for myself." He asked Parvati to stand and to walk across the courtyard and back. "She has the perfect body for a dancer. She is agile and slender and she moves with uncommon grace. Her face is expressive. She is intelligent. And I understand she has an innate gift for dance."

Meenakshi did not answer. She shifted uncomfortably on the stool facing the cot, and concentrated on not looking fearful.

"Yes, yes, yes," Auntie said enthusiastically. But the Guru went on as if she had not spoken.

"A child changes as she grows. Your Parvati has grown to become what I would call a natural talent. And she has developed a—a . . . something not easy to define. It is a spiritual level that transcends most people's way of looking at—and participating in—the world."

Still Meenakshi kept silent. But her fingers clutched and unclutched, her lips quivered, and her eyes looked stranger and stranger.

"I must make myself understood," the Guru went on. "I believe it would be shameful—it would go against nature— to waste a talent such as hers. But what I ask of you and of her is difficult—I will not keep the truth from you. It will change your life and hers enormously."

When silence met his words he continued. "I want to take her to the gurukulam in Madras. There she would study to become a devadasi—"

Auntie gasped, but the Guru held up his hand. "It is not what you are thinking," he said. "A devadasi is a servant of the gods. After the British came, they were regarded as common prostitutes. To be a devadasi is a sacred thing—as it was in ancient times. To the devadasi, dance is prayer as well as art, and it requires total devotion. If Parvati is to become a devadasi, it must be with full knowledge of what it means. I want her to come to the gurukulam soon. Her training must progress as she grows, and there is much to learn."

"What a fine thing!" Auntie exploded.

"But she's had no schooling," Meenakshi said. "She doesn't even know—" Again the Guru interrupted.

"There are students from all over India at the gurukulam. She will learn Tamil, the language of the poetry of bharata natyam. But we also speak Kannada—the language of Nandipuram. She will learn to read and write in her own language. In no time she'll be sending you letters. She will also study Sanskrit, the language of the ancient texts."

With that the Guru turned and looked at Parvati. "Do you want to be a devadasi, child?" he asked. She continued looking down at her bare brown feet without speaking.

"It means . . ." He lifted her chin so that her eyes met his directly. "It means that you would devote yourself completely to the study of classical dance and music, the Natya Shastra and the Shiva Purana . . ."

Meenakshi sat up straight and cleared her throat. "Does this mean you would take her from us?" she asked. "For . . . forever?"

The Guru looked around the courtyard. Chickens scratched here and there. Laundry fluttered in one corner. Nearby a dry hand pump stood idle and rusty, and two goats nibbled at the dust.

"She would have a rigorous life, but a good one. She would be well fed, well cared for, and well educated. And we would pay you for giving her up to us. You would not have to go to the expense of arranging a marriage for her in a few years. But her devotion must be complete. She must not marry while she is with us. Some devadasis continue in their faith afterward and choose that path their entire lives. She will wash clothes and cook and clean the toilet. Everyone at the gurukulam does. She will be respected and admired. But while she is a student she will be devoted to her studies and the gods."

"But . . ." And Meenakshi's eyes filled with tears. She swallowed hard. "Would I not see her?"

"Students are not permitted to visit their families," he replied. "We ask total devotion. The students must give up everything of their former lives . . ." He held up his hand as Meenakshi leaned forward to object. "But I believe she has the potential, the spiritual and physical and mental power to become a first-class dancer and teacher. And that means she will be in demand and you and your family will never need anything as long as you live."

Auntie sat back, her mouth and eyes open wide. The tears in Meenakshi's eyes spilled over.

"You don't have to give an answer now," the Guru said. "But Parvati should begin her studies soon, if that is what you decide."

Meenakshi sat with her hand over her mouth, weeping silently.

Parvati could barely keep still. There was so much to think about! At first all she thought of was herself dancing—not only would she be permitted to dance, it would be *demanded* of her! She thought of herself studying and working hard to be the finest dancer in all of India—in all the world! She knew she could do that. She thought of wearing a green sari with a silver border and of jasmine blossoms in her hair, and of magnificent jewelry.

And then she wondered whether she could leave her mother and her brothers and her cousins without breaking her own heart. And what of her mother's heart? She thought of how the only times she heard her mother laugh and sing were when she bathed Parvati in the courtyard, or when they walked together to the fields and river, or worked together in the kitchen. Her mother loved her more than anyone in the world, and Parvati loved her back equally.

Parvati felt torn in half, with the two things she loved the most laying equal claim to her heart.

"If you have questions," the Guru began.

"Exactly how much money, Guru-ji?" Auntie asked.

"That depends," the Guru answered.

"And on what does it depend?" Auntie demanded.

"On how well she learns, how she matures, how devoted she is, how much in demand she is later. It depends on many things. But you may rest assured that her life and the life of your entire family will be far better if she succeeds even modestly at the gurukulam. And I believe she will do uncommonly well."

Parvati was bursting with questions, but she was too shy to ask. When would she start? Would she have her own bed? Would she be allowed to talk about Shiva's dancing at the gurukulam—the one thing she was forbidden to talk about at home? But would she never see her mother again? Would she never be allowed to come home?

Eight

When Sathya returned that night, Meenakshi and Parvati sat silently as Auntie told him about the Guru's visit.

"But that's wonderful!" he said, smiling broadly at Parvati. "Do you want to go, Parvati?" he asked.

"Of course she does," Auntie said, and Uncle held up his hand.

"Let the child speak. Do you, Parvati?"

Parvati looked at her mother. She wanted to live what she knew was the truth: that dance was as much a part of her as the blood in her veins, the breath in her lungs. She would never have guessed it could cost her the person she loved most.

"It's time Parvati should give to the family," said Auntie, "rather than take. We could use the money."

Meenakshi gasped, a short, sharp, involuntary intake of breath. Parvati took her mother's hand. Since the Guru's visit Meenakshi had said little. Her eyes looked straight ahead, showing nothing of the person who lived behind them, in the same way as they had looked following Sundar's death. Parvati and her mother both knew that Parvati's going was the only chance Meenakshi would have to get away from Auntie.

And so it was only two weeks later that Parvati and her mother departed for Madras, where Parvati was to live and study with Guru Pazhayanur Muthu Kumara Pillai at his gurukulam. He came again and paid Meenakshi some money, which she handed over to Uncle Sathya. The Guru gave Uncle Sathya written instructions for getting from the train station to the gurukulam, and another set of instructions written in Tamil for the taxi driver. He assured them that more money would come, and Parvati felt very proud.

Meenakshi packed her daughter's few belongings into a bundle wrapped inside a new shawl Uncle brought her from the market in the district town: a skirt and tunic, her old dress, and a new bar of tallowy soap, its edges hard and sharp. She was to be allowed very little at the gurukulam beyond a few pieces of clothing. Her mother then wrapped the bundle inside a cloth that Parvati remembered was her father's old dhoti.

"You must remember your father," Meenakshi said, as if

reading her daughter's mind. "He was a good and kind man. He believed that if you work very hard and fulfill your duty—your dharma—good will come to you. It's important to do good simply for the sake of fulfilling your role in the natural order. You must expect nothing in return." It was the closest her mother came to lecturing Parvati about her behavior once she left home to live at the gurukulam. But Parvati understood, because that was how her mother lived.

Parvati stood before Meenakshi while her mother oiled her hair and braided it down her back. Meenakshi's hands were gentle, and Parvati's throat tightened when she thought of how she'd miss her mother and brothers. She'd miss her mother's touch—her hands rubbing the soap into her shoulders, washing her hair, even shaking her when she scolded.

Parvati was aware that her life would never be the same. But somehow she always managed to deflect the thought of it. She could not keep her mind from the dancing, or from the city, although she didn't know exactly what a city was.

Parvati dressed carefully in her new dress, white with red flowers and a large lace collar with a red ribbon through it. Her mother insisted she wear a new pair of sandals, which were too large and caused her feet to shuffle. Parvati had never worn anything on her feet before, and they rubbed blisters between her toes.

"You'll learn to look after yourself from now on," Auntie remarked from where she sat across the courtyard, eyeing Parvati critically as she cut green mangoes for a hot pickle relish.

I'll miss Auntie's hot spicy pickles, Parvati thought. But I won't miss her.

Uncle Sathya hired a jatka to drive Meenakshi and Parvati to the train that would take them to Madras. The pony and cart arrived, jingling at the edge of the village, and Parvati said goodbye to her cousins, her brothers, Auntie, the goats and chickens, in a blur that she couldn't remember afterward. Uncle Sathya stepped up to sit beside the driver, and Parvati and her mother sat with their backs to them, facing the village as it disappeared behind a shower of dust put up by the jatka. The cart followed the parade route, which was the only road that led from village to village.

The pony was small and slender, but he looked well fed, and the jatka driver clicked his tongue and snapped the reins. The pony trotted quickly and brightly, and Parvati bounced up and down on the hard seat. Meenakshi laid her hand on her daughter's arm. Parvati found it difficult to sit still the rest of the ride.

They crossed the small earthen dam and turned onto the main road. Parvati had never been so far from home before. A herd of goats darted from the side of the road into their path, and the pony shied. Automobiles sped past at high speed, sending the pony and jatka onto the rutted shoulder of the pavement. Crowded buses screeched past, and trucks loaded with sugarcane and timber bolted along with horns blaring.

Suddenly the world outside Anandanagar seemed dangerous and unpredictable, and Parvati knew she would miss the quiet safety of a village where everyone was either a relative or someone she'd known since birth.

A lacy canopy of acacia trees hung over the road. The way was crowded and noisy with lumbering wooden wagons, some filled with vegetables, others with sugarcane or bamboo. The carts clattered on wooden wheels behind teams of white bullocks with yokes lying across their necks in front of fleshy, humped shoulders. Their eyes were gentle and sweet, and their huge pink tongues licked up into their nostrils.

They passed dozens of jatkas just like the one in which they rode, and bicycles—some carrying three or four people—clinking, clattering, and raising showers of dust from the holes and ruts in the roadbed.

Parvati's mind whirled with thoughts of dancing and delivering her mother from poverty and from Auntie's anger. She would not see her mother's face again, perhaps for many years. She would not share her mother's bed, or hear her voice, and her mother would be unhappy without her.

Parvati thought of having her own room and her own bed—a place where she might dream her dreams undisturbed. She thought of lying alone, with no one to reach out to for comfort in the night. Her throat tightened and she pinched the insides of her arms to keep the tears from spilling down her cheeks.

When they got to the train station, Uncle Sathya lifted Parvati down from the seat and held her close to him for a moment, kissing both of her cheeks.

"Be a good little mango" was all that he said. Then he

climbed back up into the jatka, and the little pony turned in a narrow circle. With a click of the driver's tongue, and a flick of the end of his switch, the pony trotted away. Uncle Sathya did not look back, although Parvati stood for a long time, her arm shading her eyes, in case he should turn and wave. Finally her mother took her by the hand and gave her the bundle of her belongings and they turned toward the train station.

Chittoor was a small marketplace that had grown up around a wide platform with railroad tracks running through the center. Parvati wondered whether this was a city. Dozens of food stalls lined the road with steaming kettles of things that smelled delicious and sizzling dosai cooked over wood fires.

Meenakshi and Parvati sat under a banyan tree near the platform and waited for the train to Madras. The girl held her mother's hand, sitting beside her under the huge canopy made by the arms of the tree and its glossy, dark leaves, with trunks reaching down from the branches, an infinite cocoon of a tree.

Parvati had never seen anything like it. Among its roots were cubicles occupied by vendors. In one shop dozens of puppets hung waiting to be sold. In another a woman strung garlands of flowers for temple offerings. Beside her a man with red betel-stained teeth sold cigarettes and paan, and a thin boy in a tattered shirt sold postcards. Overhead, parrots scolded, and the unearthly call of a peacock shattered the air. Parvati could never have imagined one tree might afford so much shade and shelter.

As the hour for the train's arrival drew near, vendors pushed their carts closer to the platform. One cart was heaped high with golden mangoes. The vendor wore a dirty white dhoti and jibba and stood fanning himself. Next to him a man turned a large red wheel that pressed sugarcane into a pale brown liquid that ran into smudged and chipped glasses. Flies swarmed around the carts, buzzing lazily in the sunlight. Another vendor carried a tray suspended by leather straps around his neck and filled with uppama, rich with onions and chunks of red chilis, and a pot of spicy coconut chutney.

Parvati's mouth watered. She looked up to ask her mother if she could have some, but Meenakshi's face was so solemn and sad that Parvati bit her lips to keep from speaking. And she distracted herself by watching the crowd milling about the station.

Women passed on their way to market with large round baskets balanced atop their heads. A bullock, his fine, up-turned horns painted blue and hung with brilliant pink and green tassels, grazed beside a vegetable cart on parings left by the vendor. Two girls wearing short dresses walked past holding hands and laughing. One carried a single pineapple on her head, the other a basket with several coconuts.

Seeing the two friends filled Parvati with longing. She had always been alone, except for her mother. She wondered whether she would ever have a friend to share secrets with. Everyone had impressed upon her how serious and solitary her life at the gurukulam would be.

Meenakshi sat hunched between the knees of the banyan

tree, staring straight ahead. Parvati wanted to comfort her mother, but didn't know how.

"Amma," Parvati said softly. Meenakshi didn't answer, and Parvati knelt before her, their faces level.

"Amma, I will be a wonderful dancer," she said, her voice an urgent whisper. "The best in all of India—even the world! I promise. You will be so happy that you are my mother!" Meenakshi looked up at her daughter then and touched her face.

"I have always been happy to be your mother," she said, mildly surprised that Parvati should think otherwise.

"And you and Venkat and Venu will have plenty to eat," Parvati rushed on. "And you won't have to listen to Auntie's scolding anymore. And you will have your own house again. And Venkat will marry and bring his wife to live with you. She will be like a daughter, and she'll have sons. We will all be fine. You'll see!"

"Ji, daughter," said her mother, nodding her head in agreement. "We will all be fine, but we will no longer be a family."

"Amma!" Parvati said, unable to hide her shock. "We will always be a family. Nobody can undo a family!"

Her mother hid her face and wept, and Parvati sat down and waited for the train. There was nothing more she could say.

The day grew hotter and hotter, until it seemed there was no air to breathe. Finally, from a distance they heard a long wail and a clang and a louder clang and another still louder, and the great locomotive screeched into the station. As the engine passed, Parvati felt the vibration under her feet and in her chest, like the growl of the tiger.

Aboard the train, an old man wearing a tattered blue jacket with silver buttons over a limp white dhoti took the tickets the Guru had sent and helped them through the tightly packed crowd to find the slatted wooden bench where they were to sit the six hours to Madras. There was room for only one of them to sit. Parvati stared at the skin hanging in folds over the conductor's knees and under his chin. Meenakshi tugged her daughter away to sit on her lap. On one side a woman in a black garment that covered her head to foot held an infant and two small children. On the other side a boy balanced a loosely woven basket on his lap. Inside, three brown chickens were crowded so that their feathers poked out.

Parvati felt sad for the chickens. She stuck her finger through one of the holes and stroked the one nearest her. The frightened birds relaxed, and there was room enough for all three.

The train started slowly, pulling away from the platform, passing along the river, and crossing over a bridge. Below the trestle, dhobis squatted on the riverbank, slapping laundry against stones beside the muddy brown water. Meenakshi owned only one sari, which she washed every day when she bathed in the river. One day, Parvati thought, my mother will have dozens of saris, and she will hire a dhobi to do her washing.

The train careened along, gathering speed, and the countryside rushed by on either side. Soot and dust flew in through the windows, and as the afternoon wore on, the air grew sweltering hot. Men hung from poles at the doors on either end of the coach to scoop up fresher air from outside.

A thin man in a white jacket frayed at the cuffs and collar passed through the coach balancing a tray on his head with cups, saucers, spoons, and metal pots piled precariously. "Coffee! Coffee!" he cried in a high-pitched chant. The family across the aisle gave him two rupees, and he handed them thick, stained cups with a steaming black liquid that spilled over into chipped saucers as the train rattled from side to side.

The train slowed to enter a city, where a uniformed man with gold braid on his shoulder and a black patent leather brim on his cap was standing on a platform at an intersection, holding back traffic with short shrill bursts from a silver whistle. A few minutes later the train stopped at a station and more people crowded on. The engine clanked even at rest, waiting like an impatient horse. Cows wandered past at the outer edge of the platform, chewing placidly on bits of garbage dropped by hurrying passengers.

The train lurched forward and moved slowly past enormous advertising billboards showing men in smartly tailored suits and women wearing silk saris. Others featured smiling children holding glasses filled with unlikely-colored liquids, and holy men with masses of hair. Beyond the signs was a bazaar, its lanes lined with shops covered by tarpaulins.

Parvati slept for a long while curled against her mother, lulled by the rhythmic rocking of the train and stupefied by the heat. When she awoke it was dark, except for the lights toward the front of the train. The first thing she noticed was that the air was different, warm and damp, but not unpleasant. It smelled rich and ripe—her first breath of sea air.

Upon their arrival in Madras, Parvati was completely overcome by the sheer numbers of people awake and milling about in the middle of the night. She clung to her mother's hand as they made their way to a corner of the train station where other people lay sleeping on the cement floor. Meenakshi stood for a while, watching the crowds surge and thin as trains came and went. Never had they seen so many people, even at Dussehra. Finally, out of sheer exhaustion, they spread Meenakshi's shawl, lay down upon it, and fell asleep.

The next morning they sat where they had slept and ate the last of the bundle of puri Meenakshi had packed along with some water and a small, bruised, finger-length banana apiece. Meenakshi took out the Guru's written instructions, gathered their belongings, and folded the shawl. She followed the crowd toward the station exits, Parvati clinging to her hand. The noise of horns blaring, the hot damp air, the jostling crowds and shouting hawkers were bewildering.

Meenakshi saw a row of yellow-and-black three-wheeled vehicles off to the right, where the Guru had said they would be. They made their way across the crowded pavement, and a driver held out his hand for them to climb into his auto rickshaw. Meenakshi handed him the written instructions for reaching the gurukulam, and they settled on the hot plastic seat, which had tufts of horsehair and straw and sharp points of springs poking through. The driver handed back the paper and they putted off into the traffic.

The rickshaw crossed the city with its small horn rasping, dodging trucks and buses and cars and horse-drawn carts and carriages and pedestrians and bicycles and other rickshaws that sped in every direction with no apparent regard for what crossed their path. Parvati and Meenakshi held their breath, fearing they would be run down at any second.

They passed through avenues guarded on either side by giant palm trees, broad sweeps of lawn leading up to elaborate buildings, some as large and elegant as the Raja's palace in Nandipuram, and bungalows where Parvati imagined wealthy people must live. Then the broad avenues narrowed, the graceful palm trees disappeared, and they passed through dilapidated, dusty parts of the city, past clusters of temples, some small and intricately carved, others like mountains of stone.

And then without warning the city simply ended, and after some distance the highway gave way to a narrow, potholed road that passed between golden fields of millet, then through a forest of tall coconut palms, and again there was the ripe, salty smell of the sea air. The rickshaw slowed and turned onto a dirt track that became a sandy path lined with trees, and it seemed a long time before they stopped in front of a low, tin-roofed bungalow in a bright green clearing of the forest.

Nine

Meenakshi and Parvati stood at the bottom of the broad steps leading to the spacious veranda of the bungalow. A tall, heavy-set woman in a faded blue sari appeared at the door, tucking in strands of gray hair that had come loose from an untidy bun behind her head. She paid the auto rickshaw driver and sent him away.

"You must be Parvati from Nandipuram!" she said. "I am Indira. Welcome to the gurukulam!" As she spoke, the heads of four girls—two Parvati's age, and two older—appeared in the open window. Indira motioned to the girls to come out onto the veranda. They turned from the window, sending their braided hair flicking out behind them.

"Come, come," she said, "come meet Parvati from Nandipuram," and the girls came out shyly, bowed their heads, and pressed the palms of their hands together in namaskaram.

"This is Kamala," Indira said, gently pushing the smallest girl forward. Kamala had wide black eyes that looked too large for her small, fine-boned face. She wore a dress that she had nearly grown out of. Kamala looked down and bit her lips. "And this is Rukmani. You will be in the same class," said Indira. "They arrived yesterday."

The two older girls stepped forward.

"This is Nalini," said Indira. Nalini was of medium height and slim, with a narrow face and wide, dramatic eyes. "Nalini is our senior student, and a fine dancer," said Indira. Nalini's face shone with a dimpled smile. She bowed her head and pressed her hands together again.

"And this is Uma. She is a year behind Nalini, and there is no one in India who plays a sweeter flute." Uma looked solemnly at Parvati, then bowed her head.

Indira clapped her hands and sent the two older girls off to bring lime water and something to eat.

"Kamala and Rukmani will show you to your room," Indira said, and turned to Meenakshi. "We have a few things to discuss."

Rukmani appraised Parvati's dress and her too-large sandals, then looked straight into Parvati's eyes and didn't smile. She was taller than Parvati, and wore a shalwar kameez—a tunic with trousers underneath—and a wide cummerbund pulled tight around her waist.

Rukmani took Parvati's bundle of clothes from her hands and inclined her head toward the door.

"Go with them," Indira said, gently pushing Parvati's shoulder. "They will help you get settled." The taller girl curtsied slightly and said, "Yes, madame," and Parvati thought she must remember to call Indira "madame."

Indira touched Meenakshi's shoulder, just as she had nudged Parvati, urging her through the open doorway ahead of her, and into the bungalow.

Parvati followed Rukmani and Kamala down a broad dirt path that wound through the trees to a row of one-room huts with woven grass walls, thatched roofs, and dirt floors. The branches of the trees brushed the roofs and hung thickly over the path, so that only small patches of sky were visible. They stopped outside the open door of the third hut. The light inside was dim, despite a window, a flap of thatch propped open with a stick. A rice-straw mat covered the floor just inside the doorway.

The room was furnished with a string cot that had a hand-woven sheet folded at the foot. A mosquito coil was the only thing under the bed, and mosquito netting hung from a hoop overhead. Next to the cot was a table, low to the floor, with a pillow to sit on in front of it. A worn wooden writing tablet and a yellow candle in a dented metal dish were on top. Under the table was an enamel washbasin.

Rukmani laid Parvati's bundle on the rough strings of the cot and turned to face her.

"I come from Bangalore," she said, thrusting her chin forward. Parvati was glad she spoke Kannada. Kamala bit her lips again, and her eyes sought Parvati's. "She is from Hyderabad," Rukmani said, tilting her head toward Kamala. Parvati did not know where Hyderabad was, and so she said nothing. They must speak another language there, Parvati thought. Rukmani leaned forward and fingered the candle.

"We get two candles a week," she said, and abruptly walked out of the room. Kamala gave Parvati a quick smile over her shoulder as she followed Rukmani through the doorway.

Parvati opened the bundle her mother had wrapped inside her father's dhoti, and something fell to the dirt floor. She picked up the Shiva Nataraja statue carved by her father, which she had not seen since the day her mother had hidden it away. She stood beside the open doorway to examine the fragrant, delicate likeness of the dancing deity. It seemed for once Shiva was not looking outward with a mysterious gaze into another world. His quizzical smile seemed fixed on Parvati, as if she had arrived in the place that had been his focus all this time.

Parvati's throat tightened as she rubbed her fingers over the satiny, pale golden wood. She knew then that her mother had understood her fascination with Shiva. Perhaps Meenakshi had feared losing her daughter too soon, and that was why she had put the statue away.

The heat of the morning filtered through the leaves of the tall trees and warmed Parvati's face. Quivering pools of golden light fell on the path outside, and the damp-grass smell of thatch and the sweetness of sandalwood mingled with the ripe sea breeze.

Parvati turned and placed the statue on the table. She folded the dhoti and placed it neatly atop the sheet, and laid her clothes on the shelves at one end of the room. She looked again at the Shiva Nataraja statue and remembered how he had come to life and danced in the niche in the wall opposite her bed. She wanted him to dance again, but the Shiva Nataraja stood quiet and still.

Parvati retraced her steps to the bungalow, where she found Meenakshi sitting on a grass mat on the floor facing Indira, her hands folded in her lap, listening carefully while the older woman spoke. Indira motioned Parvati inside to sit beside her mother.

"So . . ." said Indira. "We observe strict silence from sundown until devotions the next morning, before sunrise. And at all meals. Our schedule is rigorous. There is much learning, and there is much physical training.

"And there is the household work," she went on, in a clipped, official way. "Everyone washes the lavatory, everyone cooks, everyone sweeps the floor and hauls water, and does laundry. We follow the way of Gandhi-ji here," she said. "No one is above any task."

Parvati did not know who Gandhi-ji was, although she had heard his name mentioned in hushed tones many times in the village. She had wondered if perhaps he was a god worshipped at a faraway shrine. She wanted to ask about him, but she thought better of it at that moment.

Nalini and Uma served them glasses of cool, lime-scented

water and passed a wooden tray with vadai, doughnuts made of fermented lentil flour. Parvati was hungry, and she barely managed to restrain herself from grabbing up the vadai and stuffing them into her mouth. The two older girls looked solemnly at the tray as they served, and when they had finished they put the trays down and left the room, closing the door behind them.

After a while Indira stood and excused herself from the room. When she returned she carried a neatly folded stack of clothing, which she held out to Parvati. "This is your half-sari," Indira said. "It is the clothing of a dance student in the colors of the gurukulam. You must wear it until you are old enough for a dance sari. Put it on."

Parvati went into the next room and slipped the flame-colored churidar on, and the red tunic over them. She carried the saffron-colored half-sari back for Indira to wind around her. The churidar fit comfortably, hugging her calves and following the curves of her legs, with small gathers at the knees and ankles to give plenty of room for movement.

Indira took the long half-sari and wrapped it over Parvati's shoulder and around her waist, where she cinched it tightly in a broad cummerbund.

"Take a deep breath," Indira said, and pulled the fabric tighter, tucking in the end. "There. That will remind you to keep your back straight.

"Well." Indira turned toward Meenakshi. "Arumugam will be taking the auto rickshaw to the bazaar in just a moment. He will drop you back at the train station."

Parvati wanted to show her mother her little one-room

hut, the bed with the mosquito net, where she would sleep alone, the thatched window flap propped up on its stick, the Shiva Nataraja statue on the table beside the bed—anything to keep her mother from going! But she knew it would not be allowed. And so she went with her mother out onto the veranda, holding her hand, not wanting to let it go. She kissed her goodbye quietly in front of Indira and the driver at the foot of the steps, beside which the gurukulam's auto rickshaw stood waiting.

Her mother laid her hand on Parvati's cheek for a second before climbing into the back and settling on the plastic-covered seat with her cloth bundle in her lap. They both waved tentatively as the auto rickshaw drew away, then Parvati's hand flapped harder as the distance grew between them. Parvati waved wildly and kept her eyes fastened on her mother until the auto rickshaw was a small dark speck in a rolling cloud of dust as it disappeared down the green tunnel of trees.

The first evening Indira came to each girl's room to tell her dinner was ready. Parvati had folded her old clothes and laid them on the shelves. She felt strange as she looked around the room that would be her home for many years. Equal parts of sorrow and joy filled her heart. Indira thwacked a stick against the thatched wall, beside the window.

"This is the last time you will be called for a meal," Indira said from the doorway. "From now you will come on your own."

"Yes, madame," said Parvati. She wondered how she was to know when a meal was ready if no one called. But she said nothing.

When she got to the bungalow, the girls had gathered on the veranda, and Indira led them into the dining room. Parvati, Kamala, and Rukmani sat on floor cushions around the low table with bolsters behind their backs. Uma laid a stack of metal plates and cups and spoons on the table, and Nalini passed a tray with a simple meal of rice and vegetables. Uma carried in a metal pitcher filled with water, its sides sweating clear pools onto the tabletop. When the food and drink were on the table, Uma and Nalini sat and the meal began.

No one had spoken, and Parvati remembered the silence rule. She thought of the noisy hubbub that accompanied her family's meals, with the boys reaching for food and squabbling over the choicest pieces. She wondered how she would ever get used to keeping quiet. But she managed to say nothing throughout dinner, since no one else spoke, and they all ate with an air of grave formality.

When they were finished, the girls carried their plates and cups back to the kitchen. They were just finishing up the washing and drying of pots and pans when a heavy bronze bell sounded in the courtyard in front of the bungalow. Parvati poked her head through the open kitchen window.

"No matter what you are doing, stop and come when you hear the bell!" Indira called to them. "You will soon learn to

hurry through your work to get to your studies on time."
They placed the last of the pots on the shelf and scrambled
out to the courtyard. So many rules to remember! Parvati
felt slightly panicked. Nalini caught her eye and winked,
and Parvati's troubled heart lifted. Each girl was assigned a
seat on the grass mats laid out in the courtyard. Indira spoke
first in Tamil, then repeated what she'd said in Kannada and
Hindi.

"You will learn to value economy of motion," Indira said,
the loose flesh beneath her chin wobbling. "We do not tol-
erate dawdling. And did I hear laughter coming from the
kitchen? We will have none—no laughing at any time!"

The younger students looked at each other.

"The language of the gurukulam is Tamil," Indira contin-
ued. "After two weeks we will speak nothing else." Nalini and
Uma already spoke Tamil. Parvati felt lost and strange.
Kamala sat across from her, biting her lips.

"Tomorrow you will begin Tamil lessons," said Indira. As if
sensing Parvati's panic, her voice softened. "You will learn
quickly."

She told them they would have classes five days a week.
Saturday morning they would study, and Saturday afternoon
would be devoted to cleaning and other chores. "Sunday we
rest," said Indira. "Sunday there is no silence rule."

She told them about the day students who would join them
at the gurukulam the next week. "They are not special students like you. They have no particular talent and are not
preparing to become devadasis—they hope to add music and

dance to their lists of accomplishments in order to attract good husbands. They are paying students—they are our rice and the roof over our heads. You will have limited contact with them—only on the way to and from classes and at school assemblies. Treat them like sisters when you meet. They are very important to you!"

Out of the corner of her eye Parvati saw the other girls sitting straight and still. She wondered if Indira seemed as oppressive to them. She felt as if it was hard to breathe in the woman's presence, and then remembered that her waist was cinched by the band of cloth Indira had given her. When Indira finished speaking, the Guru Pazhayanur Muthu Kumara Pillai shuffled in, his thin frame leaning heavily on a stout walking stick, and Parvati took a deep breath.

"Welcome, my students." He greeted them warmly, nodding and smiling. Speaking first in Tamil, he told them not to worry if the rules seemed strict and difficult to understand. "Before long they will be second nature to you, and you will feel at home," he said. The light from two oil lamps flickered on his face as the sun set somewhere far off, beyond the forest, turning the green, friendly clearing to a black wall of shadow. After greeting the students, the Guru excused the older girls and spoke only with those who had just arrived.

"You have taken up important work," the Guru said. "If you do all that is asked of you to the best of your ability, you will fulfill your dharma." Parvati's legs began to twitch. She stiffened them to make them still.

The Guru described the founding of the gurukulam, and Parvati's eyes grew heavy as stones. She thought of her mother boarding the train, having come all that distance without a rest or a meal before returning home.

The Guru talked about what their lessons would be like. To stay awake, she bit her tongue until it ached. Each of them would have to study one instrument. She was very tired, and hoped they would soon be dismissed. The more she tried to push away thoughts of sleep, the more her mind turned toward it.

Then the Guru introduced his daughter, Kalpana, who was to be their instructor in beginning dance. She told them that they would first study the face movements separately, then the mudra, the hand and arm movements. In different lessons they would begin to learn the basic movements of the legs and feet. Gradually they would put them together with rhythm.

Kalpana was tall and slim, with an expressive face. Her wideset almond eyes were dramatic and heavy-lidded, and her neck and arms and hands were long and slender. She moved as she talked, without appearing to move, her body parts gliding together in a liquid concert, like a school of fish, thought Parvati.

Indira handed out pieces of charcoal to do writing exercises on their wooden tablets back in their rooms. Then she told them what their duties would be for the rest of the week. And finally it was over. The Guru and Indira bade them good night. Parvati did not remember getting to her room through the dark shadows along the path from the bungalow, or lying down on her cot, or falling asleep.

The next morning Parvati awoke before the sun was up. She heard movement outside, and looked out the window in time to see Nalini run down the path, a lithe shadow in the dim light under a sky that glowed pink and blue beyond the trees.

"Hssss—sss—sst!" Parvati blew through her teeth. Nalini stopped and looked around, then crept up to Parvati's window.

"We're supposed to keep quiet before devotions," Nalini whispered. "Hurry—you're late!" And she disappeared through the shrubs along the path. Parvati had been too tired to undress before she fell asleep, and her ribs ached under the tight folds of her cummerbund. She ran out of the room with sleep still in her eyes, and followed the slapping of Nalini's sandaled feet. The cicadas whistled and sawed and frogs burped and made small staccato *toks* in their throats. Bats whirred and branches creaked as a family of monkeys shifted in their sleep.

The others had gathered outside a carved stone temple that soared above a wide, flat hill facing out over the Indian Ocean. The temple seemed to glow with its own light. Parvati strained her eyes to make out dancing figures carved on square panels on the front of the ancient structure. Inside the gate a bundle of cloth stirred as the night watchman awoke and a dog growled in his sleep.

Indira herded them through the gate guarded by two life-sized stone elephants. They passed between a set of columns and along a narrow passage that led to a covered step well behind the main part of the temple.

The step well was a square stone pool covered by a pavilion with a domed roof. A stairway narrowed as it descended into the water with steps worn smooth by the bare feet of millions of worshippers, and stone risers carved with dreamlike creatures, fish with wings and birds with scales.

Parvati felt a gentle jab in her ribs. Beside her, Nalini lifted the hem of her half-sari and walked down several steps into the water, then released her skirt to float around her knees. Parvati imitated everything the older girl did. The others had changed into old clothes for the ritual bathing.

Nalini bent forward and scooped water into her hands. Parvati did the same. They washed their hands and arms and feet and faces, and finally their mouths, drawing water into their throats, then spitting it back into the tank.

Parvati followed the others back to the platform, and they entered the first chamber of the temple. Tiny oil lamps edged the platform where a stone carving of Nandi the sacred bull reclined placidly.

Beside the doorway was a small statue of Ganesha, the elephant-headed deity, with yellow blossoms at his feet and a garland around his neck. His trunk curled above a small pot of sweets held in his left hand in a gesture of resistance to temptation. Parvati's stomach growled from hunger, and she felt several pairs of eyes slide in her direction.

They pressed their hands together before their faces and bowed briefly before Ganesha, lord of beginnings, remover of obstacles. They walked clockwise three times around the platform of the gentle-eyed Nandi, and then entered the inner sanctum, where the priest stood waiting.

Uma handed the priest their offering of a coconut, bananas, and a garland of tuberoses. The piercing-sweet fragrance of the tuberoses mingled with the smoke of burning incense, and the air in the inner sanctum was still and thick.

The priest was small, naked to the waist, with a pair of dirty, twisted sacred threads across his left shoulder. His forehead was striped with three broad ocher lines. He dipped two fingers into a pot of sacred ash and smeared them across the forehead of each of the gurukulam students, chanting softly as he worked, then finished with a red mark through the center of the ash stripes.

The inner chamber was plain, except for a bronze Shiva Nataraja, with flames of cosmic fire leaping out around him in a gold and orange display unlike anything Parvati had seen before. His feet and body moved in a blur of motion that was a rapid series of perfect poses.

Parvati looked at Nalini to her right and at Kamala to her left to see if they noticed the Nataraja dancing, but their heads were bowed, and Parvati knew they did not see. A cock crowed in the yard behind them, and the first rays of the sun fell in dark red streaks on the feet of the bronze Nataraja.

Throughout her puja, Nalini nudged Parvati along, hoping to escape Indira's attention. They walked quietly from the temple. As they turned the corner, the carved stone panels of dancing figures on the eastern wall of the temple were bathed in the soft pink light of the rising sun. Parvati stopped, transfixed. She heard the clear tones of a flute and the lilting patter of a mridangam drum. Even Nalini could not budge her, and the other girls stared at Parvati as they walked around her, standing in the middle of the well-worn path as if planted there like a banyan tree. Luckily, Indira's broad back retreated up ahead and she did not see.

Finally Nalini dragged Parvati by the hand and she followed, looking back over her shoulder at the carvings, emerging slowly from her trance.

When they entered the kitchen, Indira set them straight to their assigned morning tasks. The younger students were nervous, as none of them knew exactly what to expect. They were hungry and did not want to miss a meal.

Parvati's morning chore for the first week was carrying the red clay water pots to the pump and filling them, then stacking them back in the kitchen, where the other girls prepared breakfast. She set a kettle to boil on the strange contraption that stood against one wall in the kitchen. Nalini showed her how to light it, and Parvati jumped when a blue ring of flame popped to life accompanied by the fanning out of a chord from an unseen veena. Parvati looked at Nalini, who did not seem to have heard. And none of the others stopped what they were doing.

Nalini smiled and handed Parvati the matches. Parvati lit one and Nalini guided her hand to touch it to the stove's second burner, at the same time showing her how to turn the black knob to adjust the gas. The second ring also popped to life. Another chord spread throughout the kitchen. This time everyone turned to stare. Parvati pretended not to notice. Nalini's eyes widened and she busied herself setting out cups and dishes.

As the girls resumed their work, the texture of the silence changed, as if a dangerous beast lurked unseen in the kitchen. The blood rushed in Parvati's ears. She must keep these extraordinary happenings from the others—otherwise they would turn against her, as the people of Anandanagar had done.

Only when they were seated on the floor on either side of the low dining table did the silence resume an air of normalcy. Rukmani brought a tray stacked with steamers of idli, a plate of rice porridge, and a thick, fragrant stew of vegetables with black mustard seeds and green curry leaves. They helped themselves hungrily. Parvati was relieved. She was also hungry, and she had not known whether every meal would be like the first, with great quantities of steamed rice and plain vegetables. A plate of pineapple followed, and within a second it stood empty but for a pool of tempting sweet yellow juice.

Once again they were just putting away the cleaned pots from breakfast when the bronze bell clamored in the courtyard.

In the first few days everything seemed strange to Parvati. She, Rukmani, and Kamala spent each morning with Kalpana learning Tamil vocabulary. Early in the afternoon Parvati sat with a young woman named Kala, who drew symbols in Kannada script in charcoal on a large piece of wood. Each day the younger students met with Indira, who taught them Tamil verse. After their evening meal they went to their rooms to practice what they had learned in their classes. Parvati went to sleep at night with her head full of half-familiar words and symbols.

In the second week they added meditation and yoga to their already busy days. They sat, spines straight, and practiced breathing in through one nostril and out through the other, and finally they tried not breathing at all.

The third week they spoke only Tamil at the gurukulam. Parvati slipped into her second language naturally, and by the middle of the fourth week she forgot she was speaking a different language.

In the fourth week they met twice daily with Kalpana to begin exercising their torsos, lungs, and legs so they would be fit for dancing. They stretched their arms over their heads and bent as far as they were able, first to one side, then to the other. They stood with their arms outstretched before them, and balanced on one bent leg and then the other until their thighs burned. The others complained of stiff muscles, but Parvati's body only ached to dance, and she grew impatient with the exercises.

They were always hungry from days filled with rigorous

drills and study and running from class to dance to class to meals to their rooms, and back again for another dance lesson. Their sandals slapped against the soles of their feet, and their upper lips wore a fine mist, for they were seldom still for more than a few moments at a time.

Ten

Parvati fell quickly into the gurukulam's busy schedule. Tamil flowed from her lips freely, and she had no difficulty understanding what was expected of her. She had no trouble awakening early enough for devotions. But maintaining the silence rule was an entirely different matter.

Every day Parvati tried to ignore the bronze Shiva Nataraja dancing his perfection amid a hissing ring of fire in the inner sanctum of the temple. And every day Nalini prodded and poked, nudging Parvati through the puja and past the dancing panels on the east wall of the temple. But Indira had begun to notice the trance-like state that descended like a veil over Parvati and never lifted until she was well down the path to the bungalow after devotions.

For as long as it was Parvati's morning task to light the kitchen stove, she had to create a diversion from the veena chord that fanned out—brilliantly to Parvati's ears, but more subtly to the others—as each burner popped into blue flame. And so Parvati took to dropping a pan or humming aloud in the hope the others would not hear the music where it was impossible for music to be.

Parvati missed her family, and this also caused problems with the silence rule. At first fleeting images of her mother— the strong gentle hands, almond-shaped eyes, strong curved brow—appeared before her unbidden and left her heart throbbing with loneliness.

But after only a short time at the gurukulam the visions dimmed, and what had at first crowded into Parvati's every conscious moment would not be summoned. Parvati thought of the sari her mother wore every day. It was yellow, with blue flowers—or was it blue, with yellow flowers? The words describing her mother's face came, but the images would not. As she tried to remember, Parvati accidentally dropped a cup and saucer or pan to the floor, causing another loud disturbance. She was becoming known as the girl who dropped pots and broke dishes, the girl who made strange things happen.

Twice in the first month Indira reprimanded Parvati. The first time she called Parvati aside and spoke to her quietly, reminding her of the rules. The second time, when Parvati had broken a dish in the dining room, Indira made an example of her in the courtyard after lunch.

"Parvati," Indira said, her voice deepening to scold, "please stand." Parvati stood and faced Indira. The other students sat quietly, their eyes cast downward.

"Everyone else is able to keep the silence rule," Indira said. "What is it that you are thinking of?" She tugged roughly at Parvati's downthrust chin until finally the girl raised her head and looked Indira in the face. Something in Parvati's eyes unnerved Indira, something she hadn't seen before—a kind of knowingness that felt uncomfortable; as if Parvati saw deeply into a soul whose owner was not positive it would hold up under scrutiny.

"I was thinking of my family," Parvati said softly. She was not given to crying, but she felt a hotness in the back of her throat and behind her eyes. "In my family, meals are a time for laughter and talking," she said.

"Well, you are not with your family," Indira replied, looking aside. Indira dismissed them, and Parvati ran back to her room with her face stinging.

That night, instead of lying awake thinking about her family, as she had done since her arrival, Parvati worked at her lessons until long after dark. Every hour the night watchman passed along the path with a lantern, thumping his bamboo staff as he went. When he reached the end of the path he blew his tin whistle, then inspected the other half of the compound. It was a safe sound, and it meant that all was well in the soft, gentle night.

Parvati felt better after working late. She yawned and shook her rough khadi sheet out over the cot, preparing to wrap herself in it as protection from the night chill and the mosquitoes. Outside, the tree frogs clicked and large, lacy-winged night insects whirred. And then something different—a gentle scratch on the closed window flap. Parvati thought at first it might be one of the mischievous monkeys that hung about the gurukulam trying to make its way into her room to steal something shiny.

Parvati grabbed up the damp towel she'd brought back from her bath and hung to dry at the end of her bed, and raised it to chase the pest away. The shutter moved, and a small brown hand slipped up and under the closed flap. Parvati's breath caught in her throat and she swatted at the hand with her towel—perhaps it was an urchin from a nearby village, come to steal something. She crossed the grass floor mat to the door and flung it wide, and there stood Kamala, her hand clamped against her mouth to stifle laughter.

"What are you doing out there?" Parvati whispered in Tamil.

"I just wanted to talk," Kamala said. "I couldn't sleep."

"Come in," said Parvati, although she did not feel like making conversation at that late hour. "I don't sleep much either," she said finally. "I've always stayed awake nights thinking about dancing. I've never slept much."

"Not even as an infant?" Kamala asked. Without thinking, Parvati shook her head no. Kamala laughed, then quickly put her hand over her mouth. "Babies don't think about things," she said. "Babies sleep most of the time."

"Perhaps all the babies *you* know sleep," Parvati said, a prickle of anger sounding through her whisper. "Perhaps you don't remember thinking when you were an infant. But *I* remember everything."

"That's nonsense," said Kamala. "Babies don't remember because they can't think."

"I could think and I do remember," Parvati said firmly, and she was sorry immediately. She was lonely, too, but she did not know Kamala, and she did not know who could be trusted with personal information.

Kamala sat quietly in the dark without talking and Parvati wondered what she was thinking.

"I think that perhaps it's possible," Kamala said after a few minutes had passed. "Everyone is different. Perhaps I have only known non-remembering infants."

Shortly after, Kamala stood and backed out the door, saying she should go. Parvati decided she must not tell anyone else about the remembering. As if rings of flame that burst into musical chords were not bad enough! It would not be a good thing to give the others further reason to be suspicious of her.

Parvati had just begun to discover the many ways in which she was different from other people—after all, she was Parvati, and she had never been anyone else: how could she know what was normal for anyone other than herself?

The next day, Rukmani and Kamala walked along the path toward Parvati on their way to their rooms after lunch, laughing behind their hands and whispering.

"An infant who remembers is possessed by spirits!" Kamala whispered loudly enough for Parvati to hear. She looked up and saw Parvati, and her mouth opened as if she wanted to say something else. But she covered her mouth with her hand and laughed again, pulling Rukmani by the arm down the path, without speaking to Parvati.

The feeling was familiar. They laughed at her because she was not like them. She knew there was no way back into their favor. Perhaps Auntie was right, and she was cursed. Parvati kept walking, put them from her mind, and focused on her afternoon classes.

A few nights later, again after the night watchman had passed, Parvati sat on the floor at her low table with the candle flickering before her. Someone knocked softly at the door. She arose to open it and saw Nalini, a light shawl wrapped about her shoulders and one finger raised to her lips in a warning to be quiet.

Parvati looked outside beyond Nalini, and the compound was in total darkness. Even the kerosene lamps on the veranda of the bungalow and on the post beside the path had burned themselves out. She stepped aside and motioned Nalini in, quickly shutting the door behind them.

"What are you doing out so late?" Parvati whispered. She was happier to see Nalini than she had been to see Kamala.

"I wanted to talk," Nalini said quietly.

"Come," Parvati said, motioning her toward the bed. "Sit. Aren't you afraid there will be trouble if you're caught out so late?"

"Trouble is what I want to talk about," Nalini said. "There is something about you, Parvati . . ."

"About me?" said Parvati. But she knew what Nalini was about to say.

"I don't know exactly what it is," said Nalini. "But the others have noticed it, too."

"I know they talk," Parvati said, her eyes not wanting to meet Nalini's. "They think I'm peculiar—that I'm possessed by spirits."

Nalini didn't answer for a moment. She sat back and considered Parvati, and laid her hand gently on Parvati's arm.

"You are different," Nalini said softly. "No one moves the way you do. It's as if the music resides within your muscles and bones. But also you see things other people don't see. You don't care so much what others think. I wish you could teach me how to be like you."

"Of everyone at the gurukulam," Parvati said, "I would have chosen you for a friend. But I've never had a friend!"

"Being friends isn't so difficult," Nalini said, smiling. "I'll help you."

But the silence rule made friendships difficult and furtive: Nalini and Parvati exchanged confidences in late-night visits. Nalini tried to smooth Parvati's way at the gurukulam, pressing an extra piece of candle into her hand at the evening meal when Parvati was in danger of being penalized for squandering school supplies; walking arm in arm without speaking on the way back for an afternoon rest, or from an evening meal.

The day students came each morning by bus or bicycle or auto rickshaw from the city. These were tuition-paying students, the daughters of wealthy merchants and government servants. They wore watches and gold earrings and half-saris in brilliant gem colors with gold borders. Parvati often looked at them with envy as they walked together about the compound talking and laughing, their arms linked, three and four in a row. It was not their clothing or jewelry she envied but the easy familiarity they had together, their freedom to be in each other's company.

Parvati and the others ate and studied separately from the day students. Many of them came only once a week for their instrumental or voice or dancing lessons, and most of them did not look familiar to Parvati, even after many weeks had passed.

Parvati's rigorous schedule of devotions and lessons and chores and exercises and studying the hand and face movements and postures of bharata natyam left barely enough time to eat and sleep, never mind to think of how she missed her mother. Gradually the hollow feeling at her center began to fill with other things.

Each day Parvati and Kamala and Rukmani sat on the floor of the classroom before a large cracked mirror. The Guru sat to one side of the mirror and showed them the eight basic eye movements of bharata natyam. They practiced before the mirror endlessly, widening their eyes and looking up, then narrowing them and looking out from the corners, widening them again and looking down. It felt at times as if their eyes would come loose from their sockets and roll away.

Parvati began to be discouraged. She wanted to dance, not

to roll her eyes around in her head! They also practiced the mudra, the arm and hand motions of dance, holding one palm up and the other down, then the other up and the opposite down, then both up, then both down, then to the side—more than a hundred different hand positions in all—until they thought their hands would drop off the ends of their arms.

And they studied the movements of the feet. They stood in an awkward position with their knees bent deeply, heels apart and toes turned out. This was the position from which all the foot movements began, and standing thus developed not only the leg muscles but discipline as well. Their legs burned as they worked, and at the end of the day they ached from head to foot.

Twice daily Kalpana, the Guru's daughter, stood before them and demonstrated new foot and leg movements. They watched her, then shifted their gaze to the mirror to compare their own movements to hers. They moved awkwardly at first, having to think about how their toes pointed in relation to the angle of their knees, their bodies not yet familiar with the language of dance—with the exception of Parvati.

Her hands knew how to work with her feet, and her eyes and her head acted in perfect harmony with the rest of her. Kalpana tried not to stare, but at times she stood still and watched when Parvati carried out a series of movements in perfect balance and rhythm.

The Guru sat on a mat before the students as they tried to copy Kalpana's poses.

"No!" the Guru said, clapping his hands to catch their

attention. "No! No!" His voice was soft and they had to stand still to hear him. "Again, Kalpana. Show them. The ball of the foot hits the floor first, and the knee remains bent, like that. There. That's right. Watch Parvati. She's the only one who's got it. Now let's try it again."

The Guru praised her at first, and sometimes he had her demonstrate a series of steps. The other girls narrowed their eyes as they watched. Outside of class, Rukmani refused to look at Parvati when their paths crossed. She thrust her chin forward and walked faster. Then Kamala stopped speaking to her, and then Uma. Finally no one except Nalini spoke to her at all.

Parvati hated being singled out. But what could her feet and arms and legs and neck and head and eyes do but dance perfectly—even though she knew the others hated her for it? And then, much to Parvati's relief, the Guru stopped calling special attention to her.

They repeated the steps over and over, with the Guru beating out the rhythm with a bamboo stick on a hollow block of wood on the floor before him, until each of them had it right. The simple rhythms that the Guru tapped out were familiar to Parvati: *taiya-tai, taiya-tai. Tai, tai, taiya-tai, taiya-tai.* They seemed to match the beat of her heart as she repeated the same steps over and over with the other students. Parvati was impatient to put the dance elements together. When, she wanted to know, *when* would they finally dance?

Each week, Indira assigned new chores. Without fail Nalini was given the most favored job. Every Saturday afternoon

Nalini went with Arumugam, the gurukulam's auto rickshaw driver and fix-it man and only employee apart from Indira and the teachers, to the bazaar to do the marketing.

The students kept a large vegetable garden, but staples like oil and sugar, spices, tea, rice, lentils, and flour came from the bazaar. Only the buffalo milk was delivered each day to the kitchen door in two-quart buckets carried by an elderly man on the back of a wobbling bicycle.

One Saturday, Indira sent Arumugam to the local taxi stand to fetch a car to take all of them to the bazaar for a surprise outing.

The girls buzzed in and out of each other's rooms, talking excitedly about what to wear, braiding one another's hair. The gurukulam gave each girl a small allowance, which they had little opportunity to spend. They talked about what they would buy in the bazaar with their accumulated money—ribbons, combs, perhaps talcum powder.

Parvati put on her red-flowered dress, the good one she'd worn on the train from home. It was snug around the arms and stretched tightly across the growing plumpness of her breasts. She sighed and took the dress off and reached for her half-sari—the same one she'd worn all week—which she'd just laundered. It was still damp and unironed when she slipped into it.

Arumugam held the door of the dilapidated but well-shined black-and-yellow taxi, smiling and saluting each of them as they climbed in: Parvati, Rukmani, Kamala, Nalini, Uma, and Kalpana jammed into the back, and Indira settled comfortably in the front beside the driver. The plastic seats were sticky, and the air that blew in the open windows was damp and blew wisps of hair around their faces. The taxi bumped over the tree-shaded lane through the edge of the bird sanctuary that surrounded the gurukulam, to the main road that led into the city. Arumugam followed behind in the auto rickshaw.

Because it was not a regular weekday, the road was not congested, and Parvati looked out the window at rice paddies, groves of tall sugarcane with purple plumes, and huge plots of coconut palms that seemed to march past as they sped along. They came around a bend to find a man and boy driving a herd of water buffaloes down the middle of the road. In seconds the ponderous beasts surrounded the taxi, and Kamala and Uma pulled back, shrieking and laughing, as one buffalo stuck her broad brown nose through the window and bawled, rolling her eyes.

Traffic increased as they came closer to the city, and heavy puffs of heat and dust and diesel fumes from trucks and buses poured through the windows. The taxi's progress slowed as it negotiated city roads pitted with holes.

They got out at the end of a lane that led into the bazaar, where crowds milled about, with families doing their weekly shopping. Indira organized the girls into a line, with Kalpana leading and Indira at the back to keep them from lagging. They passed through a section of the bazaar where dozens of silk shops lined the lanes.

Kalpana moved swiftly along, looking neither left nor

right. Deeper into the covered maze of shops and crowded alleys, an embroiderer sat on a platform at the edge of the lane spinning the wheel of a sewing machine with one hand while he guided a piece of jade green silk between the machine's plate and the needle, which was threaded with strands of silver so fine they looked like water. Parvati slowed and put her hand out to touch the edge of the silk.

"One day you'll have a dance sari like that," Nalini said, falling in step beside Parvati. They passed other shops where embroiderers bent over gem-colored silk, and Parvati wondered how many girls dreamed of dancing as she did.

In another lane, workers sat before burners hammering silver and gold into medallions for the hands, hair, foreheads, and necks of dancers.

A jeweler blew through a pipette and the metal before him glowed orange. The spangle of a veena chord filled the air. By now the other students paid no attention.

When they got to the heart of the bazaar, vendors sat before pyramids of tomatoes and sweet limes and cones of bright-colored spices, and the air smelled of fruits and vegetables and fish and flowers. Their ears filled with the sounds of sweeping brooms, shouting hawkers, bargaining housewives, and rattling cartwheels. "Sweet bananas! Ripe pineapples!"

They hurried from one vendor to another, buying a bushel here, a kilo there. Arumugam appeared with a large wooden cart, heaping the bundles so high he was barely able to push, the veins sticking out like blue ropes on his spindly legs.

They left the bazaar clutching small treasures—cards of hairpins, pots of kajal, packets of sweets—and most of their small hoards of rupees still wrapped in their handkerchiefs. How lucky Nalini was to come every week, Parvati thought. But she knew Nalini must not dawdle or lag—although she found time to buy things for the others: talcum powder, ointment, aspirin—or Indira would not send her anymore.

In the first half year Parvati heard only once from her family. The mail came each Wednesday, in the hottest part of the tropical afternoon. After their midday meal Indira handed out letters on the veranda of the bungalow, and the students went back to their rooms for an hour to read their mail and to rest. Parvati went to the veranda every Wednesday, and every Wednesday she was disappointed. Finally, there was a letter from Venkat.

Clutching the letter, she ran back along the path to the brilliant-blossomed gulmohar tree that towered above the compound. She took off her sandals and tucked them into her cummerbund with the letter, then climbed the tree's thick trunk, her fingers and toes finding their grip among the twist of vines that wound upward to the giant tree's canopy.

She sat in a fork with her back against the trunk, branches of feathery leaves and flame-red blossoms floating about her and hiding her from the view of those who passed below. The writing was cramped and difficult to decipher. Venkat and Venu had been to school only one year, for they were needed to work the farm. Their mother could neither read nor write. Parvati went over the pages slowly:

We work from sunup until sundown. You would not believe how much more we produce with the seed and fertilizer we buy with the money from the gurukulam. You have saved us, sister! Each harvest of rice, sugar, and vegetables brings in a little more, so we have plenty to eat and plenty to sell.

Venu has built fish traps, and he sells fresh fish at the market. You should see how Venu has grown, sister. He is proud of the money he brings in, and his fish are the finest in the bazaar.

Amma pays Uncle Sathya rent, which he says he will put toward building us a more permanent structure. But Auntie complains it is never enough, and everyone is so busy that until now no permanent structure has been built. But our mother dreams of building a house of Deccan stone of our own one day, and that is what we all hope for.

In the meantime we have been able to make our mud room more comfortable with some chairs. Amma has also planted trees, so now there is shade over our small courtyard. And jasmine vines grow all along the garden wall, so our mother has flowers for her pujas.

Parvati reread the letter three times before slipping it back into her cummerbund. There among the gulmohar blossoms she saw their faces and heard their voices. She felt her long braid lift out behind her as Uncle Sathya twirled in circles, arms outstretched, a laughing child dangling from each elbow.

She wondered what it would have been like if her father had not died. Would her destiny still be to dance? Or would she be like her mother had been before Parvati was born— sharing the responsibilities of the farm and raising children?

The bronze bell clamored in the courtyard, and Parvati climbed down, slipped on her sandals, and ran to her first afternoon class. In the evening she wrote back, telling her family about her studies, their outing in the bazaar, and her friendship with Nalini. She wrote that she missed them, but that otherwise time flew, they were so busy. Nalini mailed the letter the next time she went to the bazaar.

A few weeks later, Uncle Sathya wrote her a short letter, in which he promised he would help Venkat and Venu build their mother a house after the monsoon. Parvati wrote her family every week then in the hope they would write more often.

Parvati had been at the gurukulam six months; the weather was gray and damp and hot and oppressive. It was not in her nature to be melancholy, but for days she felt the presence of loneliness, almost like a companion standing beside her. She wanted more than anything to dance, but the Guru counseled patience, and he prescribed the tedious exercises and memorization of the mudra, all of which she already knew.

Her father's sandalwood carving sat still and lifeless on her table. Every night before closing her eyes she looked over to see if the halo around the figure was made of sandalwood or of flame. It was always sandalwood. Parvati's heart was moved only in the mornings, when the bronze Shiva Nataraja danced in the inner sanctum of the temple.

One evening when Parvati undressed for sleep, she found a rusty bloodstain on her churidar. A dull ache throbbed in her back and low in her abdomen, and she worried that something was terribly wrong. For the next two days the bleeding grew worse. Was she ill? Would she die? She tore a faded skirt that no longer fit into strips and fashioned them into bandages of sorts that kept the blood from soiling her clothes.

During the afternoon rest period she hurried back to her room and fetched the enamel washbasin from under her table, filled it at the pump behind the main bungalow, and washed the bloody bandages with her heart beating in her throat.

As she squatted beside the basin, her hands in the bloody water, she thought of her poor little cousin Chitra and wondered whether Auntie had been right. Would she at last pay for the deaths of her cousins Chitra and Satish and all the others who had died in the cyclone in Nandipuram? Would her death make up for theirs?

But Parvati did not die. After a few days the ache went away and the bleeding stopped. Parvati worried less afterward, as day after day there was no further bleeding. When the same thing happened again some weeks later, she fell into a terror. The night the bleeding returned, she curled up on her cot and covered herself with her shawl. Surely she would not be spared this time, and most likely she would die in the night.

She looked over at the sandalwood statue of the Shiva

Nataraja, hoping to see the miracle of his dance. But only darkness surrounded her. She concentrated on not thinking of her mother, who should be there when her daughter was dying. She reviewed the mudra in her head, and after some time she fell asleep.

The next morning she awoke with a fierceness in her heart. It was time to stop waiting for the worst to happen. Parvati would not suffer because of what her aunt had said. She needed help. Since her mother was not there, she would get help from someone else. Parvati sat on her cot braiding her hair and watching the open door. She heard the slapping of Nalini's sandals on the path and rose to wave her inside.

"What is it?" Nalini asked softly, for she saw the desperation on her friend's face. Parvati took her arm and guided her through the doorway. "What is it?" Nalini asked again. For a moment Parvati was unable to speak. Nalini held her hand and pulled her gently to the cot. They sat together.

Parvati solemnly told her what had happened, her eyes and voice steady.

"Oh, Parvati," Nalini said. She moved closer and laid her palm against Parvati's cheek. "It's nothing to worry about. This is normal for every girl. Didn't your mother tell you?"

Parvati shook her head and bit her lips. She did remember her mother taking the basin and washing the small cloths, but her mother had not explained. How could she not tell her daughter such a thing? Parvati was relieved, but she was also angry. It was not a thing a girl should have to learn from anyone but her mother. She was grateful to Nalini.

"Here," said Nalini, turning Parvati's shoulders away. She

finished braiding Parvati's hair, and took a blossom from her own braid and placed it in Parvati's.

Parvati remembered her mother had taught her many important things. "Truth is light, and light is the absence of darkness," Meenakshi had told her children. For the first time Parvati knew in her heart what those words meant, and she forgave her mother for neglecting to tell her about the bleeding.

Eleven

Nalini and Parvati visited often at night. They talked of their families. Nalini's father was a businessman, a shopkeeper with seven children, who lived in a small flat in a gray building in the city of Bombay. Nalini was the third of four girls, who had slept together on straw mats on the floor of the cramped living room as they grew up. Both of her elder sisters were married.

"Thank God I was the one who had talent," she told Parvati one night. "If it had been my younger sister, I would have taken her place, looking after my mother and father into their old age, and she would be here, in my place. In any case, there is no money for either of us to marry."

Nalini never tired of hearing Parvati talk about her mother and brothers and their life in the village. She begged Parvati to tell her the story about the cobra over and over again.

"If my mother loved me as your mother loved you, I would gladly have stayed to take care of her," Nalini said. Her mother was not well. When she was not actually ill, she invented a symptom to suffer. She complained and cried and expected her daughters to wait on her. Nalini had been happy to leave home.

"All my life I have dreamed that I would meet a handsome stranger who would carry me off," Nalini said. "Somewhere far away from the crowded city, where you can trust the neighbors not to steal the laundry, or the person standing beside you on the bus not to steal your purse!"

Parvati confessed to Nalini the terrible details of the catastrophe on the day of her birth, of her poor father's death, and of how the people of Anandanagar had despised her. Nalini listened with eyes as wide as the Indian Ocean.

"But that's ridiculous!" Nalini said too loudly. She clamped her hand over her mouth and they crept to the doorway, where they stood frozen, lips parted, as they listened for footfalls outside. The night was quiet but for the chirrups of the tree frogs, punctuated by the occasional soft hoot of an owl. "How can anyone think," Nalini went on in a whisper as they turned to sit again on Parvati's string cot, "that an infant could summon a cyclone?"

Parvati told Nalini about remembering, about the Shiva Nataraja her father had carved, who danced amid flames in the darkest part of the night, and that she had known how to dance before she could walk. Nalini listened, and she believed. Parvati felt loved and safe, just as she had felt with her mother, and the hate-filled stares of the others meant nothing to her.

One Saturday Nalini came to Parvati's room after the night watchman's whistle had trilled its last and Parvati was fast asleep.

"I have met him, Parvati!" Nalini said. Parvati sat up, rubbing her eyes in the beam of a battery-powered torch that Nalini shone on the floor.

"Who?" said Parvati sleepily.

"My mysterious, handsome stranger," Nalini said. "The man who will take me away so I'll never have to live in the city again!" Parvati was instantly wide awake.

"What do you mean, you've met him?" Parvati demanded. "Where? How?"

"In the bazaar. In front of the tomato vendor. Two weeks ago. And I met him again this week. Oh, Parvati! He is *so handsome*," Nalini said, her whisper nearly squeaking with excitement. "He thinks I'm beautiful." She leaned over to Parvati's table, where a small mirror stood, a gift Nalini had brought her from the bazaar. She lifted it and shone the light on her face and inspected her reflection. "My mother always told me I was ordinary. But he said I'm beautiful! Am I, Parvati?" she asked.

Shocked as she was, Parvati could not keep from laughing. "Yes, Nalini," she said. "Your smile would chase away the monsoon. But who is this man? Will you see him again? Isn't it dangerous to meet a man—just like . . . like that?"

"My father would raise such a hullabaloo if he knew!" Nalini said, and laughed. "But I don't care. They've sent me to this place to be a . . . a nun! The gurukulam sends my parents money, and they don't need to provide for me. But I don't want to be a devadasi!"

Parvati was quiet. It had never occurred to her that anyone would be at the gurukulam against her will.

"Don't you want to dance?" Parvati asked quietly. "To teach and perform? I can't imagine life without music!"

"Oh, Parvati!" Nalini whispered. "That's why I wanted you to teach me how to be like you. You are so disciplined, so sure. I love the music, and the dance, but I can't devote my body and soul to them. I *want* to be like you, but—I can't! It is not in my nature."

"What are you going to do?" Parvati asked. The realization that Nalini might leave the gurukulam washed over her, and she felt afraid, both of losing her friend and of what might become of her.

"I don't know," Nalini said, sitting down. Parvati got up and lit the candle on the table. "I do know that I'm meeting him again next week—in the bazaar."

"You must be very, very careful," Parvati said. "If Indira finds out, she will tell your parents. You would be asked to leave the gurukulam—I'm certain of it!" Nalini nodded, but Parvati could not tell how seriously she was listening. Nalini's eyes were bright, as if she saw something far away that she wanted to run to.

"Will you promise me," Parvati asked hesitantly, "that if you decide to go you'll tell me, so that I won't worry about you? I will try to talk you out of it. But I won't tell anyone." Nalini sat still. "Promise me!" Parvati demanded.

"I can't promise," Nalini said. "If I do, your future here will be at risk, too." Parvati knew she was right.

"You mustn't worry," Nalini continued. "I am willing to take risks for what I want." She left Parvati lying on her cot staring into the darkness, a strange stew of fear and excitement, sadness and longing, boiling within her.

The following Saturday the boarding students were at their weekly chores. It was after lunch, and they were sleepy in the hot, wet stillness, thinking of their late afternoon rest as they worked. Parvati swept the courtyard, making piles of the yellow waxy leaves that had fallen during the morning rain. It seemed just as she'd swept up the last leaf another fluttered to the ground.

The sultry quiet erupted into a rapid burst of sharp, hollow reports, too sharp and too hollow to be thunder. Parvati stood upright, her broom of twigs dangling from her fingers. Rukmani ran from the bungalow, a dustcloth fluttering behind her. Uma came from the vegetable garden, her trowel in one hand and a clod of earth in the other. Kamala came from the bathroom, dripping water from a large brush. More bangs shattered the air.

Indira came from behind the bungalow, keys jangling from the large steel ring tied under the fold of her sari at her waist. Kalpana was behind her, her eyes wide with alarm.

"That's gunfire!" Kalpana said, her storyteller's voice rising with excitement. "It's coming from the bird sanctuary!" The gurukulam's perimeter was ordinarily peaceful because of the bird sanctuary, apart from the voices of monkeys and birds.

"Is someone hunting?" asked Uma.

"No!" said Kalpana. "Hunting is forbidden. Even the game wardens aren't armed. Poaching is a serious crime—the penalties are severe."

Indira came to her senses then, and herded the girls toward the bungalow, waddling from side to side and clucking like a hen shooing her chicks before her.

"Where is Nalini?" Parvati asked as they came up the steps to the veranda. Normally Nalini returned from the bazaar about midafternoon. They looked at one another, their jaws dropping. Kalpana put her hand to her mouth.

"She's not back from the market," said Uma. "She should be back. Oh! I hope she's all right!" A prickle of fear skipped across Parvati's shoulders. The lane to the main road ran through the bird sanctuary in the general direction from where the shots had been fired. They peered down the lane, through the rows of trees on either side, but there was nothing. The afternoon had resettled into its familiar torpor, and Parvati had an eerie sense that the gunshots might not really have happened.

Indira pulled the shutters over the windows and made the girls sit on the straw mats in the center of the room. A large white fan with dust-encrusted blades stirred the stifling air, clicking softly as it turned. There were no further explosions, but also absent were the songs of birds, the chatter of monkeys, the thrum of lizards, the whir of insects. It seemed everything but the fan had been shocked into silence. After an uncomfortable span of time they heard the *pucka-pucka-pucka* of the gurukulam's auto rickshaw as it came down the lane.

They rushed out to the veranda in time to see Arumugam move aside bundles that surrounded Nalini so she could extricate herself from the backseat. She handed him a stalk of bananas that she carried across her lap. Mesh sacks of mangoes and papayas sat on the rickshaw floor on either side of her feet; two crates, one of pineapples and one of coconuts, were stacked on the seat beside her. Tucked among them were sacks of lentils and chickpeas and rice and a tin of ghee.

"Are you all right?" Indira asked, hurrying down the steps with a speed that was surprising. None of them had ever seen Indira move in haste before.

"Of course," Nalini said, climbing awkwardly out from among the groceries. She looked up at them, from one face to another. "I've only been to the bazaar!" Nalini's eyes and voice were bright—abnormally bright, Parvati thought. In an excited rush of relief the girls ran down the steps from the veranda, all talking at once, telling Nalini about the gunfire.

Nalini looked puzzled and a little shocked. Parvati thought for a moment that her friend might cry.

"Mayappan!" Nalini said, her voice barely above a whisper.

"What?" they cried, echoing each other. "Who is Mayappan?" They all grabbed for bundles from the bazaar and together staggered up the steps under their burdens, through the bungalow, and into the kitchen. As they put things away,

Nalini reluctantly told them what she knew. And for once Indira made no move to silence the girls, whose eyes were vibrant with fear and excitement.

"I've heard Mayappan is leader of a band of dacoits," Nalini said. "Everyone is talking about them in the bazaar. They say he and his men steal from the rich and give to the poor. The rich say he is a murdering thief. Although no one has been injured or killed."

"Why haven't you told us about him before?" Indira asked. "Why haven't the police warned us about him?"

Once again Nalini looked distressed. Her lips parted but she seemed unable to speak for a moment, and a sheen of tears lined the rim of her lower eyelids.

"We . . . we aren't in any danger," said Nalini. "He only robs from the wealthy. And you know how people gossip in the bazaar. Those who are poor say he's a hero."

"What a foolish notion!" said Indira with a snort of indignation. "I'm sure the police are embarrassed they haven't caught him. But this—here, today—I am notifying the police and the newspapers!"

Indira hurried out the door and down the back steps, calling, "Arumugam! Arumugam! Come quickly!" Arumugam had gone off to fix leaking pipes in the kitchen. He appeared on the veranda with a wrench in one hand and a pot of grease in the other. Indira took them from him and—with the students watching from the kitchen doorway—ordered him back to town, straight to the police station, and then to the newspaper office. "Tell the police they'd better come!" Indira said.

"But why the bird sanctuary?" asked Uma, turning again to Nalini, who stood behind them in the kitchen, her arms hugging her waist. "Who would there be to rob in the jungle?"

"They say . . ." Nalini cleared her throat and went on. "They say he preys on corrupt police and government officials who have taken from rather than given to their people, and on wealthy tourists who drive cars with license plates from other states. I did see several cars from Uttar Pradesh in the parking lot when I passed the bird sanctuary on my way to the bazaar."

When Arumugam returned, he proudly produced Mr. Deep Chandra, a reporter for the national daily newspaper *The Indian Express*. Arumugam had stopped first at the police station, where the police were interviewing tourists robbed by the dacoits at the bird sanctuary. The post commander said police officers would come later to the gurukulam. Arumugam had found Mr. Deep Chandra sitting in the offices of a small Madrasi newspaper, having coffee with the editor. Indira rushed out to make their guest welcome, shouting for water from the kitchen, then remembering the kitchen was closed because the students were in their rooms.

Sleepy as they had been, most of them did not rest when their chores were finished. The rain that had threatened never materialized, and Parvati had gone to Nalini's door. Nalini did not answer her knock, and Parvati wandered down the path to the gulmohar tree. She climbed up among the branches of its canopy, where she looked down on Rukmani and Uma sitting quietly on the straw mat just inside Rukmani's doorway.

Kamala approached and knocked softly at the door, which

was left open in the hope of capturing a breeze. The others made room for her to sit with them.

The bronze bell in the courtyard clanged, and the boarding students ran to where Indira stood, her hand on the bellpull, the keys at her waist jangling in concert with the clamor. She ordered Uma to the kitchen to prepare refreshments, and Kamala to help her. The two looked over their shoulders as they obeyed, reluctant to miss anything Mr. Deep Chandra had to say.

The reporter stood before Indira in a white shirt, sleeves rolled to his elbows, wiping sweat from his forehead and bald head with a handkerchief.

"And fetch some cold water," she said, pointing her chin at Rukmani. "And, Nalini, bring the cushions out onto the veranda, where we can catch a breeze. Help her, Parvati." Nalini bowed slightly and Parvati did likewise, then followed Nalini up the veranda steps, leaving Indira to talk to Mr. Deep Chandra.

They sat and listened as the reporter told what he had learned from interviewing the tourists who had been attacked in the bird sanctuary. He had met the victims in the waiting room outside the office of the local deputy inspector general of police. They were waiting their turn to be interrogated individually by the assistant DIG. The DIG did not question them personally, because he was for the moment a guest of the dacoits, Mr. Deep Chandra explained.

Ten bandits, the victims told him, had crept up to the tower built for watching wildlife beside a pool in the bend of the river. The tourists, guests of the DIG and his wife, were in a sheltered lookout at the top of the tower. The bandits fired rifles into the air and ordered their victims to lie on the floor of the machan. They climbed the tower, and two of them collected wallets, jewelry, and purses in a large cloth sack while the other bandits aimed their rifles at the heads of the guests. The bandits tied the hands of the DIG, blindfolded him, and shoved him roughly to the edge of the platform, where one burly outlaw slung him over his shoulder and carried him down the ladder. They disappeared on foot, taking the DIG with them.

Mr. Deep Chandra said the dacoits had attacked wealthy farms farther to the south in the past. Afterward they disappeared into the jungle and were not heard of again for many weeks. Then the same thing happened all over again with an attack on a farm at the other end of the district. Until now, he said, the only success the police had was in keeping news of the attacks out of the newspapers.

"But no longer!" said Mr. Deep Chandra, laying his right hand over his heart and pointing the index finger of his left up, as if toward heaven. "This will be in tomorrow's edition of *The Indian Express!*"

The reporter asked the girls what they had heard earlier that afternoon. He questioned Nalini closely, and when he was satisfied they could add little to what he already knew, he sat back against a bolster and finished his coffee and biscuits. He enjoyed an appreciative audience, and the girls had many questions.

"Are we safe here?" asked Uma, looking anxious.

"You are not wealthy," he replied, pausing to swallow a sip of coffee and to smack his lips. "Mayappan robs only the wealthy. Perhaps he will make a donation to the gurukulam," he said with a wheezy laugh.

Parvati looked at Nalini. Her mouth was set in a tight line and her face was pale.

Mr. Deep Chandra left a short while later, borne off like royalty in the back of Arumugam's auto rickshaw.

Parvati and Nalini slipped away while everyone bade the reporter farewell. Parvati linked her arm through Nalini's and they walked together back to their rooms, the clouds boiling, a gray soup through the trees.

"Are you unwell?" Parvati asked, but Nalini shook her head, and tears formed once more along the rims of her eyes. Parvati rubbed Nalini's shoulder. "What is it?" Nalini shook her head again. A knot of fear grew around Parvati's heart. "Do you want me to come to your room?" Nalini did not reply. She put her head down and hurried off. Parvati let her friend go.

A short time later, just before the evening meal, the large bronze bell clamored again. Indira waited for them in the courtyard, her hair spun out in an unkempt halo about her head. When they were assembled she made an announcement, sounding like the All India Radio news broadcaster the girls heard when they were invited for an evening at the bungalow.

"The DIG was released unharmed this afternoon, blindfolded and shoeless, outside a village at the other end of the bird sanctuary. He has ordered these posters pasted on the walls of every village in the district, and at bus stops and tea stalls." Indira held up a sheet of grayish paper with a pen-and-ink drawing of a bearded, wild-eyed man with a bandanna tied around his head and a gun in his hand. Beneath the inexpertly drawn picture were these words:

WANTED:

THE INTACT BODY OF MAYAPPAN

DACOIT

REWARD: Rs: 10,000

The students were stunned into a silence that for once was willing.

"The police have informed us that this dacoit Mayappan is extremely dangerous. They have advised that no one should walk alone to devotions or to class or to meals—or anywhere at all. Kalpana and I will escort you everywhere."

That night Indira and Kalpana walked back with them along the path. There was no question of linking elbows and whispering as they passed under the outstretched arms of the gulmohar tree, of picking up its brilliant red blossoms and tucking them into their hair. They walked silently, in orderly pairs, back from the bungalow after their meal, their feet padding over the moss-covered path.

Later that night Parvati did not even wait for the night watchman to pass on his first round before going to Nalini, who did not answer her gentle tap. Parvati lifted the latch and the door opened. Nalini stood facing the window, looking out.

She turned slowly away from the window and climbed onto her cot in the darkness, and lay down, turning her back to Parvati. Parvati lit a candle and sat on the edge of the string cot beside Nalini. After a moment Nalini turned to face her. Her eyes were swollen from crying, her skin was pale, and her hair was disheveled.

"What is it?" Parvati asked.

"He didn't come today," Nalini whispered. "I waited as long as I could at the bazaar. But he didn't come."

"I'm sure there was a reason," Parvati said. "When two people must meet secretly, there is reason for caution." Nalini tucked her head down and hugged her knees.

"He is Mayappan." Nalini's voice was barely a whisper, and for a moment Parvati thought she had misheard. "I hardly know him, and yet I feel as if I've met the only man I could ever love. I can't bear to think he's toying with me. I know he meant it when he told me he wanted me to come away with him."

"Come away? Where?" Parvati asked. "Aren't you afraid?" Nalini shook her head no.

"He is so gentle, Parvati. You will never meet anyone so gentle as Mayappan. But"—Nalini took a deep breath—"I am afraid of the kind of life he lives, depending on poor rural villagers to feed him and his men, and to hide them. He wants me to come with him. But I'm afraid we'll be captured. Or shot."

"Nalini," Parvati said, "you mustn't go with him! Your life would be in danger. The DIG has hung posters offering a reward for his body. The people who help him are poor. They need money. Sooner or later someone will betray him!"

"I'm sorry," Nalini said. "I had to tell you. I was so afraid. Please understand, Parvati. Please forgive me!"

"Sh, sh, sh," said Parvati.

Parvati stayed with Nalini until her friend slept. As she sat on the cot stroking Nalini's back, she tried not to think about the outlaw. But the drawing on the poster kept coming to her mind. It angered her that Mayappan had asked Nalini to meet him at the bazaar, knowing he would be at the bird sanctuary robbing tourists! He was reckless—asking Nalini to give up her dancing and her safety to be an outlaw!

The other students believed Parvati was possessed by spirits. If I have extraordinary powers, she thought, let me cast a spell over Nalini so she won't want to go off with Mayappan. But she knew the magic would elude her when she most wanted to summon it.

Twelve

In the following weeks word of new attacks by the dacoits spread. Within hours of the latest incident everyone at the gurukulam had heard of Mayappan and his gang robbing a wealthy farmer, or an influential politician, or a policeman along a roadside in broad daylight. The local villagers swore they had not seen the outlaws, and did not know where they had hidden. The students spoke of little else, their eyes wide with the thrill of terror.

After the third such incident within a month, the district collector appealed to higher authorities for help. The inspector general of police put together a special force of the finest policemen and trackers in the South of India to scour the forest in search of the dacoits.

The crack police force paid local villagers for information, and when a sighting of Mayappan was reported, the police waited, hiding in the jungle. The next day he was seen in another heavily forested area of the district, and two days later he'd been spotted farther to the west. Several weeks later—and several lakhs of rupees later—the heavily armed patrols had found no sign of Mayappan and his band, and they remained at large.

Indira decided it was too dangerous for Nalini to go alone with Arumugam to the bazaar, and so she or Kalpana went along. Parvati was glad that Nalini would have no chance to meet Mayappan there.

When Parvati went to Nalini's room, her friend had little or nothing to say, and Parvati simply sat beside her on the string cot until Nalini fell asleep, and then she crept back to her own room. She tried to be patient, and hoped Nalini's heart would soon mend.

Eventually the bandit attacks around the countryside subsided, and Mayappan apparently went back to wherever he had come from. The posters began to fade on the village walls and bus stops, washed by the rain, bleached by the sun, and the frightening image of Mayappan looked less menacing.

As suddenly as the tranquillity of the gurukulam had been shattered by gunfire, normal rhythms reestablished themselves. Indira resumed plans to take the boarding students to the bird sanctuary for a holiday. They had not left the compound since their trip to the bazaar, and they were restless.

The day of their outing was clear and breezy. After devotions they returned to the gurukulam for a festive breakfast of idli and sambhar and fruit. Since it was Sunday, the silence rule was not in force. Out of habit they ate quietly, and spoke to each other formally in the dining room. Afterward, Nalini came and braided Parvati's hair, twisting a string of tuberoses in among the thick strands as she worked. Nalini was thinner and quieter, but she and Parvati had resumed their friendship.

The five students, Kalpana, and Indira walked down the narrow, shaded lane, laden with water bottles, picnic baskets, and rolls of straw matting to sit upon. At the turnoff to the sanctuary they crossed a wooden bridge over the river and walked among the giant banyan trees, watching the wading birds dip for small silver fish in the water. The air shone with a mist that made everything look soft-edged.

They ate a picnic lunch of masala dosai and fruit beside the river. Afterward, they napped on the straw mats. Parvati lay with her head in Nalini's lap, and trailed her fingers in the slow-moving water while Uma and Rukmani unrolled a large chart Indira had brought, and checked off the species of birds they had seen. They talked excitedly—they had identified twenty-four species that morning alone.

Parvati realized everyone had grown quiet, and opened one eye. The others had gathered in a semicircle around her and were peering into the water next to where she dozed. Turning her head, Parvati saw thousands of little half-moons, the gaping mouths of fish that had gathered around her in the water.

"I've never seen anything like it," said Kalpana, her voice a soft whisper. The others were silent with awe, their mouths gaping just like those of the fish.

Later, in the hottest part of the afternoon, they climbed a tower beside a still, shaded pool where the river water ran back on itself in gentle eddies. They settled in a thatched machan that completely hid them, and waited high above the jungle floor to watch the birds and monkeys and lizards gather to drink.

Cheeky black drongos flitted through the clearing, their long tail feathers following them like Chinese banners. Spoonbills swished their flat beaks in the water like dhobis rinsing clothes beside the river. And hundreds of cormorants dove for fish, then spread their wings to dry like laundry in the treetops.

Suddenly the air split with the awful popping and cracking of automatic weapons, and the cormorants gathered in their wings and sailed off across the water in a wet flap of bronze and green. From somewhere below, voices shouted, and the tower shook as heavy feet climbed the ladder to the machan. Instinctively, the girls dropped to the floor, too stunned to speak. Indira leaned out through the open shutters. Her face was ashen when she pulled her head back, and she sank to the floor.

"Dacoits!" she said. The outlaws fired their automatic rifles again, and silence hung about the machan for a second. Kalpana shouted for help, and Kamala and Uma began to cry. Indira and Kalpana gathered them into a corner of the machan. "Keep your heads down," Indira whispered, and she and Kalpana shielded them with their arms.

Nalini's eyes were wide. Parvati squeezed her hand. The first of the bandits scrambled to the top of the ladder and stood in front of the girls. Through gaps in the reeds on the floor they saw other dacoits standing watch at the bottom of the tower, guns cradled in their arms. A second burly bandit appeared at the top of the ladder.

"We won't hurt you," said the first bandit, who appeared to be the leader. He was tall and strongly made. His eyes were surprisingly soft. He motioned to the man behind him, who stayed on the ladder. Then he reached out and took Nalini by the wrist. He handled her gently, pulling her to her feet. She neither spoke nor resisted. She looked into his face.

Parvati felt as if she were in a dream. She was not frightened, but she was unable to speak or to move. This must be Mayappan, although he looked nothing like the evil-faced man on the posters, she thought. Nalini looked at her, and Parvati reached for her hand.

"No!" shouted Kalpana. "No!" Indira clutched at Nalini, but Mayappan moved quickly. He hoisted Nalini over his shoulder and carried her down the ladder. Nalini's eyes never left Parvati's until her head disappeared below the floor. Parvati leapt up to watch from the window, and Indira tried to pull her back.

The other bandits waited for Mayappan to disappear into the jungle before slipping away, one by one. Uma, Rukmani, and Kamala remained huddled in the corner and for a moment Kalpana and Indira seemed unable to move.

Parvati scrambled down the ladder and ran to the ranger station at the entrance to the bird sanctuary, the loose end of her half-sari flying back over her shoulder.

"Wait! Parvati!" she heard Indira shout after her. But Parvati knew if there was any hope of getting Nalini back she must get to the police as quickly as possible. At the ranger station she found the officer on duty asleep in his chair.

"Didn't you hear them?" she demanded. The poor fellow almost fell to the floor, his khaki-colored arms and legs leaping reflexively as Parvati shouted. "Mayappan! The dacoits! Call the police." Kalpana burst through the doorway, followed by Rukmani and Uma and Kamala, all talking at once, crying and wild-eyed.

But by the time a search was assembled, Mayappan and his men had disappeared without a trace, and Nalini with them.

The next day, just past sunrise, a warm haze hung over the jungle canopy. The bronze bell in the gurukulam courtyard rang out. The girls, returning from the temple, stopped and looked at one another. What other calamity might befall them? After yesterday nothing seemed unimaginable. They ran for the bungalow together, their sandals slapping on the path.

The deputy inspector general of police paced back and forth across the top step of the veranda. He wore a crisp khaki uniform with black braids and red merit patches, silver buttons, and a cap with a patent leather brim. His hands were crossed at the back of his waist, and he clutched a silver-headed leather riding crop in one fist. Indira stood one step down, her brow creased.

The girls arrived short of breath and with shining eyes.

"I have been asked to inform you that the DIG will question each of you privately in the sitting room," Indira said. Uma was the first to face the DIG, and Indira led the others to the courtyard, where they sat leaning against the bolsters, their hands clasped around their knees. Parvati twisted her still-damp hair and tied it in a knot at the back of her head while they waited in silence.

When it was Parvati's turn, the DIG's secretary called her in. The DIG sat behind a small desk that had been brought from Indira's room. A list of handwritten names on a long sheet of gray paper lay on its leather writing surface. The secretary sat to one side of the DIG, writing down everything that was said on a pad clipped to a board. Parvati stood before them with her hands folded.

"You were a close friend of the girl who disappeared?" the DIG asked. "Nalini," he added, looking at the paper. "Is that correct?" Parvati bit her lips between her teeth and nodded.

"I knew her better than I knew the other students," she said, hesitantly. "She was my good friend. Yes."

"Did she ever tell you anything about Mayappan, the out-law leader who has been robbing people in the forest?" Parvati's heart hammered in her ears. In Anandanagar, people did not regard the police as friends. Her instinct was to re-sist answering his questions, to protect Nalini, but it was too late for that. She must tell the truth. If there was any chance of finding Nalini and bringing her back, she had to help them.

"Yes, sir," she said. He waited while she wrestled with her-self to tell what she knew.

"And what did she tell you?" he asked somewhat impatiently. Parvati swallowed hard and took a deep breath.

"Only that she met a man in the bazaar some weeks ago. She did not say at first who he was. It was a week or two before the first robbery at the bird sanctuary. She was very drawn to him, and she believed he was drawn to her. But after the robbery she was frightened of his way of life—of his need to hide and of his being hunted."

"And you did not think to tell Guru Pazhayanur Muthu Kumara Pillai about this infraction of the rules?"

"It wasn't exactly an infraction of the rules," Parvati said, resisting the urge to turn her back on this arrogant man who used his uniform to bully people. "She met him while she was shopping for the gurukulam. It was her job to go to the bazaar each week. She did not learn until later who he was. She did nothing wrong."

"Do you think," the DIG said, "this girl went with the outlaw willingly? I must know: if this is a simple case of elopement, I don't want to put my men at risk finding her. That is her family's business. If it was a kidnapping, that is a different matter. We must have full information—it could save her life!"

"I think he came for her because she would not go with him," Parvati said. "I think he is the kind of man who takes what he wants."

She hesitated. Nalini had told her very little about Mayappan, no doubt to protect her—and him. She told the DIG everything she could think of.

After the DIG had interviewed the students, Indira kept them in the courtyard.

"We have no idea where Nalini has gone," Indira said, shaking her head sadly. "When we returned from the bird sanctuary, her room was untouched. She left it as if she expected to return. The DIG did not want us to tell you until he had spoken with each of us. Nalini had a . . . a friendship with Mayappan, but we don't know whether she was kidnapped or whether she eloped. The Guru has gone to Bombay to tell her family."

Parvati knew Nalini's family would be disappointed, if only because the gurukulam would send them no more money. It gave Parvati small comfort to know Nalini loved Mayappan. But she was still afraid for her friend.

Indira dismissed the others and asked Parvati to come into the bungalow.

"The DIG tells me you knew about Nalini's friendship with Mayappan," Indira said, pacing back and forth in front of the window. Parvati stood with her back to the door. She nodded. "Tell me what you knew."

"At first I only knew that she had met someone in the bazaar," Parvati responded. "The day of the attack on the bird sanctuary she told me that 'someone' was Mayappan."

"And why did you not tell us?"

Parvati's face colored deeply. "Madame, she was my friend," she said. "Mayappan was supposed to meet her in the bazaar that day. He did not show up. Nalini was frightened of the way he lived—afraid he would be killed. She thought he was trifling with her. I believed she would not see him again."

"Still, it was your duty to inform us," Indira said.

"I could not betray her, madame, even if it meant I must leave the gurukulam" was Parvati's reply. "I am certain Mayappan kidnapped her. Why would he take such a terrible risk if he thought she would go willingly?" Parvati's eyes were steady.

"This is serious," Indira said, but she looked away from Parvati.

"I meant no disrespect to the gurukulam or to you or the Guru," Parvati said. "I am sorry. But I would not betray my friend."

"I will take you at your word," Indira said, not unkindly. "But you must observe the rules meticulously from now on. Even the smallest infraction of the silence rule and you will be sent back to your family." Parvati nodded. "Don't forget. Not a single infraction of a single rule."

"Yes, madame," Parvati said. She bowed slightly and left the room.

Thirteen

Parvati lost herself in study and dance. Without Nalini, she was alone, but being alone felt familiar.

She practiced her abhinaya, the combined movements of head, torso, arms, and legs, before a full-length mirror in the dance classroom and meditated before classes. She had chosen to study the bamboo flute her first term, and on days when the heat and damp were oppressive she went into the jungle to play. The notes soared to the top of the canopy of trees and dove to the jungle floor, and the jungle fowl and lizards, the turtles and spotted deer, the wildcats and flycatchers, the rollers and even the crocodiles were transfixed in the sleepy afternoon air. But the flute music did not inspire the Shiva statue to dance as Parvati hoped it would.

The others called her "Monkey Queen" and "Bird Girl," laughing behind their hands, for the animals of the jungle were her only companions.

Indira summoned Parvati more than once to caution her about wandering off into the jungle. Indira worried about dacoits and crocodiles and tigers and other wild animals.

"But, madame," Parvati protested, "I am safe with the wild creatures! There are no tigers here. And Mayappan has not been heard of since Nalini disappeared. It's perfectly safe."

In the classroom the only music was the tapping of the Guru's stick on the block of wood marking time in patterns of rhythm that grew more complex: *taiya-tai, taiya-tai, tai, tai, tai-takka-tai, tai, tai, tai-takka-tai, takka-tai.*

The week came for the students' annual performance review, and everyone said it didn't seem possible a year had passed so swiftly at the gurukulam. But Parvati was impatient. Every day that she did not dance—as the girl in the green silk sari at Dussehra had danced—seemed an eternity, especially since Nalini was gone.

The day of her review, Parvati ran to the bungalow, where the Guru waited for her. Monkeys chattered and scampered beside the path, and birds flew in front of her, diving gaily. She hurried up the steps onto the veranda and stood in the doorway to catch her breath. The Guru sat on a straw pallet on the parlor floor.

"Come in, come in," the Guru said. "Sit. Please sit." He motioned to a pallet with a red cotton cushion and bolster on the floor across from him. He had not called her "child." Parvati sat.

"I am pleased with your progress," the Guru began. "No, I am in awe. You have an extraordinary gift." A shiver of excitement went through Parvati.

Indira came in carrying a tray with lime water and biscuits. She served the Guru first, then Parvati. Indira served them rather than one of the students so that no one would hear what the Guru had to say.

"I have taken more money to your mother, and I have increased the amount substantially. But as always, it is up to you. You wish to continue?"

"Yes!" Parvati blurted. "But can you tell me, please, when we will start dancing? I mean truly dancing?"

The Guru looked at her as if she had spoken in a strange language. "But you are dancing," he said. "What do you call what you are doing?"

"Studying," replied Parvati. "Exercising. I mean when do we dance—with music?"

"After a year most students are not ready to perform. There is so much to learn! A dancer from this gurukulam cannot go before the public until she is a master."

Parvati's heart ached with disappointment, but she said nothing. The Guru laughed a kindly laugh and Parvati lowered her eyes.

"But you are different," he said.

"How do you mean, 'different,' sir?" she asked. The Guru grew very serious.

"It's easy for me to see why you are impatient. The music is a part of you; it's as if you've always known how to dance."

Parvati wondered whether the Guru knew about her causing the cyclone and dancing in the fire, about the cobra and all the ways in which she was different. She looked back down at the floor for a moment, as if the answers she sought might lie imbedded in the straw mat.

"What is it?" he asked. She swallowed hard before she spoke.

"All my life people have thought of me as 'different.' People blame all sorts of things on me. It has caused my poor mother nothing but trouble. That is how I know I am different. And now you talk as if this 'differentness' is good!"

"There are those who will fear you and be jealous of your gift," the Guru said. "These people will always cause you trouble. There is nothing you can do about it. You must ignore them and work hard to live up to your ability. It is your dharma. It would go against God and nature to behave as if anything else were true.

"I feel like a father who has been reluctant to allow his daughter to grow up," he said, smiling. "You can't stay in classes with the other students. You have proved yourself to be a true devadasi. I have tried not to show favoritism. We have good students who will be fine dancers one day, but none are like you.

"Now you and I must work together to make a master of you and to prepare your arangetram—your first public appearance. You will continue your classes in literature and philosophy. The rest of the time we will work on perfecting your style and building your repertoire."

Parvati bowed her head and thanked him.

Indira came into the parlor again with a neatly piled stack of clothing. This time she gave Parvati two saris with matching blouses and churidar. Parvati's very first real saris were dancer's saris—woven specially on narrower looms than dress saris so that the feet would not tangle in the skirt. Indira also gave her a small brass lantern so that she could read and study until late into the night.

"Whenever you need oil for the lantern," Indira said, "bring me this and I will give you what you need." She handed Parvati a liter can.

The Guru pulled a blue envelope out of his cloth bag and held it out to Parvati.

"Your family sent this."

Parvati took the letter, bowed respectfully, and backed out the door. Balancing her new saris, the lantern, and the liter can, she walked as quickly as she could across the veranda and down the path to her room. She stuffed the letter into her cummerbund and left the clothing, lantern, and liter can on the shelf and ran back to the gulmohar tree, her heart pounding in rhythm with her feet. She climbed the vines that twined around its trunk, her toes easily finding little mossy pockets that held her. She drew herself up into her seat among the wide, embracing branches and unfolded Venkat's letter.

Dear sister:

With the money the Guru brought we will build our house at the opposite end of the village from Uncle Sathya. There will be

a room for Venu to sleep in, and one for Amma. And there will
be a kitchen, and a room where we take our meals. And there
will be another room for me.

I am to be married after the monsoon. Can you believe it?
I am so happy that Amma will have another daughter to help
her with running the house. And you will have a sister. Our
new house will be so much more pleasant than our crumbling
mud room at Uncle Sathya's. And none of us will have to put
up with Auntie any longer.

Parvati sat in the tree for a long time, wondering whom
Venkat was to marry. Uncle Sathya would have arranged it. It
was just like Venkat to leave out the most important detail!
The breeze carried the lemony fragrance of frangipani from
the garden.

Parvati climbed down, slipped her feet into her sandals,
and hurried back to her room to dress in the dance sari
before lunch. She remembered how Nalini had tied her sari,
and wound the long cloth around herself. She secured it at
the waist and draped it across her shoulder.

When the bronze bell rang to summon them to their noon
chores, Parvati walked toward the bungalow feeling the
strangeness of the new clothing—the clothing of a real
dancer—on her legs and against her chest and back.

When she entered the kitchen, Rukmani and Kamala whispered, their heads together at the sink. They still wore half-
saris, like the younger students who had just begun to study
at the gurukulam. They turned to stare at her. Parvati smiled,
but Rukmani lit the stove without speaking and Kamala

ducked her head and fetched the pans from the shelves without acknowledging Parvati.

That afternoon Parvati went for her first lesson with the Guru in a classroom behind the bungalow, near the row of rooms where he and Indira and Kalpana had their apartments.

Parvati had never been inside this classroom, an open pavilion with a peaked thatched roof supported by gray stone pillars. A thorny tangle of bougainvillea vines with brilliant copper flowers wound around several of the pillars and crept onto the roof. Split bamboo shades were lowered on the west side against the afternoon sun. The other shades were rolled and tied at the top, opening the pavilion to the sea breeze. The room was warm and fragrant from the sun on the thatch.

Red clay pots planted with palms stood inside the entry. The Guru sat on a straw mat on the floor, a vase of tuberoses beside him. Flames danced on more than a dozen wicks set in the small vessels of a many-tiered bronze lamp. Birds flitted in and perched atop the rolled shades. Parvati kicked off her sandals and set them on the step before entering and bowing to the Guru. The polished cement floor felt warm under her bare feet.

"The first thing a dancer must do," the Guru said, "is to honor Bhuma Devi, goddess of the earth, by asking permission to stamp the ground with your feet." He recited the prayer and showed Parvati how to touch her fingers first to the ground and then to her eyes, asking Bhuma Devi's pardon.

The rest of the hour consisted of the Guru teaching Parvati a dance. It was nritta, abstract, pure dance—without a poem or any particular meaning other than the sheer beauty of the body in motion. The expression depended on harmonizing eyes, face, chin, neck, torso, arms, legs, hands, and feet. The Guru marked time with his stick, and within an hour Parvati had learned the entire sequence of repetitions. Each pose was like a perfect statue, and the Guru tilted his head, flicking out his fingers in time with her movements to show his appreciation.

From that day on, Parvati needed little sleep. Often she stayed up late to study. Sometimes she danced in her room to the dim light of the lantern, the music full and perfect in her head.

She was no longer bothered when Kamala and Rukmani lowered their eyes and did not greet her, or when the day students stopped chattering to stare when she happened by.

She concentrated on her duty—it was dharma, the law of being, the cosmic order that she should live without friendship. She would be a true devadasi, devoted only to worship through music.

It had been more than a year since Parvati left her family in Anandanagar, and she had not seen them in all that time. In Venkat's most recent letter was an account of his marriage. It was sparse in detail, as was Venkat's way, and so she had to imagine the jewelry that Venkat had given his bride, Sumitra, the clothing she had worn, and the details of the ceremony.

Parvati reread his letter a hundred times, and could see as clearly as if she had been there the tying of the wedding pendant and the circling of the sacred fire. She saw it all in the orange light of the flames, the tears glistening in her mother's eyes, the winking of the silver threads in the wedding sari.

One day not long after Venkat's letter the Guru came to Parvati's lesson with an extra spark in his eye. His voice was high and excited as a child's.

"I have decided," he said. "It's time."

"Time for what?" Parvati asked.

"I have consulted with the priest. In another three months the time will be perfect for your arangetram. You are ready."

Parvati's mouth went dry. She was ready. She could perform publicly right now, she thought. But she was certain her family did not have the money so soon after Venkat's marriage to stage her first public performance, the important ceremony in which the student honored her family and her guru.

"My mother cannot . . ." Parvati began, but the Guru shook his head.

"It doesn't matter," he said. "There is money in the guru-kulam's budget for students whose families are unable to sponsor their daughter's arangetram. That is why we live frugally—everything is sacrificed for dancing."

The Guru and Kalpana and Indira went into a flurry of activity, renting an auditorium in the city of Madras, collecting names for the guest list, issuing invitations, selecting musicians, ordering flowers, printing the program, delivering notices to the newspapers. But for Parvati, there was nothing but the dancing. And she was happier than she ever had been before.

The Guru sent her one morning to Kalpana to try on a dance costume and jewelry. Kalpana was taller than Parvati, and the sari was too long.

"Never mind," Kalpana said. "We'll go to the bazaar and buy you one."

The next morning Arumugam drove them in the gurukulam's auto rickshaw to the bazaar. Kalpana led Parvati directly to a lane of shops with dance costumes on display. They stopped before a small, dingy shop with a single light bulb hanging from the ceiling on a wire. The proprietor sat on a white sheet on the floor near the entry, bent over a brilliant green piece of silk with a silver and blue design sewn into the hem. It was a sari he had cut and fashioned into a costume.

Kalpana leaned close to Parvati's ear. "His is the smallest, most crowded shop. But he sells his dance costumes at a very good price," she whispered. Parvati barely heard. The green silk shimmered and the silver threads sparkled as the shopkeeper turned it under the needle of the sewing machine that whirred before him.

Kalpana spoke to the shopkeeper, and he removed the costume from the sewing machine and held it up. Parvati fingered the pleats. He showed them the blouse, which was blue like the hem of the costume, with a green and silver design in the sleeves.

"A tuck here," he said, pinching the costume at the waist, and eyeing Parvati, and then the costume again. "It's almost as if I'd made it for you." He and Kalpana bargained, but Parvati did not hear, she was so absorbed in the beautiful green silk. They agreed on a price and the shopkeeper sat down at the sewing machine to make the minor adjustment. A few minutes later he folded the costume, wrapped it in brown paper, and tied it into a bundle with string.

Kalpana had to loosen Parvati's grip on the bundle in the auto rickshaw. "You'll crush it," she said, laughing. They went to Kalpana's room, and she helped Parvati into the costume, hooking the blouse and arranging the pleats. Kalpana selected jewelry for her to wear, silver medallions and chains and bangles and earrings.

Each day Parvati learned a new sequence of the varnam, the centerpiece of her first performance. The Guru almost never corrected her, stopping her only to rearrange a bit of the choreography.

The evening of the arangetram, the auditorium was filled with dancers, students, and masters, some of whom had traveled more than a day to reach Madras. The grand people of Madrasi society came in their jewels and fine silk saris. The auditorium overflowed with people who had come to see the girl from Nandipuram perform her arangetram on the simple stage decorated with a large vase of flowers from the gurukulam, a many-tiered bronze oil lamp, small clay lamps along the edge of the platform, and a framed and garlanded portrait of the late Lakshmi, wife and inspiration of the Guru Pazhayanur Muthu Kumara Pillai.

Kalpana sat in front with students from the gurukulam.

The Guru sat with the musicians to one side of the stage. The gurukulam had been able to afford everything but train tickets for Parvati's family to come to the arangetram, and Kalpana sat in for the dancer's mother.

In the beginning sequence, Parvati performed an alarippu of intricate hand and head movements and facial expressions that included her namaskaram to Bhuma Devi, asking permission to pound the earth with her feet; to Ganesha, whom she asked to remove all obstacles; to the sandalwood Shiva Nataraja, which she had placed at the end of the stage; to the Guru, asking for his blessing; to Kalpana, her honorary mother; and to the other musicians and the audience. Next came the jatisvaram, which was even more complex, and the varnam.

After the first chord of music fanned out over the hushed crowd, Parvati was not aware of anything or anyone: her schoolmates, who leaned their heads together as if to speak, but then forgot as they watched; the distinguished-looking groups that sat against bolsters, clustered tightly together on the floor of the crowded auditorium, keeping time softly with their hands against their thighs.

For Parvati there was only the music and the dance and the sacred, purifying fire that surrounded the Shiva Nataraja, who danced before her. Parvati danced the story of Neelakanta, the blue-throated, an account of Shiva swallowing poison churned up from the ocean by demons and holding it in his throat to save the earth and all humanity.

When it was over, the auditorium was as still as an empty

room for what seemed a long time. The Guru and the other musicians wiped tears from their faces, and the audience applauded thunderously.

Afterward Parvati went back to her studies, an initiated devadasi. The other students still did not speak to her, and it was as if nothing had changed. Until one day, when she arose early as usual to bathe in the step well and pray in the temple.

On that hot still morning Parvati performed her puja quickly and slipped away before the other students from the gurukulam came sleepily, one by one. The sky was blue, with high, gold-edged clouds, as she walked to the kitchen, where she spooned some curds into a bowl and whisked them with salt and water. She drank the lassi down before anyone else arrived and hurried to do her chores and exercises before meeting with the Guru.

Parvati had never requested a reprieve from her kitchen duties. But Indira saw what went on among the students, and she reassigned Parvati to sweeping the veranda and dusting the sitting room of the bungalow, which were done alone. When she had finished, Parvati went to the open-sided class-room. She wound a string of jasmine blossoms into her hair and sat on the floor with her back toward the doorway.

She folded her legs, rested her arms, wrists up, against her knees, and inhaled deeply. Just then Kalpana burst into the room, uncharacteristically breathless and wild-eyed.

"Parvati!" Kalpana said. She was hardly able to talk, she was so excited. "Parvati, come at once!" She grabbed Parvati by the wrist and pulled her to her feet. Kalpana's hair, which she usually wore in a sleek, neat coil at the nape of her neck, hung loose in damp strands about her long thin face, as if she'd just come from her bath.

It took Parvati a moment to return from her meditation.

"He has asked for you—*you!*"

"Who is *he* and what does he ask?" Parvati said, looking quizzically at Kalpana. Breathlessly—and in a disconnected way—Kalpana attempted to explain. All the while she pulled Parvati toward the bungalow.

"The Maharaja of Nandipuram!" she said, still breathless. "Maharaja Narasimha Deva!"

"But Nandipuram is where I come from—I was born in the village of Anandanagar," Parvati said, "within sight of the palace of the Maharaja Narasimha Deva!"

"There is to be a big cultural festival. And it is also the Raja's birthday, which—do you remember?—used to be celebrated with a huge festival at the onset of the monsoon. The Raja's fortunes—and the fortunes of his people—have improved. So the Raja will celebrate his birthday again with the ritual weighing and giving gold to the poor. The Prime Minister and several ambassadors and many other VIPs are invited!" said Kalpana.

Parvati remembered, because it was her birthday as well. But she said nothing.

"The Raja's secretary, Mr. Ramanujan, contacted the Guru," Kalpana went on. "He knows the gurukulam, and he asked my father, 'Who is the most talented, accomplished dancer in all of India!' " Kalpana's eyes grew very wide. "And do you know what my father told him? He said without hesitation—I was there, I heard it myself!—he said, 'Our Parvati—Parvati from Nandipuram—is the most devout, the most talented devadasi at the gurukulam—she is the most talented I have ever taught.'

"And so the Guru invited Mr. Ramanujan to your arangetram. He was so impressed with your dancing he rushed back to Nandipuram and told the Maharaja that you are indeed the finest dancer he has ever seen. And the Maharaja said, 'If she is the finest dancer, then that is who we must have!'

"Think of it, Parvati! They want you!"

Parvati's cheeks burned and her chest tightened. Of course the Guru has never taught a student like me, she thought. Because there had never before been a dancer who caused such devastation, whose feet moved in desperation to keep the earth turning, to prevent destruction!

Kalpana pulled Parvati by the arm to the doorway.

"There is no time to lose," she said. "We must prepare your clothes and your jewelry and your recital."

For the next three months Parvati's time was spent learning the dances she would perform in Nandipuram.

Fourteen

The train to Nandipuram was not at all what Parvati had expected. The Maharaja Narasimha Deva made his three personal cars available to them, plus an attendant to see to their needs.

The saloon car was furnished with carved teak tables and chairs inlaid with ivory and handsome dhurries woven in traditional designs of blue and brown and red on the floors and draped over chairs and divans and tables. At one end was a dining table and six chairs.

The other two cars were divided into sleeping compartments, storage, a small kitchen, and servants' quarters for Indira's old ayah, whose name was Vilasini.

The ayah's arms were thin and her back was bent, but Indira insisted she must accompany them. For although Vilasini had retired as Indira's servant, she had a keen eye for details. If Indira had to remain at the gurukulam, sending Vilasini with the Guru's prodigy was like sending along her own eyes and ears.

Kalpana and Parvati settled comfortably onto velvet-covered banquettes at the windows of the saloon car. It was dark when the train pulled out of the station. As the car rocked gently from side to side, Parvati thought of how she and her mother had jostled and jolted on a bare wooden-slatted bench, with hot air blowing into their faces from the window. These cars were air-conditioned, and Parvati pulled a shawl around her shoulders.

Kalpana sat quietly beside Parvati, keeping one eye on Vilasini, who held the valise with the dance costume and the case with the jewelry Parvati was to wear for her performance. The jewelry had belonged to Kalpana's mother, the late Lakshmi, who had been one of India's greatest dancers. Parvati had tried on the costume, but had not yet seen the ornaments. At Vilasini's feet was a small cloth bag that contained Parvati's belongings. Wrapped deep inside her clothes was the statue of the dancing Shiva that had been carved by her father. Vilasini also held a bundle of gifts Parvati had bought in the bazaar for her family: a bamboo flute for Venu, a set of glass bangles for Sumitra, a folding knife for Venkat, and a hairbrush for her mother.

The Guru joined them, and the Raja's bearer in a starched

white linen jacket with silver buttons brought a large silver thali for each of them. As he served them from bowls of delicately spiced vegetables and soups and a variety of breads and pickles and rice, Parvati remembered the old bearer in the threadbare jacket passing through the aisles of the train on the journey she and her mother had made together.

"When we return to Madras," the Guru said, "I want you to begin teaching some of the younger students." Parvati looked up in surprise. "You will continue your studies, of course. But you must follow the path of a master, and that is what comes next."

"Thank you, Guru-ji," Parvati said.

"We'll help you," said Kalpana. "It will be very similar to the way you learned to dance."

As Parvati listened, she thought about the mystery of dharma—how some things were very difficult to understand and a struggle to accept, while others opened as simply and naturally as a flower bloomed.

Not long afterward, as the train sailed through the darkness, Parvati pulled aside the soft linen sheet that lay atop the feather mattress, and was asleep immediately.

It was still dark when she was awakened by a bearer with a tray of hot, lime-scented water. Kalpana was not in her bed. Parvati sat up against the feather pillows and sipped from a thin porcelain cup. Vilasini knocked softly on the doorframe to tell Parvati she had a few minutes to dress before the train pulled into Chittoor station.

It seemed to Parvati that more than two years had passed

since she and her mother had waited on the Chittoor train platform. She tried to imagine how different her life might have been if the Guru had not come to Anandanagar looking for her. She had left Anandanagar a village urchin, and she was returning a devadasi.

At the gurukulam it was impossible to see her family, and she tried hard not to think too much about them. Now the Guru had insisted she must visit them for a week. "You have worked hard, and you must rest," he had said. "Since you have become a devadasi, the rules are different." But the silence rule and the habit of solitary devotion had become a part of her.

Awakening on the day she would at last see her family, it was all she could think of. She had thought of them as she'd left them: two boys and a mother who wore her sadness like a second skin. She tried to imagine them as they were now: Venu and Venkat were young men—and Venkat's wife, Sumitra, was expecting their first child. Her mother had a new house and, in Sumitra, a new daughter.

When they alit from the train, a shiny black jatka with red wheel rims and red leather seats waited under the streetlight beside the landing. The jatka pony was large and muscular and black, his patent-leather bridle adorned with a red feathered ornament that dipped and bobbed as he tossed his head. The driver—wearing a red jacket over white churidar and a turban with a red braid and feather—jumped to the ground and held the pony's bridle while the bearer loaded their trunks and valises into the back of the Maharaja's jatka.

When everyone was seated, the driver snapped his whip and the pony stepped smartly forward. The cart rolled smoothly over the paved road on wheels of rubber. By the time they reached the stone pillar that marked the boundary of Nandipuram, the horizon glowed pink as the sun rose. The road gave way to a dusty track that rolled and curved down a lacy green tunnel of acacia trees. The countryside began to look familiar to Parvati.

After a while the neat rows of acacia trees turned to tangles of scrub along the roadside, and Parvati knew she was in her home district, where the forest would never grow again. The ground looked new and raw, still unaccustomed to not being a forest, but just as Parvati remembered it.

As the jatka neared the center of Nandipuram, Parvati sat forward and looked for her village. The road widened at one point, and was lined with tall palm trees that marked the Maharaja's parade route. She saw the hill first, and craned her neck to see the Opal Palace, with its crenellated walls.

The driver shook the reins, slapping them over the rump of the pony, and the jatka turned up the steep drive to the palace. They were stopping at the palace to drop the Guru, Kalpana, Vilasini, and the valise with Parvati's costume and Lakshmi's jewelry case. Kalpana and the Guru were to stay with the Raja and his family for a week while they scoured the countryside for new prospects for the gurukulam.

The pony's hooves struck the ancient paving stones in sharp, ringing clops as the cart made its ascent. Merchants pushing carts and workers carrying tools made their way slowly up the hill to work at the palace. They moved aside to let the jatka pass, staring at the Raja's guests.

They drove through gates built high enough to admit caparisoned elephants. A pair of guards in red tunics with black patent straps across their chests stood at attention on either side. Long swords with gilt handles hung from leather scabbards that nearly touched the ground at their left ankles. The jatka stopped just inside, and Parvati, Kalpana, and the Guru stepped down under a marble portico decorated with inlaid flowers of carved lapis, carnelian, rose quartz, and tiger's-eye, with leaves of jade.

In a large open doorway beneath a painting of the rotund elephant-headed Ganesha, Mr. Ramanujan introduced himself. He was short and round, with merry eyes. He bowed deeply before the Guru, who shook hands with the Maharaja's secretary and presented Parvati. Mr. Ramanujan's throat moved up and down for a second as if he was unable to speak, and he bowed to Parvati, who stood still in astonishment.

"Never," said Mr. Ramanujan, taking her hand in his, "never have I seen such a fine dance performance." Parvati's face was hot with happy embarrassment. She smiled and bowed. "Thank you, sir," she mumbled.

"Welcome!" said Mr. Ramanujan, opening his arms expansively. He guided the Guru, Kalpana, and Parvati to the reception hall, where the Raja and his family sat on a platform amid embroidered cushions. Overhead was a cloud-painted ceiling supported by marble columns. White doves fluttered among the arms of two enormous crystal chandeliers that shimmered with hundreds of white lights.

The Rani and her daughters talked animatedly among themselves, glancing up to smile at them. The Yuvaraja, whom Parvati recognized from the processions of her childhood, sat in front of his father, swinging his legs over the edge of the platform. He wore a cream-colored lawn tunic over slim white churidar, and silver toe rings on his bare feet.

The Raja's beard was precisely clipped, and his mustaches were waxed into curls at the tips. The Yuvaraja's face was still smooth, although a band of fine, silken hair darkened his upper lip, and his eyes were outlined dramatically in black kajal. The father was small and round, while the son was tall and slender like his mother. He looked as solemn and alone as Parvati remembered him, and for some reason she felt a deep sympathy for him, just as she had when she'd seen him as a child.

Mr. Ramanujan presented the visitors from Madras, who bowed and lowered their eyes. Mr. Ramanujan announced Parvati's name last.

"What a great honor that such a promising artist has come from Nandipuram," the Raja said. She looked up at him, uncertain whether to reply. She smiled shyly, and lowered her eyes again.

"It is a great honor that you have invited me to perform in Nandipuram, Excellency," she said, hardly able to control the shaking in her voice.

"Your mother, is she well?" the Raja asked, and Parvati was

unable to speak. She nodded her head. "I remember your father fondly," he went on. "Never have I known a man who had such a way with elephants. And his carvings were exquisite. I missed him terribly after he died."

Parvati felt the back of her throat burn at the Raja's kindness, but she bowed her head deeply and managed to say, "Thank you, Excellency." When she looked up, the Yuvaraja was staring at her, and she smiled at him slightly because she didn't quite know what else to do. But he continued to stare without returning her smile.

Once back in the jatka, Parvati forgot about everything but her family. As they drew closer to Anandanagar, a row of tamarind trees lined the dusty track, their pods of sour fruit clacking in the hot, dry breeze. Just outside the village was the temple. Parvati asked the driver to stop.

A family of monkeys watched with heavy-lidded eyes as Parvati got down from the jatka and walked to the small stone structure. She had remembered it as a grand temple. She ran her hand over a weather-blackened granite column and removed her sandals at the entry.

Inside, Parvati stared at the rough stone statue of Nandi the bull. Offerings from the village women's morning puja— jasmine, pieces of coconut, and grains of saffron rice—still sat before the bull. If there had been bananas, which were customary, they had disappeared.

The statue itself was much smaller and more crudely carved than she remembered it, though the face was well formed, with gentle eyes. The Nandi's head and horns and feet were smooth and waxy from devotees touching them. Parvati offered a silent prayer, then reached forward to touch her fingers against the end of the Nandi's nose before rising to return to the jatka.

When they reached the outer edge of Anandanagar the jatka could go no farther, for the village lanes were too narrow. Parvati reached into her bag for her brother's letter and unfolded it on her lap. Venkat had drawn a small map with directions to her mother's house at the end of a curving lane on the edge of the village, opposite the hill atop which her Uncle Sathya's house sat.

But she had no need of the map, for down the lane came a gaggle of children and behind them her mother and her brothers. Meenakshi broke from the group and ran to her daughter, her arms held wide.

Parvati dropped the bundle of gifts onto the seat and jumped down from the jatka to rush into her mother's arms. Parvati had grown several inches, and she bent her head to lay it against Meenakshi's shoulder, which smelled of rough tallowy laundry soap. Meenakshi laughed and cried at the same time as she raised her daughter's face and held it between her hands. The changes Parvati saw in her mother were subtle—a few graying strands of hair, fine lines that crinkled around her eyes and mouth. And her mother looked very small.

When Parvati looked up again, a handsome boy slightly taller than herself was smiling an enormous white smile. She could scarcely believe it was Venu, who when she last saw him still wore tattered short pants. Behind him stood Venkat, tall and serious, and beside him his delicate, shy wife, Sumitra.

Parvati hugged each of her relatives, and then hugged them all again. Seeing them after such a long time untied the wrappings of her heart, and she grieved suddenly and openly for herself having grown up without them. They laughed gently at her tears, for not one of them had ever seen her cry.

Venu gathered Parvati's bags from the jatka. Meenakshi brushed her daughter's cheeks dry, and they all began to talk at once about what she must come and see first—the field, where Venkat had rebuilt the soil and cultivated a fine crop of sugarcane; the herd of water buffaloes that provided enough milk for the entire village; the family plot of vegetables; the new path to the river; or the fish that Venu cultivated in cages at the edge of the river.

Village children followed them in a noisy procession along the lane to Meenakshi's house. As word spread that Parvati— now a famous dancer—was in Anandanagar again, adults joined the procession just to catch a glimpse of her.

The village looked far more prosperous than Parvati remembered it. Beside each front door was a toddy palm, and on each doorstep stood a red clay pot planted with orange and yellow flowers, and still another with plantings of basil and mint and curry bushes and other herbs for cooking. The mud walls were well cared for, and the roofs were covered with curved red clay tiles.

The wooden gate to the courtyard of her mother's house was painted bright blue. The hinges squeaked as the gate swung wide, and Meenakshi showed Parvati the house. It was made of stone with a tiled roof. The rooms were spacious and each had at least one window with wooden shutters to close at night. The main room had two windows and a door on each outside wall. At one end of the house were rooms where her mother and Venu slept, and at the other end was a room for Venkat and Sumitra.

Behind the house and across the courtyard was a kitchen with a chopping block made from a thick section of tree trunk, stone mortars and pestles for grinding spices, a stone basin for washing dishes and vegetables, and a counter along one side. The walls were whitewashed and decorated with small sunbursts and drawings of animals in earthen colors. Pots and baskets sat neatly stacked on shelves. Whisks and spatulas and wooden spoons hung from a pegged wooden rack. Dried palm fronds lay in one corner waiting to kindle wood from a generous pile beside the stove. A warm and spicy smell came from the oven.

The roof tiles overhead clattered and a monkey peered through a space between the tiles with one bright black eye. His tail hung down through another hole that served as a vent for smoke from the cooking fire. Meenakshi flicked a cloth at him to make him go away.

"They rearrange the roof every day!" she said, folding the cloth and putting it on the counter. Meenakshi touched everything in the kitchen lightly with her fingertips as she showed it to Parvati, who felt her mother's happiness.

They sat on woven grass pallets in the shade of the veranda

that ran the length of the house. The breeze from the court-yard was warm and scented with rain, for the monsoon had already begun farther to the south.

Sumitra came out carrying trays with strong coffee and milk in thick steaming cups. Meenakshi handed the cups around while Sumitra rushed back inside and returned with spicy dumplings and a tart tamarind sauce, which she passed around the table. Parvati tasted one, and it melted hotly on her tongue. She smiled.

"Sumitra is a wonderful cook," Meenakshi said quietly, and they all agreed. The girl smiled with pleasure and looked down at her hands. She was small, with large, intelligent eyes and even white teeth. Her belly showed roundly under her sari.

Parvati was to be with her family for one week, before going to the palace to prepare for her program. It seemed such a short time.

"You are not drinking your coffee," said her mother.

"Devadasis don't take coffee," Parvati replied. Meenakshi brought her a lassi, mixed with sugar. Venkat and Venu returned to their work. Meenakshi, Sumitra, and Parvati sat with their backs against the wall of the house, pulling their feet in as the sun advanced, hugging their knees, talking and laughing for the rest of the afternoon.

Parvati looked at her mother and sister-in-law with long-ing. She wanted to stay and watch Sumitra's belly grow, to be there for the birth, to help Meenakshi care for the infant and its mother. She wanted to watch her brothers' crops grow. She wanted to be a part of her family again. And she reminded herself that it was precisely because she was not a member of her family in the sense that she wanted to be that such a good life had become possible for them.

Meenakshi had invited Uncle Sathya and Auntie, Mahesh, and Mohan and his wife, Asha, to eat with them that evening. Venkat went to fetch them, and when they arrived Uncle Sathya pretended he was going to lift Parvati into the air as he'd done when she'd left, and they all laughed. Auntie had grown fat, and her hair was half gray and half black. Her mouth looked puckered and caved in like a cut melon that had sat too long in the sun.

Mohan greeted Parvati warmly and introduced his tall, plump wife, who held a small boy on her hip, their son, Suresh. Asha smiled warmly and set the boy down. He toddled off in bare feet, shaking a stick at the chickens in the yard.

Venkat and Venu went inside to fetch chairs and a string cot so everyone would have a place to sit on the veranda.

"Have you been out to see the miracle your brothers have wrought in the fields?" Uncle Sathya asked. The men talked enthusiastically and loudly about crops and politics.

Asha joined Meenakshi and Sumitra in talking about saris they had purchased from a new silk shop in the bazaar two weeks earlier.

"They're so fine they feel like water between your fingers," said Sumitra.

"And yet you can't see even a shadow through them, they're woven so tightly," said Asha.

"And you know, that clever fellow," said Meenakshi, "he's

undercut Mysore Silk Mills with his prices. He will do very well!"

Parvati listened with wonder. In all the time she'd lived at home her mother had never even owned a silk sari, and now she talked as if she bought a dozen every day.

"You have never seen such a blue!" Sumitra said, laying her hand easily on her sister-in-law's arm. "It's like the sky!" Parvati loved having been taken into the warm circle of the women, and already Venkat's wife seemed as if she had always been a sister.

Auntie sat beside Asha and said very little. She looked about her at the spacious, well-tended house and yard and pursed her lips. When the talk turned to the reason Parvati had returned to Nandipuram, Auntie's mouth puckered more deeply and she tilted her head back and looked down the length of her nose at her niece with narrowed eyes.

Sumitra and Meenakshi got up reluctantly and went to the kitchen to finish preparations for dinner. Parvati and Asha stood to go with them.

"You have little enough time to spend with your broth-ers—they are in the fields or at the river day and night—and your aunt and uncle," Meenakshi said. "Asha, please stay with Parvati and you two get to know each other." Asha and Par-vati protested, but Meenakshi would not allow them in the kitchen.

"Have you been well, Auntie?" Parvati asked. Until then her aunt had pretended not to hear whenever Parvati had spoken.

"Ummh," Auntie said, looking away and folding her arms. She seemed to be engrossed in the conversation of the men.

"Amma and I have been trying to reduce," Asha said quickly, sliding her eyes toward her mother-in-law. "I gained so much weight when Suresh was born, and I couldn't take it off by myself, so she's helping me." Parvati accepted her comment with a smile. But she remembered all too well how her aunt had looked at her with blame in her eyes, and she knew nothing had changed.

In the days that followed, Meenakshi and Sumitra wanted to know how Parvati spent every second of every day at the gurukulam, whether she had friends, what her room was like, what she ate, whether Indira was as bossy and officious as she had seemed to Meenakshi.

Parvati told them about everything except Nalini and Mayappan. Nalini's loss was still painful, and Parvati didn't want her family to worry.

Each morning Parvati arose early and went to the temple. She and her mother shared the wide cot in Meenakshi's room, and the groan of the strings awoke them at dawn. They wrapped their saris in silence and went to their puja together, not talking in the warm humid morning.

In the weeks before the monsoon, the nights were hardly cooler than the days, and the air felt like a solid substance. Early morning was the only time its weight was bearable, and then it caressed their skin, and the dust was cool and powdery between their toes.

Parvati fit into the quiet rhythm of her family's days as if she never had gone away. She swept the floors and veranda and courtyard every morning in the pearly light with the roosters crowing and the buffaloes nosing their fodder. After the midday meal everyone rested until they were awakened by peacocks screeching in the lanes.

The second morning Parvati and Sumitra walked down the palm-lined path to the river to wash clothes. They hiked their saris up between their legs, tucking them in around their waists to keep dry, and waded into the mud until the water was above their knees, deep enough to wet the laundry. They brought it back to the ghat to soap it and beat it against the large flat stone, talking all the while.

After the clothes had been rinsed and wrung, Parvati and Sumitra laid them on the rocks to dry and sat in the shade with their feet in the water. Parvati lifted the smaller basket of clean laundry and set it atop Sumitra's head, carrying the heavier one herself. As they walked along the edge of the water back to the village, Sumitra saw the fish following them and laughed, but she said nothing. Parvati draped her arm over her new sister's shoulder, and left it there as they walked home.

Fifteen

Parvati and Sumitra went to the bazaar every day to deliver vegetables from Meenakshi's garden for the grocer to sell, and to buy things they needed.

One day Sumitra felt dizzy. Parvati settled her sister-in-law on a cot on the veranda and drew the bamboo shade down, dousing it with water so the breeze would cool her. Parvati set off for the bazaar alone with a large round basket piled high with small red tomatoes and green chili peppers atop her head.

"Parvati!" Sumitra called as she went through the gate. "Please bring me some pineapple. I want pineapple more than anything!" Parvati promised she would, and Sumitra sank back against the cushions. Her face was as pale as the sun in the misty monsoon sky.

After delivering her basket of tomatoes and chilis to the grocer, Parvati made her way toward a narrow stall in the part of the lane where the fruit vendors plied their wares. The air was stifling hot under the awning and the smell of pineapple was almost overpowering. Bees hovered in buzzing gray clouds around the stall, which was piled with a six-foot pyramid of ripe yellow pineapples. The vendor, a jolly fat man in a dhoti, cut the skin of one dripping fruit in a single spiral peel with a large knife and offered a piece to Parvati.

"Have it!" he said. "You will not find a sweeter pineapple in all of Nandipuram!" Parvati laughed and took the piece he offered. It was so sweet and filled with juice that she bought two whole pineapples.

She put the fruit in her basket and hoisted it to her head. As she turned toward home she thought she saw a familiar face in the crowd. Parvati's heart leapt from her chest to her throat. She scanned the faces of the shoppers, and saw some that she had known all her life, and others she'd never seen before. This was a face she knew well—but not in Nandipuram. It was the face of a woman who looked like a Gypsy—a stranger, with dark eyes that were wary and hard. But it couldn't have been, Parvati thought, because the face she had recognized was Nalini's.

She hurried along the lane, looking down little side alleys as she went, and she thought surely she was mistaken. Then she saw Venu coming toward her. She waved and he walked home with her. For the rest of the week Parvati was haunted by the vision of Nalini, even though she had decided she only imagined seeing her friend.

Sumitra didn't open her eyes when she heard Parvati's voice. "Did you bring the pineapple?" she asked, her face still ashen against the bright red print of the pillow behind her head. Parvati quickly washed, peeled, and sliced one of the pineapples and brought it out to the veranda on a plate along with a cool wet cloth. She helped Sumitra sit up and wiped her face with the cloth.

Sumitra grabbed the plate from Parvati's hands and pushed an entire round of pineapple into her mouth, the juice dripping down her chin. She ate another, and then another, hardly bothering to chew, then sank back onto the pillow with a sigh. Parvati wiped her sister-in-law's face and hands with the cloth, but the girl was sound asleep.

Sumitra awoke a while later, full of energy in the hot still afternoon. Parvati had just fallen asleep on her mother's bed when she heard her sister-in-law's voice beside her in the room.

"Are we going to the river to wash clothes?" Sumitra asked. She fanned Parvati's face with a round palm fan that lay on a table near the cot.

"The sun is too high," Parvati said. "Not two hours ago you were fainting. You should rest for the afternoon. We can wash clothes tomorrow." Sumitra laughed and Parvati looked at her through one sleep-blurred eye. "Really," she said. "You were quite ill not two hours ago."

Sumitra tugged at her hand and finally pulled Parvati reluctantly to her feet.

Parvati carried all of the clothes herself, and just managed not to be short with Sumitra, who sang and chattered as they walked. Halfway to the river Parvati had an odd sensation at the back of her ribs, as if someone was watching. She turned quickly, nearly tipping the basket of laundry from her head. But no one was on the path behind her, and she thought perhaps she was mistaken.

While they waited in the shade for the clothes to dry, a brain-fever bird sounded its maddening shriek. Several yards from the riverbank a tall young man cast a fishing net over the water, sending up a spray of droplets.

Parvati squinted at him—he was about her age. He was naked to the waist, apart from the three white sacred threads looped over his left shoulder and around his waist. The threads were worn by priests and rulers. Parvati's people were of the caste destined to serve others. The young man wore a simple dhoti and stood hip-deep in the river, sparkles of water on his brown shoulders.

Parvati stared at the figure in the brilliant glare of the sun on the water. His back was turned toward her, but she recognized the set of his slender shoulders and the dangle of his long arms. Everything about him looked intensely concentrated and utterly alone. There was no lawn tunic, and when he turned toward her no kajal darkened the eyes. But Parvati felt certain she was looking at the son of the Maharaja Narasimha Deva.

He looked once toward the shore, and Parvati thought perhaps he'd seen her. She raised her hand to shade her eyes. He stared for a moment, then turned his back and waded off downstream with his nets.

What would the Yuvaraja be doing out fishing in the river, she wondered. And why was he alone, dressed like a fisherman?

Two days later Sumitra was too ill again to go with Parvati to the river, and so she went alone. She tucked up her sari, and waded out into the water to wet the clothes before bringing them back to the broad flat rock to soap them. She rinsed the garments, then slung them over her shoulder. The water felt cool as it dripped down her back. Parvati felt the tickle of the small fish that gathered around her, brushing up against her and nibbling at her legs and feet. She splashed water at them and they darted away before crowding around her again.

"How can I catch fish when they're all swimming around you?" a voice asked from across the water. Parvati looked up. Several yards from where she stood was the Yuvaraja, his net draped over his shoulder, the end of it fanned out behind him in the current. Parvati's pulse hammered in her throat for a moment. She focused her attention on the wet clothes, and turned toward the riverbank, her voice stuck in her throat.

"Wait!" said the Yuvaraja. But Parvati made her way quickly toward shore. The fish scattered and swam off. "Come back!" the Yuvaraja shouted. It was not a good thing to talk to a man—someone she did not know—when she was alone, even if he was the Yuvaraja. Parvati hurriedly piled the wet clothes in her basket and hoisted it to her head. She looked up once before retreating up the riverbank. The Yuvaraja stood in the river scowling, his hands on his hips. "I'm not dangerous!" he shouted after her.

The next morning Parvati took her mother's vegetables to the market and bought more pineapple for Sumitra before heading back down the lane to her mother's house. The monkeys scampered along behind her, plucking at her sari. She talked to them as she went, the pineapples balanced on her head inside the basket.

Suddenly Parvati felt the presence of someone behind her. Without warning, she whirled around and the Yuvaraja almost collided with her.

"Why are you following me?" she demanded.

"I must talk to you," the Yuvaraja said, his voice urgent.

"I'm sorry," Parvati said, and turned again toward home. But the Yuvaraja hurried in front of her and stopped. This time Parvati almost collided with him.

"I am the Yuvaraja!" he said, his voice imperious. "You must do as I say!"

Parvati brushed past him, but again he hurried around in front of her.

"Please," he said, his voice sounding more desperate than commanding.

"I can't," Parvati said. "I'm sorry."

"It's important that we talk." His eyes, which just a moment earlier had looked haughty and demanding, begged her.

"No," she said softly. He let her go, and Parvati hurried down the lane without looking back. Once inside her mother's courtyard, she leaned against the gate and took a deep breath. Her heart pounded.

That night was her last night at home. Parvati wanted to reel back the time—to gather it in again and relive it. After the evening meal, when the others had gone to bed, she walked in her mother's garden. The scent of night-blooming jasmine wafted from the wall and the air felt like a soft blanket against her skin. String squeaked against wood as someone lay down inside the house. Parvati leaned her elbows on the gate and looked out into the dark lane. Lanterns cast golden pools here and there from doorways and windows, and suddenly Parvati knew she was not alone. She jumped back from the gate with a sharp intake of breath. The Yuvaraja stood before her with his finger pressed against his lips. This time he was dressed simply in a jibba and drawstring trousers.

"Please!" he whispered. "I must talk to you. It's very important." Parvati took another step backward, and the gate squeaked softly as he opened it. "I'll only stay a minute," he persisted. "Please!" Parvati looked up the lane and back at the house. It appeared everyone had gone to sleep.

"I shouldn't," she said. And yet . . . She motioned him to a small bench against the wall behind the kitchen, where her mother and Sumitra mixed flour and water and peeled onions. She was afraid to light a lantern, but she was uncomfortable sitting there alone with a stranger.

"What is it?" she asked, her voice barely a whisper. The Yuvaraja sat beside her on the bench. He leaned his head back against the wall and took a deep breath. As her eyes grew accustomed to dim light from other houses in the lane outside the garden gate, Parvati could see he was smiling. He'd always looked sober, even sad, when she'd seen him before. His smile was lovely.

"I'm sorry," he said. "I am Rama."

"I know who you are," she said. "I mean, I know you are the Raja's son—I didn't know your name. I am Parvati."

"And I know who you are," he said. "Thank you for not giving me away at the river. I could see you recognized me, and I was afraid you would call attention to me. Does anyone know you saw me?"

"I told no one," she said. "Why were you dressed like that? And why didn't you want anyone to see you?"

"I'm not allowed out of the palace grounds," he said. "I never have been. I've never had friends, and I never have any fun." Parvati nodded. He cocked his head as if he expected her to say something, but she was silent.

"Don't people recognize you?" Parvati asked after a while. "Hasn't anyone ever told your father that you fish in the river?"

"No one expects me to go out, so no one has recognized me," he said. "You're the first and only one. Everyone thinks of me dressed in my official togs with that ridiculous eye black—they don't recognize a simple fisherman. They come from villages upstream and downstream to fish all along the river. Anywhere but there or in the bazaars people would be curious about a stranger."

Parvati wanted to ask so many questions. But she was uneasy sitting with the Yuvaraja in her mother's garden.

"I must go inside," she said.

"No, wait!" Rama said. "Can I see you again?"

"This is my last night at home," Parvati said. "I will be at the palace tomorrow."

"I'll come see you there," Rama said, his voice brightening.

"No," said Parvati. "I'll be with the Guru and his daughter and the ayah."

"Parvati?" It was Meenakshi's voice, sounding sleepy, from inside the house. "Are you coming?"

"Yes, Amma," she said. "I must go now," she whispered. He put his hand on her arm.

"Promise I can see you again."

"I can't!" said Parvati, standing.

"Promise!" said Rama. Parvati nodded then and turned to go. Rama smiled and she couldn't resist smiling back. His look could change so quickly from desperate to happy, she thought.

The next morning, before the jatka arrived to take Parvati to the Opal Palace, the sun shone hot and white over the village. Parvati stood beside her mother, who poured a batter of fermented rice and lentil flour and water into large, thin pools on the griddle. Overhead a family of monkeys clattered across the tiles.

"When will you come again?" Meenakshi asked, lifting the edges of the dosai with a spatula.

"I wasn't supposed to visit at all," Parvati replied. "But now that I'm to be a teacher at the gurukulam perhaps I can come once or twice a year. I don't want to ask too much." Her mother nodded but said nothing.

After they had eaten, Venu came running down the lane and through the front gate.

"The jatka is here!" he called. Parvati's cloth bag sat on the top step. Sumitra lay on the cot on the veranda, looking pale again.

"You must get a pineapple for her every day," Parvati said to her mother. Her throat tightened. She had never known how happy having a sister might have made her.

Sumitra's eyelids fluttered and she raised herself on her elbows. She smiled at Parvati and asked her to come after the baby had arrived. "It can't be soon enough," she said, and sank back to the pillow. Parvati gave her sister-in-law a hug, brushed Sumitra's hair back from her damp forehead, and kissed her again. Parvati said goodbye to Venkat, who stayed with his wife while the others went to see Parvati off.

Venu carried her cloth bag, which bulged now with two new saris, one silk and one cotton, that her mother and Sumitra had given her. He handed it up to the jatka driver. Parvati kissed her mother and touched her brother's finger-tips and face.

It was difficult to say goodbye. She had savored the week, but still it had gone too quickly. Parvati had followed the Guru's advice. She had not danced, and she had tried not to think about it at all. Now it was all she could think of. It took her mind away from the pain of leaving.

Sixteen

The jatka pulled up behind a sedan under an arched cupola that covered the main entrance to the palace, and a minibus filled with men in brightly colored turbans drew up behind them. The Maharani and her daughters—Mira, who was a few years older than Parvati, and Gita, who was just a year older—greeted the arriving guests, who included other performers. Parvati stepped down from the jatka, and a servant took her bag. She waited in line with the others as the Maharani spoke briefly to each person.

When it was Parvati's turn, the Maharani took her hand and held it in her own. "We are so glad to have you back in Nandipuram," the Maharani said. Parvati bowed her head slightly and the Maharani sent her daughters to show her to her room. The servant followed with her bag.

Mira and Gita chattered about the other guests: royalty, government officials and foreign diplomats from New Delhi, and famous musicians and dancers from all over India. "Those men who came behind you," said Gita, "are from Rajasthan—they have played before the Queen in London!"

Parvati listened and looked about in awe as they walked. The floors were inlaid with medallions of malachite and lapis and carnelian. Crystal chandeliers hung every twenty feet, and between them were plain brass sconces.

They arrived outside a massive wooden door, where Indira's ayah, Vilasini, stood waiting. The ayah leaned heavily against the door, and it opened slowly. Vilasini had warmed to Parvati, for having been chosen to perform for the Maharaja elevated the girl closer to the level of Lakshmi, whom Vilasini considered to be of the station she was destined to serve. Parvati removed her sandals as she entered.

The walls of her room were pale purple, with peeling paint and a patchy sheen of mold. At one end of the room a narrow doorway led to a white-tiled bathroom. Two wooden chairs and a table sat under the high, deep window well, through which watery sunlight spilled onto the white marble floor. An armoire stood beside the door and an ancient teak fan turned slowly overhead. The bed was polished brass with pink and green linens that looked as if they had been washed hundreds of times. A small fireplace was centered on the wall opposite the bed. The room seemed to Parvati at once elegant and dilapidated and captivating.

After ordering lime and water and making sure Parvati was comfortable, the Rani's daughters and Vilasini left her. Parvati opened the armoire to put her clothes away.

On the shelves inside were her costume, wrapped in tissue paper, the locked case with the jewelry for her performance, extra bedding and linen, and two folded saris that she did not recognize. She emptied her cloth bag and laid her belongings on an empty shelf, closed the armoire door, and placed the Shiva Nataraja on the table.

Parvati changed into a dance sari to meditate and practice. She was sitting comfortably on the floor, her legs folded in the lotus position and her back to the window, deep in meditation, when a knock came at the heavy wooden door. At first she did not hear it, but when it was repeated more insistently, she said, "Come in," then realized the door might be too thick for her voice to be heard on the other side.

It was probably Kalpana, she thought, and rose to open the door. Standing before her in a white jibba of homespun cotton and a pair of matching drawstring pajama trousers was Rama.

At first she was too surprised to speak. When the Yuvaraja looked over his shoulder and down the corridor first in one direction and then in the other, she came to her senses. This was not like Venu coming to ask if she wanted to see his fish traps! It was hardly proper for the son of the Maharaja to come to her bedroom door.

"What do you want?" she asked.

"I must talk to you," the Yuvaraja said, his voice an urgent whisper.

"I'm sorry," Parvati said, and pushed the door to close it. But the Yuvaraja wedged his foot against it to hold it open. "If the Guru knew I was talking to you . . ."

"I also would be in trouble," Rama said.

Parvati was afraid someone would come down the corridor and see him, and so she stepped aside to let him in. She closed the door and leaned against it, her heart beating hard.

"Thank you," he said. "Why are you afraid to let me in?"

Parvati didn't want to do something she was sure the Guru would not approve of. But how could he disapprove of the Yuvaraja?

"How do you get away?" she asked. "Doesn't anyone miss you when you're out for an entire afternoon?"

He smiled mysteriously. "I am not at liberty to say," he replied, lifting his chin and looking down his nose at her.

"Well, you should go," Parvati said coolly, and turned to reopen the door. Rama's eyes widened and he closed the door again.

"Please," he said. "We really must talk."

"What is so important that we must talk about?" she asked.

"It's rather complicated," the Yuvaraja said. When Parvati said nothing, he hurried on. "It's about your father and some very odd coincidences."

Parvati checked the door, and it was latched securely.

There was a lock, but no key. "Anyone could come in," she said. In spite of herself she wanted to hear what Rama had to say. Still she blocked his way into the room.

"Servants always knock," he said. The window was high and deep enough that it was impossible to see inside from the courtyard. And she knew she would take the risk. She pointed to the chair where she wanted him to sit.

Rama smiled widely and watched her walk around the table to sit in the other chair. He reached forward and picked up the Shiva Nataraja.

"Your father carved this," he said, touching the palm of the raised hand and the hooded eyes of the statue with his fingertip.

"How did you know?" Parvati asked. "It's . . ." She hesitated, remembering to be cautious about the statue's magic. "It's very special to me," she said.

"I know," Rama said, "because my father owns many of your father's carvings. Did you know that our fathers knew each other?"

"So the Raja said," Parvati replied, not meaning for so much skepticism to sound in her voice. She had assumed the Maharaja was being polite when he said how much he'd missed her father.

"Your father saved my father's life," Rama said. Parvati squinted her eyes. "Truly!" he said. And he told her the story.

One day when Sundar was a young man, the Raja had invited foreigners who were studying India's forestry industry to watch the mahouts train young elephants to work in the timber harvest.

As the guests sat beneath a tree near the clearing where the elephants were kept, servants fanned them with woven palm punkas. The Raja asked Sundar to explain to the visitors how the elephants were captured, trained, and cared for. Sundar asked the mahouts to bring a young elephant they were working with and the Raja translated what he said into English for the visitors. Sundar explained that this elephant had been snared only a month earlier.

The men chained the young bull elephant by his back legs to two large trees. They shouted a command at him over and over, and when the young bull did not understand—for how could he?—they beat him with bamboo sticks. The elephant raised his trunk and trumpeted, first in fear, appealing to them to stop the beating.

"It's a terrible thing to watch," Rama said. "It sounds cruel, but it is necessary to teach the elephants to obey the mahouts. If they do not fear, they will not obey."

"I could train an elephant to do as I asked without beating it," Parvati said, her voice low with indignation.

"And so could your father," Rama said. "But what these people wanted was a demonstration of how it is done, not how a wizard does it!"

Parvati colored. Her father was not a wizard. But she said nothing, and Rama resumed his story.

The young elephant, who was deceptively strong for his size and age, broke the chains on his legs. In a rage he looked about him, trunk upraised, and charged the mahouts, who ran off in different directions. It was not the first time such a thing had happened, and they knew the beast would be confused if they all went their separate ways. But Sundar stood his ground beside the Raja and his guests, who were frozen to the spot. With the objects of his rage gone off, the elephant turned toward those who stayed in one place.

Swaying backward and forward, he churned the dirt with his massive front foot, and sprayed up curtains of dust with his trunk. Then he lifted his trunk high and ran toward them, gathering speed as he went.

Sundar stepped between the charging beast and the foreigners and calmly bent, scooped up two handfuls of loose dust, and scattered it into the sun, in front of the elephant's face. Stunned, the elephant stopped and backed away. Swaying from side to side and raising his trunk to sniff the air, the elephant was calm once again.

"My father was convinced your father had charmed the elephant," Rama said. "He showed tremendous courage. Then, as if charming a rogue were not enough, your father walked calmly to the elephant, led him back to where he had been confined earlier, and shackled him again—and he was docile as a lamb!"

"I never heard this story," Parvati said. "Could it be that my mother didn't know about it?"

"Your father was a modest man," Rama said. "After he had secured the elephant, your father came back to where my father and his guests watched, still very shaken. Sundar apologized for the elephant's behavior and asked my father's forgiveness for himself, and also for the elephant. He promised it would not happen again.

" 'This is a young elephant, who has only been with us a short time, Excellency,' your father said to mine. 'It was my fault. He was not ready for a demonstration. I will personally take over his training, and nothing like this will happen ever again.' You see, Sundar knew that, having threatened the Maharaja's life, the elephant was likely to be shot, and your father could not bear for that to happen. This is the elephant my father chooses to ride each year in the Dussehra procession."

"Thank you for that story about my father," she said. She wanted to ask him a thousand questions about her father, but there was a knock at the door.

"May I come tonight?" he whispered. "I haven't told you what I came to tell . . ." Parvati had jumped up and gone to the door.

"Just a moment," she said loudly, her mouth close to the door.

"I don't think so," she whispered, turning back toward Rama, but it was difficult to keep regret from her voice.

"I'll see you tonight," he whispered, and opened the armoire. She couldn't help smiling at his persistence.

She thought he meant to hide inside, and so she closed the armoire door behind him and went back to the bedroom door, opening it slowly. Kalpana stood before her.

"I'm in the next room along the hall," Kalpana said. "Did you look in your armoire?"

"Yes," Parvati said. "I . . . That is, I put my clothes away."

"The saris!" Kalpana said. "They're gifts from the Maharani—didn't you see them?" She went to the armoire, and Parvati stood frozen, unable to stop her. When Kalpana opened the armoire door, the clothing sat undisturbed on the shelves—but no Rama! Kalpana reached in and brought out the two silk saris, the clothing Parvati had assumed someone had left behind. "You can tell by the weave they're from Kanchipuram," said Kalpana. Parvati peered inside, but the armoire was empty except for her clothing, the costume and jewelry case, and an extra blanket.

Parvati couldn't imagine where Rama had gone, and she still couldn't trust her voice.

They took the saris to the window to examine in the light. One was shot silk that looked red when turned this way and black turned that way, with gold, red, black, and green threads woven into an intricate pattern along the hem and border.

"Perhaps they thought we would not have the proper clothing," Kalpana said, refolding the sari neatly.

"And if this is the proper clothing, they were right!" Parvati said, finally able to speak. She unfolded the other sari, a brilliant blue silk with a paisley border of green, dark blue, and gold.

Kalpana took the sari from Parvati, folded it carefully, and opened the door of the armoire again. Once again Parvati's heart flew into her mouth. But again, there was not a sign of Rama.

"We have two days to practice," said Kalpana, closing the armoire. "There are meetings and dance demonstrations and speeches for two days. Then on the third day is the Raja's birthday celebration. You will perform that evening."

"Where are we to practice?" Parvati asked.

"I'll meet you at the room at the end of the corridor in ten minutes," Kalpana said. At the doorway she pointed to a closed door at the end of the corridor. Parvati nodded, and Kalpana left her. Parvati waited a moment and went to the armoire.

She opened the door, but the armoire was empty. Nothing was disturbed. She knocked on the back panel, behind the shelves that held her belongings, but the wood there sounded solid. She swung open the heavy, carved bedroom door and looked down the corridor. Nothing stood against the wall next to the armoire and no one was in sight. Somehow he had gotten out—but how?

Parvati met Kalpana in the room at the end of the corridor, where a stage had been erected. The air was pungent with the smell of freshly cut wood. The windows on either side of the long room were open and the breeze was cooler than the still air in the corridor.

"This is the size of the area where you will perform," Kalpana said. "You'll share the stage with the musicians. Tomorrow you'll dance with them—they're very good. You'll have just one session with them before the performance." She sat on the floor facing the stage and motioned Parvati up onto it.

Kalpana struck her stick against the wooden block to mark out the rhythm of Parvati's dance. She hummed the music in parts. Kalpana had a fine and versatile voice, and Parvati was lost in the music for the rest of the afternoon.

When they had finished, Kalpana went looking for the Guru, and Parvati returned to her room to rest. She thought about Rama and wondered how he had gotten out of the armoire.

A bearer carrying a silver tray with lime water and a plate of sweet biscuits and fried savories knocked at the door. He wore a turban that had been stiffly starched and arranged into an elaborately pleated fan with a gold edge. The bearer placed the tray on the table beside the window. "Would there be anything else, miss?" he asked. She said no, thanked him, and closed the door behind him. Then she went back to the armoire, but still she could find no door, no way the Yuvaraja could have escaped.

Parvati nibbled at the savories and drank some lime water. She did not like knowing Rama could come and go through her armoire. As she ate, she decided she could not allow him to return. She must find a way to tell him. It wasn't that she didn't want to see him—or even that she cared so much that it wasn't proper. But the Guru had trusted her to perform at the palace. She could not let him down.

She set her tray outside the door so that the bearer would not disturb her when he came back for it.

In two days she would perform before an audience of dignitaries and artists. She needed to meditate and rehearse. She had no time for anything else. If Rama came back that evening she would tell him she could not be distracted.

Seventeen

That evening, after a quiet dinner, Kalpana, the Guru, and Parvati sat together in Kalpana's room. The Guru told stories about performances he and Lakshmi had given before India's first Prime Minister, Jawaharlal Nehru, and Lord Mountbatten, the Viceroy at the time of India's independence.

"This Raja was there—he saw us," the Guru said.

"Surely he's not that old," Kalpana said. Her father laughed.

"Independence was a little more than fifty years ago, daughter, not five hundred years ago! He was a boy then, as the Yuvaraja is now. I think he took a fancy to your mother, but of course we were married . . ." His voice trailed off and his eyes looked far away.

"The Raja is still one of India's most beloved leaders," he said. "When his father was Maharaja, he was one of the most highly regarded princes, although Nandipuram rated only a thirteen-gun salute. Like his father, this Raja has improved schools, made donations to temples, and helped families in need. That is why people honor him. They still call him 'Maharaja' and they come to him for advice. After the cyclone fourteen years ago he converted the ruined land to agriculture, and he and his people have flourished."

After the Guru said good night and returned to his room, Parvati and Kalpana sat for a while. Parvati was quiet.

"Aren't you feeling well?" Kalpana asked. "You've been quiet all day."

"I miss my family," Parvati said. "It was wonderful to see them, but the time was too short. I don't know when I'll see them again." She did not want to think about Rama, but she could not quite banish him from her mind.

Kalpana laid her hand on Parvati's. "What you are doing is very important," she said. "To have a talent like yours is an enormous responsibility. It can also pay great rewards."

Parvati smiled. "I'm grateful for my talent and the money it's brought my family. But sometimes it is lonely."

"Very lonely," Kalpana agreed. "But in two days, after your performance before the Maharaja, you will know better why we make these sacrifices. So—shall we rehearse in the morning?" They agreed to meet after breakfast and again with the musicians in the afternoon.

Parvati was weary when she closed the door to her room. A small electric lamp was lit on the table beside the Shiva

Nataraja. She picked up the statue and rubbed the fragrant wood, thinking of her mother. She decided to write her a letter before going to sleep. She opened the armoire and reached inside for the paper in her cloth bag. She thought she saw a faint movement, and a neatly folded towel fell from its shelf to the floor. Parvati drew back, and a small sound escaped from her throat.

Rama climbed from behind the shelves of the armoire, stepping up, as if over a sill at the top of a stairway. He held a finger to his lips, and moved stealthily to the door and listened for a moment before turning to Parvati.

At first she was angry. "You can't just appear in my room whenever you like!" she said. "This is an important performance, and you . . ." But the sight of him made her happy and she could not be angry for more than a minute.

"Sssshhh!" Rama said, putting his finger to his lips again and listening at the door. He wore a cream-colored silk achkan and a salmon turban. A string of large, perfect pearls hung about his neck. His eyes were rimmed with kajal.

When he was satisfied no one was in the corridor outside the door, Rama crossed the room and sat in one of the chairs beneath the window.

"Have you been hiding in there all this time?" Parvati asked. But he couldn't have changed clothes if he had been. She felt silly. "How did you get in and out?"

Rama acted as if he hadn't heard her questions. "I'll only stay a minute. I want to tell you why I'm confined," he said. "I've never told anyone—but I've never had a friend to confide in." And he told her a story that took her breath away.

"I was born on my father's birthday," he began. "And the things that happened on that day were so terrible and extraordinary I have remembered everything from the moment of my birth. Within a few hours palm trees were flying like arrows, and the forest that my father once owned—and his father before him, and so on, back more generations than anyone can remember—was ruined in the worst storm in Nandipuram's history. It was the only cyclone ever, the storm in which your father died."

"Why are you telling me this?" Parvati asked.

"Before we can be friends, I must tell you I caused the storm that killed your father. I couldn't bear for you to find out later. If you do not want to be friends, you must tell me now."

"No!" she said. "It wasn't your fault." She spoke intensely, but in a near whisper. "It was *my* fault."

Rama held up his hand. "You don't need to be kind. I've always known I have destructive powers."

"Listen," Parvati said. "I was also born on the day of the cyclone. And I remember everything from the moment of my birth!" Rama looked at her with disbelief. She told him of her mother staying behind while everyone went to the Raja's birthday feast, of the crow, and of how her family had survived the storm.

"It's a coincidence we were born the same day," Rama said. "But there is more. Soon after my birth I fell deathly ill. Neither milk nor water would stay in my stomach, and I writhed in pain. My flesh began to waste away, and everyone was afraid I would die. Then one by one every child in the palace fell ill with the same affliction. And one by one the children died. Only I survived."

"But that was because of the cyclone, not because of you!" Parvati said. "*I* was responsible for the illness." She told him her aunt and others believed she and her mother had laid claim to all the good health in Anandanagar, and that was why everyone else fell ill. "They even blamed me for your illness!"

Rama hesitated a moment. "There is more," he said. "As if the misfortune of everyone else were not enough, I also seem to have been given extraordinary powers. It's hard for me to explain, but I will show you. From my infancy everyone believed I would make other children ill, and so I was kept away from them. And long after I was well, my father employed two servants to carry me from place to place, from morning till night. For seven years I was never allowed to walk anywhere!"

"When did you learn to walk?" Parvati asked.

"I've always known how to walk," he replied. "That was part of my gift! When I was still an infant, while everyone else slept I climbed from my cradle and walked about the palace. But my father has always been overly protective. He doesn't rule any longer, yet he persists with the dhoom-dham and folderol of royalty. There is no need for the son of a former Raja to be coddled and protected as I have been. It was inhumane even when the Yuvaraja was heir to the throne. Now that we're ordinary citizens it shouldn't be allowed!"

They sat silent for a moment while each absorbed what the other had said.

"You can't reason with your father?" she asked.

"My father says, 'This is your dharma, just as it was mine.' But his father still ruled when he was a boy, so there was reason for him to be treated differently. My father doesn't rule, nor will I. I don't believe it's my dharma to prepare for something that will never happen."

"I, too, was born with strange gifts," Parvati said. "When I was small I didn't know that I was different from everyone else. But my gifts are my dharma. It's difficult to talk about. It makes other people uncomfortable, and so I've learned to be secretive about these things, even though I value them. One of my gifts is dance. You'll see that soon enough. The others I cannot summon at will. They are a kind of . . . well, I call it magic. But I have no power over them."

"Why do you think *you* caused the cyclone?" he asked, sticking his chin out.

"Perhaps for the same reason you think *you* were the cause!" Parvati said, matching his tone. And they looked at one another in amazement that each laid claim to the most shameful secret of the other's life. They laughed and laughed, until their stomachs were weak.

Parvati noticed a gecko clinging to the underside of the windowsill, his head turned to look at her. She put her hand under the window ledge, a few inches from where the gecko sat. He turned his head sideways, dipping it to examine her hand for a second before jumping onto her palm.

"How did you get him to do that?" Rama asked. Parvati smiled and lifted her hand closer to her face.

"This is my friend," she said to the gecko, who cocked his head as if listening. "Go sit on his shoulder." Parvati put her hand beside Rama's left shoulder and the gecko jumped onto him. Rama shivered slightly, although he couldn't feel the tiny lizard's feet on the fabric of his achkan. The gecko was not afraid, and sat there while they talked.

"That's part of my gift," Parvati said. "I have always talked to the animals, and they've always talked to me. We are creatures of the same substance. But people think it's odd, and even frightening." She leaned forward for the gecko to jump back onto her hand. But the creature stayed on Rama's shoulder, and Parvati was delighted. "You understand, and he knows that you do."

Parvati gazed into Rama's face, and he looked back at her with steady eyes for a long moment.

"In any case," he said, breaking the spell, "I wanted to make sure you still want to be friends. Do you?"

"Does anyone ever say no to you?" she asked. He lowered his eyes, and she laughed.

"You would be surprised," he said.

"I want to be your friend," Parvati said, not hiding the emotion in her voice. "I feel suddenly as if I have found the friend I've longed for all my life."

Rama smiled and took her hand and held it in both of his. "I feel exactly the same way," he said. "Tomorrow I want to take you on a tour of the palace."

"No!" Parvati said. "It's one thing to meet—but if we go about the palace someone is bound to see us, and—"

"No one will see us!" he whispered. "You don't think I've lived all my life locked behind doors without learning a thing or two, do you?"

"I don't know," she said. "There's too much at risk."

"Promise me you'll come with me," he said. But Parvati refused until he promised to tell her about the armoire.

"You can come and go any time you want!" she said.

Rama's face colored.

"I will never come again through the armoire unless you know I'm coming," he said. "I promise. I will be back tomorrow afternoon. I will tell you everything then."

With that he stood and crossed to the armoire. Parvati followed, but he turned and grinned at her.

"I'll explain tomorrow." He disappeared into the armoire, the gecko still on his shoulder, and closed the door behind him.

Eighteen

That night Parvati lay in her bed and thought of the Yuvaraja and his gifts. Was it all a strange coincidence? Had they both caused the cyclone and the suffering? Was there a cosmic design at work, in which a deeper meaning lay? Their births might have occurred at the same minute of the same hour. Somehow Parvati believed this was so. But what of their gifts? Perhaps Rama's gifts were more ordinary than he imagined.

Perhaps her own gifts were as ordinary as she had imagined them to be when she was small. Perhaps she was like Lakshmi, a dancer of great ability and talent who devoted her life to her art. Perhaps her "gift"—the dance magic—was simply the knowledge that her body was an instrument of music, and the confidence that gave her. But what of the magic of the Shiva Nataraja? Perhaps that was a gift from her father.

She fell asleep thinking Rama had other gifts of which he was not aware: a smile that transformed his brooding face in an instant and filled it with light and mischief, his musical laugh . . .

The next morning she awoke when the sun was just coming over the horizon, and flung open the shutters at the window. She stood on a chair to look down through the gulmohar branches to the courtyard. Parvati was inexplicably happy, and she thought of Rama again and remembered why.

Sitting on a branch outside the open window were two monkeys. One was an old female with grizzled hair. The younger one might have been the other's adolescent child. Parvati beckoned to the monkeys. They stared at her with bright eyes for a moment, then swung easily across to the window ledge. The older monkey reached up and plucked a brilliant red blossom and laid it on the ledge within Parvati's reach.

Parvati climbed down and lit a small candle beside the feet of the Shiva Nataraja, laid the blossom beside the candle, and offered a prayer.

She had just finished when Vilasini knocked. Parvati let her in, and the old ayah went through the narrow doorway to the bathroom and ran hot water in the large tub. While Parvati bathed with perfumed soap, Vilasini unwrapped Lakshmi's costume from the tissue paper. She unlocked the case, took the jewelry from it, and laid the pieces out on the bed.

When Parvati stepped out of her bath, Vilasini wrapped a towel about her and dried her like a child, briskly rubbing her arms and legs and body. Parvati protested, but the old ayah went about her duty as if she didn't hear. She powdered Parvati and held out a white dressing gown, and Parvati tied it about herself. Vilasini led her by the hand into the bedroom, where Kalpana sat waiting on a chair beneath the window.

On the bed was a red-and-yellow silk sari that had been sewn into a dance costume. Vilasini shook out the short blouse, unfastened the small row of hooks up the back, and held it for Parvati to slip into. The silk of the blouse was the color of the nasturtiums that shimmered in the sunlight beside her mother's front doorstep. Vilasini hooked the back. The short sleeves were banded with gold and a deep red the color of the rose petals strewn before the Raja. The sari was the same dark red with gold bands woven into the hem and the border, which hung in a pleated fan down the front of the costume from her waist. The fabric was arranged around the legs like a sari tied by a farm woman, with each leg encased separately in silk.

Kalpana braided Parvati's hair. Vilasini slipped five narrow gold bangles onto each of Parvati's wrists, and fastened a rope of pearls with an emerald-and-ruby-studded pendant so it hung to the middle of her chest. Kalpana tied about her throat a band of gold beads and a small enameled pendant with pearls dangling from its edges. A harp-shaped gold clip was fastened in her hair, and from it a thread-thin gold chain was attached to an earring encrusted with jewels that covered her ear like a helmet. Another pendant hung on her forehead from a headband of gold mesh. Vilasini fastened a nose ring with a clip that pinched the skin between her nostrils and made her eyes water for a moment.

The two women worked, winding around and around Parvati, one going under the other's arms, and back again. Vilasini strapped leather cuffs to her ankles, each with four rows of brass bells. Beneath them she clasped gold-beaded ankle chains.

"You must practice in the costume," Kalpana said, turning Parvati and adjusting a pleat here and a pendant there until she was satisfied. "The costume is tighter than what you're used to, and the jewelry is heavy," she said.

Kalpana moved the table back and stood away from Parvati.

"You look like Lakshmi when she was young!" Tears sprang to her eyes. Vilasini nodded and fished a handkerchief out of her waist for Kalpana. After she wiped her eyes, Kalpana was all business again, sitting on the edge of the table and clapping out the rhythm for Parvati to practice poses.

Parvati liked the weight and the tightness of the costume. They imposed a slight restraint that reminded her she was performing. But when it seemed she had only danced a few seconds, Kalpana stopped her.

"I wanted to be sure it fit. Now change into your cotton sari and save this so it will be fresh for your performance," she said.

Vilasini helped Parvati out of the costume and shook out one of the plain cotton dance saris she wore at the gurukulam. Parvati wound it about herself and fastened the end tightly around her waist. She practiced in the room at the end of the corridor the entire morning with Kalpana. Her head guided her dancing—the magic did not manifest itself.

Parvati wore the jewelry while she practiced to accustom herself to its weight. By the end of the rehearsal, her cotton sari was damp with perspiration, but she did not want to stop. Kalpana insisted she must go back to her room to rest. Vilasini gave her the key to the case for the jewelry on a small silver safety pin.

"Pin it inside your blouse," Vilasini whispered through the spaces in her long teeth. "Lock Lakshmi's jewels in the case and put it in your armoire until it's time to dress for your performance tomorrow. You must guard them with your life!" She patted Parvati on the hand and left her. Parvati pinned the key as Vilasini had told her, and the cool metal warmed against her skin.

Parvati closed her bedroom door, went to the table beneath the window, and removed the jewelry, examining each piece as she took it off. The stones sparkled in the bright light from the window. Each facet of every stone was a small and perfect miracle. She held the stones up to the light and put her face close to them, touching each piece with the end of her finger. The gold headband glowed like a lizard sunning itself beside the river.

She heard the sound of branches clattering and looked outside. There, just beyond the window, were the two monkeys, their faces crowded side by side and peering in at her. She laughed and they scampered farther back among the gulmohar branches, still watching her with their bright eyes.

Parvati took the jewelry case from the armoire, unlocked it, and pinned the key back inside her blouse. The case was lined with red velvet, and each piece had its own lambskin pouch. Thick velvet-covered pads protected the jewelry.

When she had replaced the case in the armoire, Parvati lay down to rest. She fell asleep almost immediately. A light tapping from inside the armoire awoke her. She went to the door and listened. The tapping continued and she unlatched the door. Rama emerged wearing his fisherman's clothing. He was smiling broadly.

"You promised you wouldn't come without letting me know!" she said.

"I said I'd come today," he said, lowering his eyes.

"Tonight we are touring the palace," he said. Parvati began to protest, but he shook his head. "No one will see us. You must trust me."

"Why should I trust you when you won't tell me how you come and go without being seen?" she asked. She felt a nudge at her heart. After years of keeping to herself, of strict discipline and devotion to her dancing, she longed for Rama's friendship and for adventure.

"I will explain," he said. "I want you to know coming with me is safe. After my illness I was not allowed to go anywhere or do anything. I had no exercise, no fresh air. They fed me nourishing broths and plain rice and steamed vegetables—"

"That sounds cruel!" Parvati said.

"It was," he said. "The ayah sent me off to sleep before anyone else. When she left me alone in the nursery, I got up and explored every hallway, room, and closet. I found a door that led to a back corridor that's no longer used. The servants said there were ghosts in that part of the palace—the spirits of dead children poisoned during the reign of one of our ancestors.

"That corridor opened a whole world for me. It leads to an outside gate through which I could leave the palace and come back without being seen. And to the passage that ends up in your armoire and other hidden places. It led me to discover my special powers." He hesitated. "You do believe me, don't you?"

"About your gifts?" she asked. "Of course. My whole life I've had people not believe me. I'm not one to disbelieve!"

"I discovered them five years ago, just after my upanayana, when the second birth of enlightenment occurs through the ceremony of the sacred threads. I was nine, and my parents held a big celebration. I had to ride through the streets on the elephant. You know—dhoom-dham and folderol!"

"I remember seeing you," said Parvati. "Your head was shaved except for one bit in the back, and you wore only a small piece of cloth around your waist."

That evening, Rama went on, when the ceremony was over he was sent to bed early. Many of his cousins stayed overnight at the palace, and he didn't want to leave the celebration feast. His ayah insisted. Reluctantly he said good night and went off to the nursery. But he had an adventure in mind, a visit to the villages, where the people continued to celebrate his upanayana.

"I slipped out of the nursery and through a series of doors into the secret corridor." That night for the first time he heard voices in the corridor. It was narrow and there was no place to hide. Rama saw a light coming toward him, and he retreated to the door that led to the nursery. But he had come too far, and it was clear he'd be caught. He stood his ground as two cousins came down the center of the old passageway, one holding a kerosene lantern in front of him.

"Uncle says this is where they were killed," his cousin Sethu was saying. The two young men, who were five or six years older than Rama, joked about the ghosts, but Rama could see they were uncomfortable. Rama stood directly in their path, thinking what he would say to them. But they almost ran into him before he jumped out of the way. Clearly, they had not seen him, and he stared at their retreating backs in astonishment.

"So, you see," he said to Parvati, "I was surprised when you recognized me at the river. Because either people do not see me at all, or they see me as someone completely different—a fisherman or a peon—but not as the Yuvaraja."

"Are you certain they don't see you?" Parvati asked. "Is it

possible people know you've been confined to the palace all your life? Perhaps they overlook your coming and going without your father's knowledge because they feel sorry for you."

"That was what I thought at first. But people in the palace would not disobey my father, no matter how much they might sympathize with me. He's a very kind man, but he's used to having his way. No one will see us when we tour the palace."

"I haven't made up my mind yet," she said. "Now I must rehearse with the musicians."

"And I must study." Rama folded his arms over his chest. "But you must agree to come with me tonight."

She did believe him.

"How do I know I won't be seen?" she asked.

"You'll have to trust me," he said.

"I will." Parvati was hesitant. But she wanted him to leave. "I'll come with you tonight." He grinned again and disappeared into the armoire.

Parvati hurried to Kalpana's room and they went together to the reception hall where the Raja had first greeted them on their arrival in Nandipuram. A stage had been erected in the center of the hall, in front of the draped and cushioned platform where the Raja and his family had sat.

Parvati stepped onto the stage, where the musicians sat on a large red silk carpet, tuning their instruments. Brass lampstands with small receptacles filled with oil waited to be lit. Panels of embroidered fabric and strings of white lights draped the stage, and hundreds of fat round bolsters were strewn about the floor for the audience to recline against.

From the very first chord of the veena Parvati was transfixed. It felt as if the mridangam drum had lodged in her heart and its rhythm pulsed through her veins. Her fingers matched every note the flute sang, and once again she felt the magic of possibilities.

That evening the Maharaja invited Parvati and the other performers and guests for a feast. Vilasini came to Parvati's room to help her dress. She ran the bath, but this time Parvati closed the bathroom door and latched it so that the ayah could not intrude. She lay back in the perfumed water and thought about Rama.

Vilasini knocked at the door and interrupted Parvati, who sighed and climbed out of the bath, dried herself, and came out wrapped in the dressing gown. Vilasini had laid out the magnificent red-and-black shot-silk sari the Maharani had given her. Vilasini had also put out some of Lakshmi's jewelry, a ruby pendant on a rope of pearls and gold beads, and a pair of ruby earrings, great globes of red stone that sparkled simply at the ends of her earlobes, and gold bangles. Vilasini wrapped Parvati's hair into an elaborate chignon at the back of her neck and pinned a garland of jasmine around it.

When she was dressed, Parvati looked at her reflection in a large mirror with a peeling silver frame that hung on the wall. She could hardly believe her eyes. A woman looked back from the mirror—a woman with Parvati's face, wearing

Lakshmi's jewelry. A strange shiver of excitement crept up her spine.

There was a knock at the door and Parvati opened it to Kalpana, who sucked in her breath in surprise.

"You look magnificent!" she said. Parvati smiled. Kalpana walked around Parvati, admiring the sari. Kalpana was also very striking, tall and elegant in a purple sari with a rich gold border, her gift from the Maharani.

"I hardly recognize us!" Parvati said, laughing. They walked together to the dining hall through the long corridors, their feet tapping softly on the marble. Parvati kept falling into tumults of thought. Kalpana spoke to her several times, and she answered, but she could not remember what either of them said.

Outside the dining hall, in a milling crowd, they met the Guru, who wore his simple homespun jibba and dhoti, freshly laundered, starched, and pleated. His white hair stood out around his face, which always radiated energy and peace. They entered the dining hall through a pair of large glass doors flanked by pages dressed in blue achkans.

Crystal chandeliers hung from glass domes in the ceiling over a long dining table covered with white linen and sprinkled with red rose petals. Flowers in vases stood beside each of the room's dozens of sculptured columns, and everywhere tiers of tiny flames danced on the arms of brass oil lamps.

The Guru and Kalpana seemed unaware that the rooms of the palace were any different from the plaster-walled rooms of the bungalow at the gurukulam. They smiled at the other guests, speaking to everyone they met, and looked perfectly at home.

At one side of the dining hall eight musicians played on a carpeted stage. The mridangam drum set the fast pace, and a violin slid easily over notes answered by a woman's smoky voice that moved through the music like liquid silver.

Just inside the door the Raja, the Rani, Gita, Mira, and Rama sat on a stage so that their faces were slightly elevated above the line of people who passed before them, bowing and greeting each member of the royal family.

Parvati's eyes went directly to Rama, who wore a pale yellow turban pinned with a topaz and pearl brooch and a plume from a golden peacock. On the middle finger of his right hand was a large yellow diamond ring. His eyes were rimmed with kajal and his look was imperious. When he saw Parvati his face softened and his jaw dropped. He stared for a moment before looking away.

Among the performers who had come for the cultural festival were Rajput sword dancers from the desert area of Bikaner in Rajasthan, Kathakali dancers from Kerala, Odissi performers from the eastern state of Orissa, puppeteers and jugglers from Gwalior, and even a jazz band from Bombay. They all mingled with foreigners and dignitaries who had traveled from abroad and the North of India.

Parvati stood in line behind Kalpana to greet the Maharaja and his family. The Raja and his wife nodded to each guest and spoke graciously. Gita smiled and Mira winked at Parvati. She stood before Rama and bowed slightly, and felt her cheeks and neck grow warm. He looked out over her head, barely acknowledging her greeting.

When they were seated, waiters in long, starched tunics and red turbans served platter after platter: prawn curry, Malabar fish curry, fragrant vegetables, mounds of scented rice, plates of pickles, steaming breads, soups, sauces—more food than Parvati had ever seen.

Parvati tasted one or two vegetable dishes, but her mind was on Rama.

Nineteen

When the banquet was over, Parvati and Kalpana walked back along the corridor the way they had come. Kalpana talked animatedly about the other guests, but Parvati was quiet. When Kalpana realized Parvati was not listening, she fell silent, and the swish of their silk saris and the soft tap of their leather soles on the marble were the only sounds in the corridor.

Parvati worried that her friendship with Rama would have serious consequences. How could meeting the Yuvaraja secretly in her room be part of her dharma? She did not want to embarrass the Guru and the gurukulam and her family. But at the same time she thought of the Yuvaraja's touch on her hand.

Kalpana looked at her through narrowed eyes when she said good night. Parvati recognized the look that she had first seen in her mother's eyes when she was a child. It was a look that said something inexplicable was at work.

"I'm sorry I haven't been good company," Parvati said.

Kalpana did not wait for an explanation but kissed Parvati's cheek. "I hope you sleep soundly," she said, and Parvati smiled at her gratefully. "Everything will go well tomorrow if you relax and are rested."

When finally she was alone, Parvati opened the armoire, unpinned the key, and took out the costume and jewelry. She undressed quickly, hooked the blouse of the costume halfway, wriggled into it, fastened the rest of the hooks, and pulled on the rest of the costume. She braided her hair over her shoulder, securing the jasmine garland with hairpins, and added a hair ornament to the pearl and ruby pendant, earrings, and bangles she had worn earlier, locked the case, and put everything away in the armoire.

When Rama tapped at the armoire door a few minutes later, she was examining herself in the mirror on the wall. She did look like Lakshmi, whose photograph hung in the bungalow at the gurukulam.

"Are you ready?" Rama asked as she opened the armoire. He still had on the clothes he'd worn at dinner.

He noticed her costume.

"You look like the devadasis carved on the walls at Chidambaram," he said, his voice soft.

"I am a devadasi," Parvati said. "I have sacrificed everything to dance. Dance is my life. And that is why I cannot do something silly like a midnight tour of the palace with you! Instead I will show you my magic, the magic of dance."

He took her hand and pulled her over to sit on the chairs beside the window. A soft warm breeze touched their faces.

"Please come with me," Rama said. "No one will see you. I'm certain!"

Rama crossed to Parvati's bed, gathered up the pillows that sat on the coverlet, and stuffed them under the sheets. He smoothed the sheet over them and arranged the mosquito netting around the bed so the fans moved it rhythmically, and it looked as if the pillows breathed.

"It's such an old trick," he said, "but it always works."

"How do you know I, too, will go unseen?" Parvati asked. "I can't take such a risk!"

"Please!" Rama said. "Believe me!"

"I want to," she said. "But too much is at stake. I've made up my mind." Just then there was a knock at her bedroom door. Parvati jumped, but Rama held up his hand and touched his forefinger to his lips to signal her to be quiet. Kalpana stuck her head inside the room, then turned and spoke to Vilasini, who was behind her in the hallway.

"She's asleep," Kalpana said. "The poor child was so tired when we came back she must have gotten into her bed immediately." Kalpana closed the door softly and pulled it until the latch caught.

"There!" said Rama triumphantly. "You see? That's how it happens!" Parvati was speechless. "So," he said. "Are you ready?" She could think of no other argument against going with him. She removed the leather cuffs with the brass bells from her ankles and shut them away. She nodded and followed Rama into the armoire.

The passageway was dark and dank and bitter with the smell of bats. Dust and cobwebs brushed against their faces as they descended into an old stairwell. Parvati walked close behind Rama. She wished she weren't wearing Lakshmi's costume. They followed another corridor on the main level only a few minutes before they came to a wooden door. Rama worked expertly on the lock with a small metal pick, and the door clicked open. They came into a narrow servants' passage between the pantry and dining hall, and Rama relocked the door behind them.

He went first, poking his head into the darkened dining hall. The marble floor had been swept and mopped just minutes before, and streaks of damp shone darkly.

"Come," he said. "I want to show you how they hung the chandeliers. They're lead crystal and gold—each one weighs more than a ton." The chandeliers were suspended from whimsical glass domes.

Rama led her to a curved stairway. They emerged on the roof, where a damp breeze blew gently. Overhead the stars shone here and there, for clouds had begun to gather. The monsoon rains were to begin the next day, and the weather had already changed.

He explained how the chandeliers had been hung from a cage of steel beams over the domes by elephants that had lifted them into place by pulleys. He showed her the ramps where the elephants carried water to concrete tanks on the roof, and explained how gravity caused the fountains to flow in the gardens.

For two hours Rama showed Parvati about the palace, from his grandmother's bedroom, in the middle of which sat a huge silver and teak four-poster bed, to the trophy room, where the magnificent heads of tigers, elephants, lions, leopards, and deer hung on three stories of wall that soared from the stone floor to the vaulted ceiling.

"I don't like it here," Parvati said with a shudder. "The ghosts of these animals all around . . ." Rama took her hand and led her to the gem vault, which was protected by an electronic alarm system, where the state jewels were kept, and the garage, where a dozen old sedans sat under a canopy of dust.

As they went from room to room they ran into two servants, who appeared not to see them. Otherwise they had no need to call upon Rama's gifts.

"There is too much to see for one night," Rama said. "I think we should go back. You must rest for tomorrow. And we must leave more for next time."

"You're right," she said. But she thought it likely there would not be another time for them. She kept the thought to herself.

"What will you do when you've finished your studies?" she asked as they walked back.

"I want to study medicine in America," he said. "But my

father thinks I should stay here and manage our land. Since the forests were destroyed, most of the land is in agriculture. I'm not much interested in farming." Parvati thought how Venkat would love to have such land to manage.

Parvati's room was undisturbed. She had left the small electric lamp burning on the table under the window, and in its golden pool of light the Shiva Nataraja glowed softly.

"Sit here, please," she said to Rama, gesturing to one of the chairs beside the table.

Parvati took the leather cuffs with brass bells from the armoire and strapped them around her ankles again. Then she went to the fireplace and laid a small fire with wood from a brass bin beside the hearth. She lit a long taper and touched it to the kindling.

As the flames sprang to life, a magical, spiraling chord from a veena filled the room, and a mridangam drum lilted in a complex rhythm, and a harmonium droned. Parvati bent forward and touched the floor, then touched her eyes and murmured her request for permission from Bhuma Devi to punish the earth with her feet, and the raga began.

Parvati danced the possibilities into being—the possibility of friendship, the happiness of her family, Rama's freedom—and they spun beneath her feet. The magic washed over her and around her and carried her to a place she'd never been before.

When the dance ended and the last chord of the veena still hung in the air, Rama sat still with tears glistening in his eyes. Parvati bowed from the waist with her hands pressed together in front of her. Rama took her by the shoulders. He kissed her gently on the lips, and for a brief moment the possibilities were all she could think of. It was a moment without time, like a moment in dance when the unfolding was all that mattered. And then it was over.

We are of different worlds, she thought. In the established order of things, Rama should not stand near enough to Parvati to look into her face. To kiss her was unthinkable.

She touched her hand to her mouth.

"What is it?" he asked.

"You are twice-born," she said, speaking of his high status, his caste, everything that separated them.

"Yes," Rama said. "But you are twice-blessed. I come from the past—a moldy relic. Your life's work is the lifting of the spirit. Your dharma is to develop your talent, to realize yourself. How I envy you!" His voice broke.

Parvati touched his cheek.

"And what of your dharma?" she asked. "Your father is more than a farmer. He is a spiritual leader. If I was born to dance, you were born to lead."

Rama took her hand and kissed her fingers, and Parvati let the warm feeling blossom in the pit of her stomach.

"Will you come away with me?" he whispered. He held her face between his hands and looked into her eyes, asking her to see the possibilities in what he asked. "I will be a doctor in America and you can teach children to dance."

For the first time Parvati saw destiny as a terrible burden.

Twenty

In that instant a clamor went up in the corridor outside
Parvati's room, and the moment dissolved in less than the
blink of an eye. A bell clanged, and shouting reverberated
from the marble walls beyond the door. Parvati's heart began
to thunder in her chest. Someone pounded on the door, and
Parvati and Rama were jolted into action.

Rama leapt for the armoire. Parvati tore the jewelry from
her hair, neck, wrists, fingers, and ears. She unfastened the
hooks she could reach on her costume, wriggled out of it
half-undone, and grabbed the dressing gown on the brass
bedpost. Tying the white gown around herself, she tossed the
costume inside the armoire. She unstrapped the bells from

her ankles, tossed them into the armoire atop the costume, and shut the door quickly. The pounding from the corridor grew more insistent. She ripped the garland of jasmine from her hair.

Parvati glanced quickly around the room. The jewelry! She grabbed it up from the chair and table, and just as the door flew open she shoved it and the jasmine garland into the recess of the window well, and slammed the shutters closed.

"There!" said Kalpana, pointing at the embers burning themselves out on the grate. Her hair hung in loose strands around her sleep-creased face. The head bearer grabbed up a red can of fire retardant from outside the door, and a burst of foam spewed over the embers.

"Didn't you smell the smoke?" Kalpana asked. "What were you thinking of, building a fire? I was afraid your room had caught fire . . ."

"I was—chilled," Parvati stammered, realizing as the words came out of her mouth that it was an uncomfortably warm night. "I couldn't sleep, and . . ."

Kalpana looked around the room. The pillows that Rama had stuffed beneath the sheet still gave the appearance of someone sleeping in the bed. A swatch of the nasturtium-colored silk of her costume peeped out from the bottom of the armoire door. Parvati knew Kalpana saw the pillows and the protruding piece of costume, but Kalpana said nothing.

"It's strange there's no smoke in here." Kalpana sniffed the air.

"This is a very old palace, madame," the head bearer said.

"All fireplace vents in this wing must be open for the chimney system to draw smoke out. We close them because of mosquitoes as the monsoon approaches. When a fire is lit in one room, the smoke finds its way to other rooms that have open vents. One of the servants must have opened just these two flues, knowing these rooms would have guests."

"I'm so sorry," Parvati said, still numb with surprise and fear. "I had no idea . . ."

"It's all right," Kalpana said, turning to her. "When my room filled with smoke I was frightened. I was certain something terrible had happened."

"Nothing terrible has happened," said Parvati. "Since there's smoke in your room, do you want to sleep in here?"

Kalpana sat with Parvati while the servants aired out her room. Parvati's heart continued to beat hard. Kalpana looked again at the pillows under the covers, and at the costume peeping out from the armoire door, and back at Parvati, as if she expected an explanation. Parvati considered trying to explain. What could she say that would not cause the Guru to send her away? And shame her family? And cause Rama trouble?

"Parvati," Kalpana said gently, "where have you been? Why did you light a fire? And why is your costume caught in the armoire door?"

"I . . . was restless," Parvati said. "I went exploring the palace. I took out my costume. And I made a fire. I've always loved fire, and I just felt like making one on the hearth. I assumed since there was wood it was all right . . ."

"But this is odd behavior," Kalpana said. "Is it because you can't sleep? Perhaps you're nervous about your performance."

"Perhaps." Because Kalpana had always been kind, it pained Parvati not to be completely truthful with her. She took Kalpana's hand and pressed it and looked into her face.

"I am sorry. Truly," Parvati said, and meant it with her entire being. Kalpana smiled.

"You would tell me if there was something wrong? If you were in any kind of trouble?" Parvati nodded, but she felt even more miserable.

There was a knock at the door and Parvati opened it. The head bearer came in and addressed Kalpana.

"Your room is clear, madame," he said. "We've changed the linens. Please come and see."

Kalpana rose and said good night to Parvati, who let her hand go reluctantly.

"Come back if it still smells of smoke," Parvati said.

"No more fires," said Kalpana with a smile. She looked briefly again at the pillows under the covers. A tight little cluster of lines crinkled around the corners of her eyes, and Parvati remembered her mother and the scolding she'd given when Parvati had danced amid the flames in the courtyard at Anandanagar.

"Do go to sleep," Kalpana said. "Tomorrow is an important day. Good night." Parvati nodded and tried to smile, and closed the door behind Kalpana. When she was alone again, her hands and knees shook and her heart would not be quiet.

She went to the armoire and took out her costume. She inspected the rows of tiny hooks and straightened the pleats and put it back in its place and got into bed. Her arms and legs continued to tremble for a long time.

She had risked everything. Everything! The honor of her family. The trust of the Guru. The respect of the Maharaja and his family. Her own future. She had never known such feelings as those she had for Rama. For the first time Parvati understood how Nalini could have considered giving up everything for Mayappan. The feelings had sprung upon her from nowhere, and suddenly Rama meant so much to her. But did he mean so much that she'd give up her life of dancing?

She had no answer. She only knew she would do the same thing if she had the chance to explore the palace with Rama again. Yet going away with him would mean giving up everything else, as Nalini had done. But there was an important difference. Nalini was dependent upon a man who had taken her by force, with no regard for her safety or happiness. Parvati realized then the Gypsy woman she'd seen in the bazaar might indeed have been Nalini. Life with Mayappan would have hardened her.

Parvati knew Rama was gentle, and he cared for her. If they went away together, they would need and respect each other. But all that Parvati knew about duty told her she must not turn her back on it. Her duty was to dance—to fulfill her potential.

She imagined going on with her life at the gurukulam, and

never seeing Rama again. The thought of seeing him the next day amid the dhoom-dham and folderol of his father's birthday celebration, knowing they would never talk and laugh and touch again as they had that night—it was too much to bear.

Parvati tried to sleep but couldn't. She spent the night memorizing every second she had spent with Rama, imprinting on her heart every word and gesture. Still, the thought of never seeing him again seemed impossible.

She could not imagine life without him, nor could she imagine it without dancing. When I am an old woman, she thought, will I believe I made the right choice?

Sometime shortly after dawn, Parvati fell asleep. She awoke with a start when a watery beam of sunlight fell across her face through a crack in the shuttered window. Again Parvati remembered the night before and her heart was in her mouth.

Then for the first time she remembered the jewelry she had left in the window well. She leapt out of bed and threw open the shutters. The jewelry was gone! She climbed up on the chair and looked deeper into the window well, from front to back and along both sides—nothing but the withered garland of jasmine!

Parvati leaned her head against the shutter. She felt as if she might be sick to her stomach. She leaned forward to look out the window. No one was there beneath the gulmohar tree.

Someone must have climbed the tree in the night and stolen the jewelry. Who would think of finding jewelry in the window well? Parvati thought of the familiar face in the bazaar—of Nalini. Mayappan was known for his boldness—would he risk stealing money and jewels from wealthy people at a celebration heavily guarded by palace security and police? She knew that he would.

Someone had come into the room while she slept—that much was clear. If it had been Nalini and Mayappan, the jewelry was lost. She sat in the chair to think. But that made matters worse. She remembered Indira's warning: even a minor infraction of the rules would result in her expulsion from the gurukulam. The jewelry was far from minor. And it would be far worse to be dismissed as a teacher than as a student. Parvati put her face in her hands.

Someone knocked at her door. "Come in," Parvati said. It was Vilasini, followed by the bearer with hot water and lime, fruit, and vadai. Vilasini said good morning and went to run Parvati's bath.

Parvati's knees shook, and Vilasini gave her an odd little look. As soon as the old ayah left the bathroom, Parvati closed the door and got into the tub. She lay there, up to her chin in warm water, feeling more terrible than she had ever felt. Her eyes were swollen and her head was light and fuzzy with sleeplessness. And there was a deep well of emptiness where her heart had been.

She could not imagine summoning the energy and feeling to dance that evening—it seemed the magic had abandoned her.

Perhaps the missing jewelry meant she no longer had a

choice—she would be dismissed from the gurukulam, and she and Rama could go away together. The thought of letting everyone down—the Guru and Kalpana, the Raja, her family—took away all joy at the thought of being with Rama.

Perhaps someone else—a servant?—had opened the shutters, seen the jewelry, and decided to keep it for safety. Perhaps that person would return this morning and put the jewelry back while she was at the Raja's birthday celebration. She would wait and see what happened.

Vilasini had laid out the green, blue, and gold sari the Rani had given her and a pearl and emerald necklace. Parvati's heart lurched when she saw the pearls. Then she remembered each piece of jewelry had its own separate lambskin pouch. Vilasini did not have to open any of the empty pouches to find what she wanted.

Parvati dressed carefully and braided her hair, then wound the long thick braid into a chignon. Vilasini pinned lemon-scented frangipani blossoms into the shining coil of hair, and left when Kalpana knocked at the door.

"That sari is even more beautiful on you than the other!" Kalpana said. Parvati held her hand for a second. She wanted to tell Kalpana about the jewelry, but decided to wait.

They walked through the palace corridors, joining dozens of other guests and performers on their way to the celebration. The air was hot, heavy with the promise of rain. The ceremony was traditionally held outdoors in the durbar hall, a pavilion where the Maharaja had met for centuries with the people of his state.

The pavilion was attached to the palace wall through a wide doorway from a hallway on the main floor. It opened onto the parade ground, already crowded with the people of Nandipuram wanting to see the Raja, his family, officials, and important guests. At one end of the parade ground was a pandal, where the feast would be served.

When Parvati and Kalpana came through the doorway into the pavilion, the heat and dampness pressed down on them. Fans hanging on long stems from the vaulted ceiling turned lazily. Young women posted under the marble arch shook rose water from silver containers over the guests, and girls carrying baskets threw handfuls of rose petals before their feet.

Everyone in the pavilion had an assigned seat, and when Parvati had taken her place she looked out over the colorful patchwork on the parade ground searching for her family, but there were too many people.

On either side of the broad stage at the front of the pavilion stood enormous oil lamps, palms in red clay pots, tall urns with flowers, and enlarged photographs of the Maharaja's father, who had died some thirty years before. Everything was draped with garlands of flowers. Music filled the hall, and the sweetness of the air made Parvati's stomach churn.

A dozen men in white marched in step onto the stage, and the crowd fell silent. The men raised sunset-pink conch shells to their lips and sounded a fanfare. Everyone stood, and the Maharani walked in, followed by Mira and Gita. They sat in gilt chairs. Rama came next, looking haughty and immovable. Parvati could not keep her eyes from him.

The crowd cheered as four servants rolled a wide, velvet-covered chair onto the stage. The Raja sat in the chair, his mustaches curled and waxed. He wore ceremonial robes of gold and silk tapestry, heavy velvet epaulets with gold embroidered medallions and dozens of strands of pearls about his neck. Behind the Raja stood a round, sharp-faced man in a gray-and-white pin-striped achkan.

"That's the treasurer of the Raja's enterprise," Kalpana whispered. "He sat across the table from us at dinner last night—do you remember?" But Parvati did not.

Another fanfare issued from the conch shells and a large teak-and-silver contraption was wheeled onto the stage, a balance scale with two silver pans dangling from chains on either arm. The Raja's robes were so heavy it took two men to help him move from the chair to a red velvet cushion in one of the scale's silver pans.

The pin-striped man stepped foward and picked up a sapphire-blue lambskin sack from a heap of bulging gem-colored bags and sifted dozens of gold coins onto the raised silver pan opposite the Maharaja. Then he reached for another sack, and emptied it, and another.

When the mound of gold reached a weight that balanced the Raja in midair, a servant brought a stepladder. The treasurer climbed until his face was even with the balance arm. He bent forward and peered at the small mercury level embedded in the teak, and dropped another coin onto the pile in the pan. When the Raja and the mound of gold weighed exactly the same, the treasurer nodded and a roar went up from the crowd. At the same instant, a clap of thunder sounded and the monsoon rains broke, sending everyone in the parade ground running for cover.

People came away from the long, heavily piled tables under the bright pandal carrying banana-leaf plates covered with sweet rice. Children held fistfuls of boiled candy and biscuits, and ran squealing and laughing through streaming curtains of water. Adults turned their faces to the sky and let the rain run down their necks and over their shoulders.

While the people of Nandipuram rejoiced, Parvati's heart grew darker. She thought of the impossibility of her love for Rama and of the missing jewelry. And she thought again of Nalini.

Twenty-one

Parvati slipped away when the crowd pressed forward and separated her from Kalpana. The pavilion was so noisy it was impossible to hear above the din of voices and music. Parvati moved quickly through the crowd, and the profusion of colored clothing throbbed before her aching eyes.

When she reached the corridor, she ran and didn't stop until she came to her room. She flung open the door, went straight to the window, and threw back the shutters. She stepped up onto the chair that sat under the window and saw that the well remained white and empty in the gloom of the monsoon afternoon.

Parvati sat heavily on the chair. Outside, the rain had steadied to a hissing downpour. She had five hours before she was to perform, perhaps three hours before she had to dress. She could wait no longer. She had to tell Kalpana and the Guru about the missing jewelry immediately so a search could be mounted. If Nalini was caught . . . She could not think about it.

She looked up, and in the doorway was Rama.

"Where have you been? I was worried," he said, and looked at her closely. "What's wrong?"

"Lakshmi's jewelry," she said, "the jewelry I was to wear for my performance—the jewelry I wore last night—it's gone!"

"Gone? Gone where?"

She told him what had happened. Her throat was tight, so that it hurt to talk. He looked at her in disbelief.

"But that's not possible!" he said.

"I assure you, it is," she said.

"My father pays everyone on the palace staff well," Rama said. "He goes to great pains to let them know they are trusted and valued. In the history of my family's rule there have been murders over the throne. But there has never been a theft in this palace!"

"This may be different," Parvati said. She told him about Nalini and the day she thought she had seen her in the bazaar. "If Nalini and Mayappan are here, then anything is possible," she said.

Rama took her hands and held them.

"I am going to get the palace security chief," he said. "You must tell him exactly what happened—everything."

"I don't want you to get into trouble," she said.

"Don't worry. It would be good for my father to know I haven't been cloistered in the palace all this time. I've often thought about telling him. Perhaps he'll loosen his grip on me."

Parvati looked at their hands clasped together.

"Meeting you—having you for a friend—has made me so happy." Her voice quavered. "I don't want it to end like this!"

"We will find the jewelry," he said. "Don't worry. You do what you must do. I will talk to the security people."

Rama's knowing gave Parvati courage. She set out to find Kalpana and the Guru to tell them what had happened, and met them walking together, arm in arm, along one of the corridors.

"Where did you go?" Kalpana asked.

"I must talk to you," Parvati said. "Please. Come to my room." Kalpana and her father looked at each other, but they said nothing and followed Parvati. She asked them to sit in the chairs under the window. She folded her hands in front of her and composed herself before speaking. Kalpana and the Guru waited patiently.

"I was not entirely truthful with you last night," Parvati said, looking at Kalpana, who sat forward in her chair. "I toured the palace with the Yuvaraja. I'm afraid I did some-thing . . . irresponsible. I wanted to dance for him, and so I put on my costume and the jewelry. When I heard the com-motion in the hallway I didn't know who it was. I hid the jewelry behind the window shutters. In the confusion I forgot it was there. When I remembered this morning, it was gone."

Kalpana's hands flew up to her mouth. The Guru looked at the floor.

"All of it?" he asked. Parvati shook her head. She told him which pieces she'd worn. He nodded. He looked dazed.

"Why didn't you tell us so we might look for it? Perhaps the palace security people can help," said Kalpana.

"Rama—the Yuvaraja—is talking to them now. He says there has never been a theft in the palace. But there is more." Parvati told them about Nalini in the bazaar.

"Are you certain it was Nalini?" Kalpana asked.

Parvati shook her head. "It was just the briefest glimpse," she said miserably.

"But without a key to lock your door, anyone could have come in," Kalpana said.

"I didn't sleep at all last night," Parvati said. "It was light when I dozed off this morning. I heard nothing—no one—all night."

"Whoever it was may have come from outside," Kalpana said, standing on her toes to look out the window. The rain fell steadily, and silvery drops of water hung from the lintel. "They could have climbed the tree up to your window without your knowing."

"But who would climb up to the window? No one could have known the jewelry would be there."

"Vilasini!" said Kalpana. "Perhaps she heard or saw something. Did you ask her?"

Parvati shook her head and Kalpana went to find the ayah, leaving the Guru and Parvati alone.

"I'm so sorry. I thought if I said nothing it would reappear. Perhaps I simply did not have the courage to tell you," she said to the Guru. "You entrusted me with the most valuable things you had and I did something stupid and unworthy. I would understand if you want me to leave the gurukulam." She looked up at the Guru, who had been studying her quietly.

"You have made a serious mistake," he said. "Yes, the jewelry is valuable—irreplaceable, in fact. But it is not the most valuable thing. The gurukulam is more valuable, and the students. And you are the most valuable student. If I thought you had jeopardized the institution or the other students, perhaps I would ask you to leave the gurukulam. But I don't think that."

"I don't know what to do." Parvati looked at the floor, and the Guru thought for a moment before speaking.

"What you must do is what your heart tells you," he said. "You are no longer just a student, and the rules of the gurukulam no longer apply in the same way as before. You are a person of free will. Do you love this boy?"

"I believe so," Parvati said.

"If your heart tells you that you should marry this boy—Rama—then that is a matter for you and him and your families to decide."

"But how am I to know what is the right thing to do?" she asked.

The Guru smiled and laid his hand against her cheek.

"That is a basic human frailty—we always want to know what will happen if we do one thing rather than another. Not knowing is the mystery of destiny. If you are still for a moment, no doubt you will hear your heart tell you what you must do. It would say something like this: Have a rest, Parvati. Get up and eat something light—perhaps just sweet lime juice. Dress in your dance costume, and whatever jewelry Kalpana selects for you to wear. Then dance as you've never danced in your life. Destiny is not so complicated."

Kalpana came back into the room. "Vilasini says she saw nothing unusual, heard nothing at all last night," she said.

At that moment there was a knock at the door. Kalpana opened it. Rama and a tall slim man dressed in a khaki uniform stood outside.

The man in the uniform removed his patent-leather-brimmed hat, and he and Rama came into the room.

"This is Mr. Prasad," Rama said. "He is chief of security. Perhaps he can help."

"Please," said Mr. Prasad, "please sit." Kalpana sat beside her father, but Parvati remained standing. "So. Please. Tell me what happened."

Parvati told Mr. Prasad about taking off the jewelry and putting it in the window well and discovering that it was gone. And she told him about the possibility that she had seen Nalini.

"Theft is all but unheard of in the palace," Mr. Prasad said. "I would be surprised if it was stolen—by anyone here, at least. Of course, at the moment there are many visitors."

"Mayappan is clever and bold," said Kalpana. "He has robbed hundreds of people right under the noses of the police."

"I've heard of him," Mr. Prasad said. "So far as I know, Mayappan has not operated outside of Tamil Nadu. I would be surprised if he had come here. Of course, anything is possible. I will look into it."

"Actually," said Rama, "there *are* thieves here in the palace." Everyone turned to look at him. "The monkeys hang about looking for a teaspoon or something shiny to steal. It happens often. Finding where they hide things is the problem."

"I will also question the bearers and the other servants," Mr. Prasad said. "Perhaps they saw someone in the corridors last night. Or perhaps they know where the monkeys put their silver spoons. I will report back." They thanked him and he left the room, followed by Rama.

"I don't know if I can," Parvati said when she and Kalpana and the Guru were alone again. They turned and looked at her. "Dance this evening."

"Can?" asked the Guru. "If there is anything that you *can* do, it's dance! You have a genius." He regarded Parvati with his gentle black eyes. "That is what you were put on earth to do." He stood stiffly and shuffled toward the door.

"I'm going to leave you," he said. "Kalpana will decide what jewelry you should wear. I will come back an hour before the performance so we can go down together. I am going to have my nap now."

"Don't worry," Kalpana said when her father was gone. "We'll find the jewelry. Mr. Prasad seems confident it wasn't stolen." Parvati nodded. Kalpana hurried to unlock the jewelry case and selected another pair of earrings, a pendant, hair ornament, and bracelets.

"After you rest," she said, "send Vilasini for me and I will come help you dress." Parvati nodded, and Kalpana kissed her on the cheek. "Don't worry."

Parvati shut the door and leaned against it. The image of the Guru shuffling out of the room stayed with her—the glint in his eye as he told her to eat lightly before she danced. She crossed to the window and sat in the chair. The gecko was on the windowsill, his throat pulsing yellow as he looked for insects taking refuge from the rain. Parvati held out her hand. The gecko raised up on his legs and looked at her, cocking his head. Then he skittered across the windowsill and disappeared.

What is this magic that comes and goes, she wondered.

She stood and looked out the window. Not a single monkey, not a single bird. She whistled, hoping one of the creatures she'd befriended would come to her. But none did. There are so many questions without answers, she thought. Where had her knowledge of music come from? What was the magic that always had been part of her? And where had it gone?

She lay on her bed, and immediately fell asleep.

Some time later, a gentle tapping on the armoire door awakened her. She opened the door and Rama stepped out.

"You were born to dance, Parvati," he said. "For people like us, there are so few friendships. That makes it difficult. Who knows? One day when I am a doctor and you are a famous dancer, perhaps we will meet again. We both know what the right thing is. Dance like Shiva!"

Parvati was unable to speak. Tears wet her cheeks, and Rama took her face in his hands and kissed her twice, once on each cheek. He climbed back into the armoire and was gone.

An urgent banging on the door awakened Parvati a while later. She arose in a haze of sleep and opened the door to Kalpana.

"I've been knocking for five minutes!" Kalpana said. "Come—it's time for you to dress." Vilasini scurried in and ran the bathwater. There was no question of a quiet bath. Kalpana and Vilasini came in and out of the bathroom a dozen times.

Parvati thought of Rama's visit—what he'd said had made perfect sense. Or had she only dreamed he'd come to her? She felt calm and rested, as if she'd slept an entire night. But the sensation of weeping . . . She wrapped the dressing gown around her and walked toward the bed, and could see the pillow was still wet with her tears.

"You'll have time to sleep afterward," Kalpana said, turning her and splashing powder over her body. As nervous as Kalpana was, you might have thought it was *her* performance, Parvati thought. They wove around her, placing jewelry on her arms and neck, and pinning jasmine in her hair.

Then it was time for makeup. Parvati turned to sit in the chair.

"No!" said Kalpana. "Don't sit!" Parvati felt as if they were performing strange rituals on someone else. She saw that other person, an infant wrapped in her father's dhoti, gazing at the Shiva Nataraja, imagining the sacred dance that destroyed and created the earth in a perpetual cycle.

Vilasini, who had done Lakshmi's makeup for years, stood on a stool working on Parvati's face. Parvati kept her eyes closed for a long time while the old ayah drew thick lines in black wax pencil across Parvati's eyelids and painted her lips, hands, and feet red.

Finally it was time to go, and there was another knock on the door. Vilasini opened it to the Guru, who stood just across the threshold looking at Parvati.

"You look like Lakshmi," he said, his voice soft.

Rama appeared over the Guru's shoulder, and Mr. Prasad was behind him.

"Did you find it?" Parvati asked, standing on her toes to see Rama. She wanted to touch his face. He smiled and held up a flannel bag.

"Where was it?" she asked.

The Guru clasped his hands before his face. "Thank God, thank God," he said, over and over, taking the red flannel bag from the Yuvaraja.

"The monkeys that stay in the palace grounds sleep out in the trees beyond the stable," Rama said, pushing into the room and standing close to Parvati. "Some bangles may still be missing. These were in the hollows of the trees. Now you can dance with a clear mind." He leaned over and whispered into her ear, "Dance like Shiva!"

Then Rama left, leaving only the Guru and Kalpana with Parvati.

"You look perfect," Kalpana said. "Now it's up to you."

Parvati did not remember the walk to the reception hall, or her first glimpse of the audience waiting expectantly, or the sound of the musicians tuning their instruments, or Rama sitting in front with the Guru and Kalpana.

She thought of what she might call upon to transport her through the dance. To her, the dance was movement of spirit as well as body. Her training should carry her body, she thought. She would have to pray for the other.

She walked as if her feet did not belong to her, and she stepped onto the stage as if some strange force propelled her. When she touched first the floor and then her eyes and pressed her hands together and prayed to Bhuma Devi to grant permission to strike the earth with her feet, she also asked for the earth to turn beneath them and remind her of all that had ever moved her.

She raised her eyes, and her arms and one leg, just as she had done when she was a child about to fall into the dust. The chord of the veena fanned out and enveloped her, and the pulse of the mridangam drum infected her blood and thumped within her bones. She summoned the energy from the cosmic fire at the depth of her being, and from the great well of the souls around her. The air whistled, and the wind from a thousand monsoons dampened her face. Each flick of a finger and roll of an eye was a frozen perfect moment.

"This is it," a voice said softly in her ear, and she knew it was the voice of Shiva. "You are the magic of possibilities."

GLOSSARY

(Pronunciation guide: underlined vowels are long vowels; vowels with "h" at the end are short vowels; italicized syllables are accented. English spellings of Hindi, Tamil, and Sanskrit words are phonetic.)

abhinaya (ah-bh<u>e</u>-*nah*-yah) Combined expressive movements of the head, arms, hands, and body in bharata natyam.

achkan (*ahch*-kahn) Fitted, knee-length coat with a short stand-up collar worn by men.

alarippu (ah-lah-*rih*-p<u>u</u>) Opening sequence in a bharata natyam dance recital.

amma (*ahm*-mah) Mother.

arangetram (ah-ruhn-*geht*-rahm) Dance student's first performance in honor of the guru and the student's parents.

auto rickshaw (ah-t<u>o</u> *rihk*-shah) A three-wheeled taxi with a seat for a driver and a passenger seat behind; usually painted black and yellow.

ayah (*ah*-yah) Maidservant, often a children's caretaker.

bharata natyam (bhah-*rah*-tah *nah*-tyahm) Sacred Hindu classical dance that originated in the South Indian state of Tamil Nadu.

Bhuma Devi (*bhu*-mah *deh*-ve) Hindu goddess, mother of the earth.

bungalow (*buhn*-guh-lo) Single-story house with veranda.

champakam (*chahm*-pah-kahm) White, pink, and yellow blossoms often used as temple offerings.

churidar (*chuh*-rih-dahr) Trousers with a drawstring waist, cut on the bias to fit calves and ankles snugly.

dacoit (dah-*koyt*) Member of a band of robbers.

devadasi (deh-vah-*dah*-se) A servant of the gods; one entirely devoted to the sacred art of classical dance.

dharma (*dhahr*-mah) Natural law; duty; universal law that holds all life together.

dhobi (*dho*-be) Washerman.

dhoom-dham (*dhum*-dhahm) Noise and pomp surrounding former Indian royalty.

dhoti (*dho*-te) Plain white cloth worn by men wrapped around the waist.

dhurrie (*dhuhr*-re) Woven cotton or wool rug.

dosai (*do*-si) Skillet-fried pancake made of fermented lentil and rice flours and water.

drongo (*drohn*-go) Black crowlike bird with long, graceful tail plumes.

durbar (*duhr*-bahr) Ceremonial reception hall, in former times for the Raja's court officials.

Dussehra (dus-*shehr*-ah) Ten-day Hindu festival celebrating the victory of the goddess Durga over the demon Mahishasura.

Ganesha (gahn-*esh*-ah) Elephant-headed Hindu god of good fortune; remover of obstacles; son of Shiva.

ghat (ghaht) Rock or cement platform on a riverbank; used for doing laundry or performing religious rituals such as burning the dead and consigning them to the river.

gulmohar (gul-mo-*hahr*) Large tree with brilliant red blossoms.

guru (*gu*-ru) Master, teacher.

gurukulam (gu-ru-*kul*-ahm) School where students live and study with the guru.

howdah (*how*-dah) Platform seat, often with a canopy, on which passengers ride an elephant.

idli (*ihd*-le) Steamed bread of a fermented mix of water and rice and lentil flour.

jatisvaram (jah-tihs-*vahr*-ahm) Second movement in a bharata natyam dance piece—more complex than the opening alarippu.

jatka (*jaht*-kah) Horse-drawn cart.

ji (je) Affectionate term of respect when added to the end of a name or title; also, a positive response or term showing agreement.

jibba (*jihb*-bah) Long cotton shirt pulled over the head; usually collarless.

kajal (*kahj*-ahl) Black oil worn around the eyes to enhance them.

Kathakali (*kah*-thah-*kah*-le) Classical dance drama from Kerala in South India.

khadi (*khad*-de) Hand-loomed cotton cloth.

Krishna (*krihsh*-nah) Playful, blue-skinned Hindu god.

lakh (lahkh) One hundred thousand.

lassi (*lahs*-se) Drink made by whisking water into yogurt, with sugar or salt.

machan (*mah*-chahn) Enclosed elevated shelter used to hunt or view wildlife.

maharaja (mah-hah-*rah*-jah) "Great ruler"; a high-ranking Indian prince.

maharani (mah-hah-*rah*-ne̲) Queen, wife of a maharaja.

mahatma (mah-*haht*-mah) Great spiritual leader; popular title of Mohandas Gandhi.

Mahishasura (mah-*hish*-ah-*suhr*-ah) A powerful demon in Hindu mythology.

mahout (mah-*ho̲u̲t*) Driver and keeper of elephants.

masala dosai (mah-*sahl*-ah do̲-si̲) Flavored potato and onion mixture wrapped in thin skillet-fried bread made from fermented lentil and rice flour.

mridangam (mre̲h-*dahn*-gahm) Melodic drum with a leather head at each end.

mudra (*muh*-drah) Hand and arm movements in bharata natyam classical dance.

namaskaram (nah-mahs-*kahr*-ahm) Greeting among Hindus in South India in which the hands are pressed together in front of the face and the head is bowed.

Nandi (*nahn*-de̲) "The Joyful"; the sacred bull, the vehicle or mount of Lord Shiva; shown kneeling, he is the symbol of the perfect devotee.

Nataraja (nah-tah-*rah*-jah) Dancing incarnation of Lord Shiva.

Natya Shastra (*naht*-yah *shah*-strah) Ancient treatise on Indian classical dance.

neem (ne̲m) Large deciduous tree thought to have medicinal properties.

nritta (*nrih*-tah) Pure dance form, rhythm and motion not intended as dramatization.

Odissi (o-*dihs*-se) Classical dance form from the eastern Indian state of Orissa.

paan (pahn) Mixture of betel nut and spices, wrapped in a betel leaf and eaten as a digestive aid.

palanquin (pah-*lahn*-kwihn) Seat on poles carried by bearers or on a platform by an animal; now used mainly for ceremonial purposes.

pandal (*pahn*-dahl) Bright colored tent used for festivals and celebrations.

peepul (*pe*-puhl) Sacred tree of the ficus, or fig, family with small, brilliant green leaves.

peon (*pe*-ahn) Low-ranking office worker who runs errands.

puja (*pu*-jah) Worship or devotion paid to a Hindu god at a temple or before a shrine at home.

punka (*puhn*-kah) Fan, often made from a palm leaf.

Puranas (puh-*rah*-nahz) Ancient folktales that have a strong influence on the lives of Hindus.

puri (*pu*-re) Fried puffed bread.

raja (*rah*-jah) Ruler of one of India's former princely states.

rani (*rah*-ne) Queen of one of India's former princely states.

sambhar (*sahm*-bhahr) Thin peppery soup poured over rice.

sari (*sah*-re) Long piece of cloth wrapped at the waist and drawn over one shoulder, worn by women on the Indian subcontinent.

shalwar kameez (shahl-*wahr* kah-*mez*) Loose trousers with a tunic worn over the top.

shikar (shih-*kahr*) Organized hunt.

shikari (shih-*kahr*-e̱) Someone who participates in a shikar.

Shiva (*she̱*-vah) Hindu god of destruction and re-creation; Lord of the dance; one of the three major Hindu gods (with Brahma and Vishnu).

Shiva Purana (*she̱*-vah puh-*rah*-nah) Ancient Hindu texts about Lord Shiva.

thali (*thah*-le̱) South Indian meal served on a round metal tray with small helpings of rice, pickles, soups, spiced vegetables, relishes, and puri.

toddy palm (*tahd*-de̱ pahlm) Palm tree tapped for liquid that is fermented to make an alcoholic beverage.

topee (to̱-*pe̱*) Light hard hat worn especially by Westerners to protect the head from the sun.

upanayana (u̱-*pahn*-ah-*yah*-nah) Hindu ceremony in which upper-caste boys receive sacred threads to wear over the left shoulder to symbolize spiritual rebirth.

uppama (up-*ah*-mah) Stir-fried snack made of ground wheat or semolina.

vadai (vah-*di̱*) Salty doughnut.

varnam (*vahr*-nahm) Highly complex dance sequence that serves as the centerpiece of a bharata natyam performance.

veena (ve̱-nah) Long, wooden stringed instrument.

yuvaraja (yu̱-vah-*rah*-jah) Son and heir of the raja.